Gustavus Geo

A Manual of the Development of Art

Outlook

Gustavus George Zerffi

A Manual of the Historical Development of Art

1. Auflage | ISBN: 978-3-73261-744-9

Erscheinungsort: Paderborn, Deutschland

Erscheinungsjahr: 2018

Outlook Verlag GmbH, Paderborn.

Reproduction of the original.

Gustavus George Zerffi

A Manual of the Historical Development of Art

Outlook

A MANUAL OF THE

HISTORICAL DEVELOPMENT

OF ART.

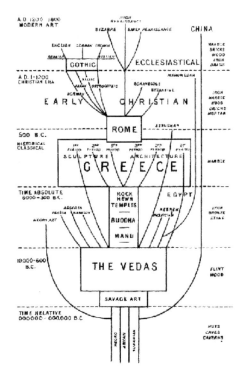

CHART
OF THE
HISTORICAL DEVELOPMENT OF ART.

A MANUAL

OF THE HISTORICAL

DEVELOPMENT OF ART

Pre-historic—Ancient—Classic—Early Christian

WITH SPECIAL REFERENCE TO

ARCHITECTURE, SCULPTURE, PAINTING, AND ORNAMENTATION

BY

G. G. ZERFFI, PH.D., F.R.S.L.

ONE OF THE LECTURERS OF H. M. DEPARTMENT OF SCIENCE AND ART.

LONDON:
HARDWICKE & BOGUE, 192 PICCADILLY, W.
1876.

LONDON: PRINTED BY
SPOTTISWOODE AND CO., NEW-STREET SQUARE
AND PARLIAMENT STREET

The right of translation is reserved.

This Book is Inscribed

TO

E. J. POYNTER, ESQ., R.A.

DIRECTOR OF THE ART TRAINING SCHOOLS,

SOUTH KENSINGTON,

IN RECOGNITION OF HIS GENIUS AS A PAINTER,

AND OF

HIS UNTIRING EFFORTS IN PROMOTING

HIGHER ART EDUCATION.

PREFACE.

An experience of more than eight years as Lecturer on the 'Historical Development of Art,' at the National Art Training School, South Kensington, has convinced me of the necessity for a short and concise Manual, which should serve both the public and students as a guide to the study of the history of art. In all our educational establishments, colleges, and ladies' schools, the study of art-history, which ought to form one of the most important subjects of our educational system, is entirely neglected. To suggest and to excite to such a study is the aim of this book. It would be impossible to exhaust in a short volume even that section of the subject which I propose to treat, and the most that can be done is to give outlines, which must be filled in by further studies.

Art is at last assuming a better position with us, thanks to the influence of the lamented Prince Consort, to whom we undoubtedly owe the revival of the culture of sciences and arts, and the indefatigable exertions of the Government, aided by munificent grants of Parliament. But much more is to be desired from the public. If the 'National Association for the Promotion of Social Science' is a faithful mirror of our intellectual stand-point, we certainly have not yet attained a very high position as an artistic national body. For twenty years the Association has met and has discussed a variety of topics, and this year, for the *first* time, it occurred to the learned socialists that there was such a factor in humanity as art, and the congress allowed an art-section to be opened under the presidency of Mr. E. J. Poynter, R.A., the director of the 'National Art Training School.' *Four* questions were proposed for discussion, and I gave anticipatory answers to these, before the congress was opened, in my introductory lecture to the students of the Art Training School. These answers will serve as so many reasons for the issue of this book, and I therefore reproduce them here, with the questions to which they refer.

1. 'What are the best methods of securing the improvement of Street Architecture, especially as regards its connection with public buildings?'

Answer.—Architects must be trained in art-history to prevent them from committing glaring anachronisms in brick, mortar, stone, iron, wood, or any other building material. Our street architecture cannot improve so long as we allow any *original* genius to *copy* mediæval oddities, and revive by-gone monstrosities at random, in perfect contradiction to the spirit of our times.

2. 'How best can the encouragement of Mural Decoration, especially Frescoes, be secured?'

Answer.—This might be attained by enlarging the area of national interest beyond horse-racing, pigeon-shooting, and deer-stalking, the buying of old china, mediæval candlesticks, ewers and salvers, or of old pictures, that can scarcely be seen; and extending our general art-support to our own talented artists, even though they may not all be Michael Angelos or Raphaels. We could allow them to decorate the walls of our town-houses, public buildings, chapels, churches, banks, and museums. We must, however, first train their minds to a correct appreciation of art-history, of the world's history, and of the glorious History of England, thus enriching their imaginations with the illustrious deeds of the past, in which they may mirror our present state, and foreshadow a continually progressing glorious future. For there is a mysterious and marvellous 'one-ness' in the religious, social, and artistic development of humanity which I have tried in the pages of this book continually to point out.

No civilised and wealthy country on the surface of our globe, can boast of more heroic deeds on sea and land, in and out of Parliament; of more splendid conquests by warlike and peaceful means than ours. The Wars of the Roses, the colonisation of America, the occupation of India, the peopling of Australia, the struggles of conformists and non-conformists, of Cavaliers and Roundheads, of Churchmen and Puritans, of Independents and Royalists, of Papists and Covenanters, of Iconoclasts and Free-thinkers, all offer stirring scenes; and yet, if we want to see on canvas pictures of our past, we must turn to France or Germany for them. I am sorry to say that until lately the Iconoclasts have borne all before them. As, however, the 'National Association' has at length consented to allow the discussion of art, and as words are in general precursors of deeds, we may expect some results from our awakened interest in art-matters.

3. 'What is the influence of academies upon the art of the nation?'

Answer.—Academies have no influence whatever, if the nation itself takes no interest in art, and has no art-education from a general, theoretical, and historical point of view. So long as art is considered a mere luxury, because a house does not keep out cold and wet better, if it be outwardly decorated; so long as it is thought that a parlour need but have red curtains to be a parlour; that our walls may be covered with any description of hideously- shaped, realistically-wrought Chinese or Japanese flowers, if they are only kept in greenish or brownish neutral tints; so long as we fancy that our wainscotings may be bright light, though the paper above be dark; and that a window is admirable, if only provided with a pointed arch, and some trefoil or quatrefoil to keep out as much light as possible; academies can do nothing. So long as we neglect higher esthetical culture and training in our public schools, our academy will but reflect this neglect. In reviewing the past I have throughout endeavoured to show the close connection of art-forms with the general, social, religious, intellectual, and moral conditions of the different nations and periods in which they appeared. It is erroneous to suppose that art has only to treat of straight or waving lines, of triangles, squares, and circles, of imitations of flowers, animals, and men, of nature and nothing but nature. The study of art comprises man in all his thoughts and actions, and has to add to this the phenomena of the whole outer world, from crystallisations to the heavenly vault, studded with innumerable stars at night, or glowing with light and life in colours at day-time. If our academy were to take this to heart, and expand its curriculum so as to have the students taught the beauties of Greek, English, and German poetry, we should not be obliged to turn to foreigners for worthy illustrations of our immortal Shakespeare, Milton, or even Tennyson. The art-historian knows that academies neither produced a Pheidias nor a Praxiteles, neither a Raphael nor an Albert Dürer; neither a Rubens nor a Holbein; neither a Gainsborough nor a Hogarth; neither a Canova nor a Flaxman. For art-academies, as mere outgrowths of fashion, unless rooted in the earnest, artistic spirit of a nation, only foster mannerism, pander to the general bad taste of the wealthy classes, and one-sidedly cultivate portrait-painting, whilst they shut out landscape or historical figure- painting. Academies have rarely encouraged grand ideas; they create a kind of parlour or bed-room art, with nice, but very small, sentiments, water-colour effusions and flower imitations, in which the Chinese surpass us by far. So long as our academy will have great names on its programmes, as nominal lecturers, so called because they do not lecture; so long as it will systematically neglect to teach our rising artists Universal History, Art History, Archæology, Comparative Mythology, Symbolism, Iconography, Esthetics from a higher scientific point, and Psychology with special reference to artistic composition, and so long as these subjects are ignored in our general educational establishments, we shall in vain try to compete at large with other nations, however many isolated great artists we may produce. Artists in all ages reflected in their products the general sentiments of the times in which they lived, and of the people for whom they worked; every page of this book bears out this assertion. Art is a mighty civiliser of humanity and elevates the whole of our earthly existence, for it purifies passions and pacifies our mind. Art is the eternally-active genius of humanity. Let our academy acknowledge this, and it will at least try to imitate the Art Training School at South Kensington, which has continually worked in the direction of enlarging the range of the studies of its students.

4. 'What is the influence upon society of Decorative Art and Art-workmanship in all household details?'

Answer.—If this question had been asked with an eye to business, we might answer that decorative art makes trade brisk, induces people to buy ornaments, and fills the pockets of dealers in curiosities. But this is not our aim. So long as we fail to look upon art as an earnest and serious study, as important and necessary to our social wellbeing as either ethics or science, the influence of decorative art must be confined to enticing people to plaster their walls with all sorts of China plate, or pay dearly for Japanese trays, screens, or cupboards, because they have not learnt to distinguish between the quaint and the comical, the beautiful and the ugly. Their taste is still on a level with that of untrained children, who have plenty of money in their pockets, do not know what to buy, and rush to purchase the ugliest monstrosities. If half the money that is wasted in these directions were to be devoted to the encouragement of our hard-working rising artists, we might soon boast of still greater successes than we can proudly point to, despite the adverse circumstances under which artists have to labour amongst us. Art with us is still looked upon as an extravagance, a luxury, as it was with the Romans of old, and this produces a craving for oddities. We hang up big china cockatoos, or place big china dogs, or stags with big china antlers, on our hearth-rugs. We have coarse china frogs and lizards, crabs or lobsters, from which we eat our fruit or fish; or a life-like salmon with staring eyes is brought on our table, its back takes off, and we scoop out the real cooked salmon with which its inside is filled. Form of dish, association of ideas, and action of the host are more worthy of anthropophagi than civilised beings of the nineteenth century. So long as art-history and esthetics are not made regular studies, not only in art-schools but also in general educational establishments, and especially ladies' schools, our national consciousness of art in general and the requirements of our age in particular cannot improve. Art is a branch of human knowledge, ingenuity, and creative force in which ladies, trained to appreciate beauty, might be made better 'helps,' than in the kitchen, the pantry, or the larder. The national wealth of France consists in the nation's superiority in taste and artistic skill. The French arrange a few artificial flowers with an exquisite understanding of the juxtaposition of colours and the combination of forms, and make us pay for a 'bouquet' on a bonnet from fifty to sixty francs, whilst the raw material costs from five to six francs; they do the same in terra-cotta, bronze, or iron. So long as everyone with us thinks himself justified in having his own bad taste gratified, because he can pay for it, decorative artists will serve that bad taste in all our household details. Art- history comprises not merely measurements of temples, heights of spires in feet, or of statues in cubits and inches.

We have of late years made gigantic strides in the advancement of street-architecture, though we do not yet know how to create perspective views of artistic beauty; we still indulge too much in mediæval crookedness and unintelligible windings. We still decorate too gaudily, or, falling into the other extreme, too much in neutral colours; but we are beginning to understand that man does not live on stone and brick alone, but also on taste in arranging and decorating the stone. London, with the exception of some of our monstrous railway bridges and railway stations, begins to look worthy of its position as the centre of the world's commerce. Our streets have lately put on some stately 'Sunday clothing' in terra-cotta, Portland cement, and iron railings. Our glass and china, our furniture and carpets, begin to have more variegated patterns, though I am sorry to hear that foreigners are still generally appointed as the principal modellers. I base this assertion on the Report on the National Competition of the Works of Schools of Art for 1876, in which the examiners say: 'Our want of that workman-like power over the material, which is so noticeable in all French productions in modelling, is still very conspicuous. As long as this continues a large proportion of the decorative figure or ornamental designs in relief made for the English market will be in the hands of foreign artists.' The panacea of this evil will and can only be a higher intellectual training, not merely of the faculty of imitating and combining given forms in nature, but of endowing them with ideal beauty, fostered by a correct study of art-history.

There are no illustrations to this work, but I have annexed a long list of illustrated works on art. My aim in teaching, and writing, has been consistently to induce my hearers and readers to think and study for themselves. Bad or even good wood-cuts are by no means essential in art-books, for we possess in the British, Christy's, and South Kensington Museums such invaluable art-collections, that we may write books without illustrations if we can induce readers and students to verify what we say by a diligent study of these specimens. Theoretical generalisation ought always to precede our special studies. We only then know when we are able to systematise, to group, to draw analogies, or to arrange our details according to some general principle. If we enter on any study without having prepared our mind to grasp the connecting links in an artistic or scientific subject, our knowledge of an incoherent mass of details will only dwarf our understanding, instead of brightening and clearing it, and we shall become technically-trained machines, instead of self-conscious and self-reasoning creators in any branch of art. The Art Library at the South Kensington Museum is, without any exaggeration, the completest in the world; it abounds in the best illustrated works of all nations. Art-books with bad or indifferent illustrations, or even with good illustrations, are not so much needed as art-books with unbiased theories, esthetical principles, and philosophical ideas, which may awaken the power of reasoning in both readers and students. It is only too often the case that, in seeing bad illustrations, the student imagines he knows everything about the work spoken of and produced in outlines. He must, however, go and see for himself. Art has its own fairy domain and its own most catholic realm, in which everyone is welcome who can contribute to the improvement, delight, and happiness of man. To induce readers and students to visit, with some fore-thought and fore-knowledge, our vast and unparalleled art-collections, and to convince them, that to detach the study of art from a correct appreciation of the ideas that engendered its forms, is an impossibility, was the task I set myself in writing the pages of this book.

LONDON: *October 1876.*

MANUAL

OF THE

HISTORICAL DEVELOPMENT OF

ART

CHAPTER I.

PROLEGOMENA.

Gazing at the heavens on a starry night, we see, in addition to myriads of sparkling worlds floating in the air, a great quantity of nebulæ—either decayed systems of worlds, or worlds in formation. Worlds which have lost their centre of gravity and fallen to pieces; or worlds which are seeking, according to the general law of gravitation, to form a central body by the attraction of cosmical ether. The one phenomenon is that of destruction, the other that of new formation.

This double process is continually repeating itself in the development of art. Consciously or unconsciously, the artists of the different nations, at different periods, devote themselves to the dissolution or reconstruction of artistic products. To become acquainted with this process, to trace the elements from which art is built up, or the influences which engender a dissolution of artistic forms, is of the greatest importance.

Art must be looked upon as the phenomenal result of certain religious, social, intellectual, and natural conditions. To trace these conditions, their origin, influence, and gradual development, by means of a critical and historical investigation into the causes which produced them, will be our task. For art is like a mirror: whatever looks into it is reflected by it. If a poor, untrained imagination stares into it, no one must be astonished that poor and distorted images result.

It is usually accepted as a truism that the essence of art is the reproduction of nature. Wherever, then, nature were reflected in the 'Art- mirror,' we should have the best work of art. But this is not so. For art has to reflect the phenomena of the makrokosm as a subjectively-conceived mikrokosm. We do not see matters as they really are, as each thing is surrounded by a thick fog of incidental, objective, and subjective peculiarities. This fog must be cleared away, to show us nature in the bright colours of intellectual and self-conscious idealisation.

Nature furnishes us with mortar and stones for the building, but the architect's intellectual power has to arrange these elements, and to bring them into an artistic shape. Nature furnishes us with flowers, trees, animals and men; but the ornamental designer or painter has to reproduce and to group them so as to impress the forms of nature with an intellectual vitality.

Before the artist proceeds to his work he must become thoroughly conscious of the distinction between the SUBLIME and the BEAUTIFUL. It is essential that he should draw a strict line of demarcation between the two conceptions; in order not to waste his energies on the reproduction of objects which are beyond the powers of art.

During the long period of the cosmical formation of the earth, when mountains were towered upon mountains, rocks upheaved, islands submerged; when air, water, fire, and solid matter seemed engaged in never- ending conflict—nature was *sublime*. The dynamic force appeared to be the only element, and the counterbalancing static force was without influence. Gradually vegetable and animal life, in their first crude forms, commenced to show themselves.

Zoophites were developed into megatheriums and mastodons. Mammoths and elks sported on plains which now form the mountain tops of our continents. Scarcely visible coral animals were still engaged in constructing mountain chains, and a luxuriant vegetation covered the small continents. Such transformations, convulsions, and changes are gigantic, grand, awe-inspiring—sublime, but not beautiful. Whenever nature is at work, disturbing the air with electric currents or shaking huge mountains, so that they bow their lofty summits, or when the dry soil is rent asunder, and sends forth streams of glowing lava, we are in the presence of the sublime, not of the beautiful. Whenever man's nature is overawed, whenever he is made to feel his impotence by the phenomena of nature, he faces the sublime. In art, only a few divinely-gifted and chosen geniuses have ever reached the sublime.

When, however, the cosmical forces had expended their exuberant powers—when a diversified climate had produced those plants and animals that surround us—when man appeared on this revolving planet, and by degrees reached self-consciousness as his highest development—then only beauty acquired existence and dominion on earth. Without men capable of understanding what is beautiful, art would have no meaning.

The aim of science is to vanquish error; the province of industry to subdue matter, and the vocation of art to produce beauty. The artist must not neglect science, for he has to be truthful, as error is ugly; he must make himself well acquainted with matter, for he has to use, to transform, and to modify it; and, finally, he has to hallow this scientifically-treated matter by impressing it with the stamp of ideal beauty.

The attainment of this, the perfection of art, has been slow and gradual. Though art, like all the inventions, took its origin in want and necessity, the *utilitarian* spirit is the very bane of art, for art flourishes only under the influence of the very highest intellectual culture.

Nature produces like art; but the products of nature are the unconscious effects of the immutable law of causation. The products of art are the results of the conscious intellectual power of the artist. It is the free, yet well-regulated, consciousness of the artist that elevates his productions into works of art. Undoubtedly the great store-house of the artist is nature; he learns from nature how to ornament, but he has to discern, to combine, to adapt, to select, his forms. The whole success of the artist, in whatever branch he works, must depend on an earnest and severe use of the word CHOICE.

'He is truly great who knows the value of everything, and distinguishes what is more or less great, and what is most estimable, so as to begin from that, and to apply the genius, and fix the desires upon the execution of things worthy and great.' This mode of thinking was followed by the most celebrated and enlightened artists from the ancient Greeks to our own time. They knew to distinguish that which was most worthy in nature, and to this they directed their study, diligence, and industry. Inferior geniuses, because they are attached to mediocrity, believe that a mere clinging to nature constitutes all art; and the lowest artists are enchanted with the minutiæ of little works, taking them for principal things; so that human ignorance passes from the trifling to the useless, from the useless to the ugly, and from the ugly to the false and chimerical.

In treating of the historical development of art, to enable artists to distinguish and to choose the best, and not only to imitate but to create consciously for themselves, it is necessary to make them *theoretically* acquainted with the progress of art.

To trace historically the changes art had to undergo is necessary for all really self-conscious artists. Art with us is still looked upon as entirely subject to individual taste. Everyone thinks himself competent to have an opinion on products of art. '*De gustibus non est disputandum*' is heard not only in our drawing-rooms, but also in art-circles. This false and utterly untenable adage is the cause of the chaotic anarchy in our art-world.

So little as there can be differences in truth, can there be differences in beauty. It is the duty of philosophy to strive for truth; it is the task of the theoretical artist to point out what is beautiful.

We may treat art from three different points of view:—

1. From a *realistic* point of view, taking nature and geometry as its basis.

2. From an *historical* point of view; showing by antiquarian and

archæological researches its gradual development.

3. From a *critical* point of view; propounding abstract principles of speculative philosophy and esthetics as applied to art.

A.

The *realistic* school has in later years had an immense influence with us. Art-critics have almost gone so far as to demand from the artist a correct rendering of the very stratification of rocks; or of the different kinds of soil, to such a degree that the farmer should be able to recognise the ground in which to sow oats or wheat. Pictures, according to these estheticists, should be geological maps, mineralogical collections, and, so far as flowers are concerned, perfect herbariums. When this school takes up the archæological view, it clings with indomitable tenacity to given forms, and checks imagination. Art is then only to be handled as the Greeks or Romans practised it. Either the Gothic or the Renaissance style is to be slavishly imitated. This school has one great drawback: it considers all things natural beautiful, and looks upon an imitation of that which *was* as better than an exertion of the self-creative originality of the artist.

B.

The *historical* school endeavours to bring before our eyes the past, so as to enable us to understand the present, and to influence the future of art. This school has followed two divergent directions, the Antique and the Gothic, the classical or romantic; the one holding that everything beautiful must be based upon Greek patterns; the other that all beauty is confined to the Gothic. The writers of these two schools bewilder the students; either driving them into a cold, soulless imitation of classic forms, or forcing them to sacrifice everything to trefoils, pinnacles, tracery, finials, buttresses, thin spires, painted windows, and pointed arches.

C.

The *critical* school indulges in tall phrases, mere hypothetical paradoxes, often startling the world with speculations of the wildest sort. Art-critics frequently roam in the spheres of surmises; they have their good points, but often neglect reality, or the historical ground; they sacrifice everything to the idea, which is with them the only productive basis of everything existing in art.

We shall try to be realistic, as it would be vain to attempt to detach art from the influences of nature; for art borrows its principal elements from the impressions of natural phenomena. We shall be historical, and point out the progressive development of art; and, lastly, we shall endeavour to be critical. Speculative philosophy has its merits in art. Esthetical criticism suggests new ideas, and new ideas engender new forms. We shall endeavour to adopt from each of the three schools what is best. Our age is an age of eclecticism in art. We must, however, try to prepare for a period of original vitality, which can only be done by avoiding one-sidedness and heedless originality. We shall try to suggest and to excite in our readers new thoughts. As music speaks in sounds, poetry in words, so art in forms; but music, poetry, and art are subject to certain rules, without which harmony would become dissonance, poetry an inflated prose, and art a tasteless entity, of which quaintness will be the only distinguishing attribute. What we call our sense of beauty is based on those laws which make the existence of the universe possible.

The Greeks used for beauty in art the same word, as for order, or the perfect arrangement of the universe. The word κόσμος {kosmos} (from which we have 'cosmetic,' any beautifying application) may teach us how we should look upon works of art, which ought to be a reflection of the general laws ruling nature.

Two forces guide our material and intellectual life. We possess two means of acquiring knowledge and of practising art: reason and experience. Impressions from without are the everlasting source of all our conceptions. Hunger and thirst drive us to seek nourishment, to become fishers, hunters, herdsmen, or agriculturists. Cold and heat force us to seek a shelter, to construct wigwams, huts, dwellings on piles, cottages, houses, palaces, and temples.

Though order and harmony prevail in the outer world, every atom of the universe is endowed with an unconscious will or life of its own. Atoms seek atoms according to inherent laws, or fly from or annihilate one another. The whole process of life around us appears to be one never-ending struggle. Apparently there rules only the law of chance and might; what cannot conquer is conquered.

History is one long catalogue of appearing and disappearing nations, of devouring and devoured kingdoms and empires. It is as though generation after generation had emerged from the spectral past into the sanguinary present, to destroy or to be destroyed. This conflict in the outer world is seconded by everlasting conflicts in our inner world. Fear, hope, love— passions of all kinds, imagination and reality, ignorance and knowledge, pride and humility, prejudice and wisdom, form an intellectual hurricane not less destructive than the warfare of the cosmical elements. Religion, Science, and Art, this divine triad, step in. Religion excites in us the hope of higher and better morals; science creates consciousness of the laws according to which we are governed; the link between cause and effect is traced, and the rule of arbitrary chance narrowed. Lastly, art throws its beautifying halo on everything. Thus these three are instrumental in elevating our mind, expanding our intellectual powers, and bringing harmony and beauty into the eternal conflict. Faith is the element of religion, experience the element of knowledge, and beauty the element of art. Whilst faith and experience are possible without an artistic elevation of the mind, art must combine the elements of religion and science, and form through beauty a visible link between these elements.

The sublime, as we have said, rules in the universe. Clouds chase one another and are subject to everlasting changes. Trees cover the surface of our globe, forming woods at random. Mountains are towered up, as if hurled together by chance. Seas form a bewildering variety of coasts. Streams wind their paths through mountains and valleys with capricious irregularity. All these phenomena confuse and oppress us, they engender an incomprehensible, indistinct feeling in us. But so soon as we begin with our intellectual force to sift, to separate, and to detach single phenomena from the general mass—as soon as *choice* begins to work, the isolated phenomenon displays at once its symmetrical beauty.

This is the case with crystallisations, the *first* artistic products of unconscious nature. If we look at a vast plain covered with snow, a feeling of sublime cold and wretchedness overcomes us; but if we take up one isolated snow-flake, and place it under a microscope, we find that the elements of the crystallised drop of water surround with harmonious regularity a common centre, which is the body, from which radiate as integral parts the diversified forms of the flake. In studying snow-flakes, we find that the three dimensions of space—height, breadth, and depth, limited by symmetry, proportion and direction—are the principal elements of every form which in itself has to represent a detached total. In all the crystallisations there is one 'momentum' of formation—the centre, from which all the parts emanate perfectly well-balanced and complete in themselves. The elements of which all artistic works, whether natural or produced by men, are composed, are the straight line and the waving line. With these elements we can obtain the three principal conditions of every work of art—symmetry, proportion, and direction. Snow-flakes may be used in any direction, and therefore they may be set down as without distinct direction. The rays with their radiation, however, are formed according to the principal law of the universe. They represent the *dynamic* force; they strive at isolation from the centre which must be looked upon as their *static* momentum. Thus in the first artistic products of nature positive and negative, or rather dynamic and static forces are clearly perceptible. The horizontal line is the representative of the static, whilst the vertical line is the indicator of the dynamic force.

SYMMETRY *is a perfect equality of form to the right and left of a vertical line on a horizontal base.*

EURYTHMY *consists in a repetition of variegated forms.*

In order to produce eurythmy we must confine symmetry within a certain compass; for this purpose we have the *frame*. Our doors are nothing but frames for the entering or departing individuals; as our windows are frames for the landscape, sky, or walls on which we look, or for ourselves when seen from without. The frame, whether it be real or imaginary, as the correct limitation of forms, is of the very highest importance in decorative and pictorial art.

Eurythmy may be alternating. This alternating principle is observed in metopes and triglyphs. The alternation may be interrupted by a cæsura (a mark or sign of rest). Masks, heads of lions, or any other figures may form the cæsura, as decorative elements in the long lines of the tops of houses, palaces, or temples. The cæsura, combined with eurythmy and symmetry, will give us the best patterns for flat decorations, as in carpets, paper-hangings, keramic works and metal or wood ornaments.

Applying what we have said of crystallisations to plants and animals, we find that symmetry is undoubtedly the predominant element in every flower. The plant developes itself from the ground, which is its horizontal basis. It shoots up generally in a vertical direction, as a radiation from our globe. In trees the branches, leaves, flowers, and fruits are clustered around a central line in eurythmical proportion. In flowers symmetry predominates, whilst in trees eurythmy prevails. In considering the branches of a tree in relation to its trunk, we find the same symmetry and eurythmy, though the direction be changed. We can study these forms best in plants of the coal formation—the Sigillaria, Stigmaria, Lepidodendra, and Calamites; and in ferns, fir-trees, cedars, &c.

In the palm tree we see most distinctly the working of the conflicting forces of nature. The dynamic force of vitality drives the stem upwards, and the static force of gravitation towards a common centre is expressed in the beautifully-drooping curves of the leaves. Symmetry is further to be observed in the lowest animals, in polyps, radiata, &c., but never in higher species, in which it is not planimetrical (viz., cannot be treated on a plane) but linear, none of them being perfectly regular in any of the three dimensions of space.

Man is altogether different from the products of the mineral or vegetable kingdoms, which give us the prototypes of conventional art. Man is not in all directions symmetrical in the strict sense of the word. He has not two heads, two noses, or two mouths. The component elements in man are different. His very nature revolts against a planimetrical treatment. This was perfectly understood by the masters of arabesque, who have always turned man half into a fish, a plant, a serpent, a tendril, or some other form adapted for planimetrical treatment. Eurythmy and *Proportion* are the elements of higher organic forms—to which must be added direction or *Action*, and finally *Expression*.

In most of the lower animals the vertebræ are horizontal, and coincident with the moving direction of the whole creature. In man, on the other hand, the vertebræ are vertical, in opposition to the moving direction which is horizontal; so that the vertebræ and line of motion are at right angles.

In men, detached as they are from their horizontal basis, the soil—carrying their static force with them, and able to change it either from below, upwards, or from front to back—*direction* is of a complicated nature, and must be well studied, so as not to produce incongruities.

If a woman or man were painted with the most beautiful and expressive face, but having it twisted round, so as to crown the spine, we should turn from it with disgust, as anyone endowed with the sense of beauty turns from acrobats, because the natural laws of gravitation and symmetry would be violated. This illustration may serve to prove, that there are laws in art with which we must make ourselves acquainted, and that the mere 'right of taste,' in the general sense of the words, cannot promote the understanding and appreciation of our artistic productions.

Next to direction we have to take into account *motion*. This element is in animals and men produced by their inherent dynamic force, counteracted by the body itself, which represents the static force, or the '*vis inertiæ*,' chaining them to the centre of gravitation in the earth.

Motion again leads to *expression* and *action*.

Expression is the effect of the conflicting static or dynamic (passive or active) state of the mind, so far as this state is revealed in the lineaments of the face.

Action is the effect of the same conflicting force so far as it is expressed in the limbs and the position of the body.

A third force, which is often used unconsciously, necessarily grows out of these elements—the controlling or ruling element, or, as Vitruvius has it, '*the principle of authority*.' This element points out the preponderance of certain forms as the visible representatives of the general principles which we have stated, bringing into the *variety* of details, harmony and *unity*. This controlling element stands to the surrounding and united parts in the same relation as the key-note to a harmonious melody. Without that key-note no harmony—without the controlling element no beauty, were possible.

Having proceeded step by step from the formation of matter in crystals to man, we may set down the following as the five principal elements necessary to beauty in art:—

1. Symmetry.
2. Eurythmy.
3. Proportion.
4. Direction or motion.
5. Expression.

α. Symmetry has already been amply treated.

β. Eurythmy is either stereometric or planimetric. It is stereometric in balls and in regular solid bodies, such as the tetrahedron, a figure of four equal triangular faces, or the polyhedron, a figure with many sides. These forms are symmetrical without any controlling element. Such an element shows itself first in the ellipsoid—distinct from the oval—in the prism, and the pyramid. Planimetric eurythmy preponderates in snow-crystals, flowers, plants, trees, and the lowest animals.

The controlling element shows itself in the grouping of the single parts round a common centre, which is often distinguished by a contrast in forms or colours. It is unconsciously expressed by a sign or mark.

Ornamentation takes its origin in the effort to express, to designate, or to mark out the controlling element. The ornamented object has only then a meaning, when it expresses visibly the hidden idea of the controlling element, say the idea of fastening or keeping together, as in clasps, brooches, buckles; or the idea of equilibrium, as in earrings. Such signs or marks were very early used, and are spread all over our globe; they developed into the rough tombs in Phrygia, Greece and Italy; took a higher form in Central America and Assyria; became crystallised in the Pyramids; and attained the highest perfection in the tombs of Mausolus, Augustus, and Hadrian. The mark or sign is also used in games, as on race-courses, in the stadium, the circus, or the amphitheatre. A more distinct expression is gained when the mark or sign, as divine statue, altar, &c., is surrounded by rhythmically-arranged circles or encompassing walls, as the visible expression of the union of the many, or variety, for one religious or ceremonial purpose. The mark or sign reflects, on the one hand, the idea of harmony, whilst, on the other, the rhythmically-arranged surroundings form an impressive total, heightening the force of the controlling element. This law explains the awe, veneration, mysterious feeling, and secret fear with which men at all times have looked upon the central mark or sign, whether in the simple stone-circles of Abury, Stonehenge, and Carnac, the rock-hewn temples of India, the temples of Egypt, Greece, and Rome, or the synagogues and churches of our own times.

Next to the controlling element, we must take into consideration the grouping of the whole object on a horizontal basis around a vertical axis. This axis becomes the seat of the linear, symmetrical, controlling element. It is especially marked by richly ornamented reliefs or by gaudier colours, so pronounced that the other parts of the ornamented object appear as mere accompaniments of the horizontal and vertical lines. Remarkable in their incongruity, but often unsurpassed in the application of this principle, are the tattooed heads of savages, in which the linear central line is ornamented symmetrically on both sides of the face—the prominent parts being marked by spirals to make them appear still more prominent.

γ. Proportion, as an element of art, cannot work by itself, but must be considered in relation to its parts and the controlling element. Proportion consists of a basis, a middle piece, and a dominant. To illustrate this, we have in plants and trees, the root (basis), the stem or trunk (middle piece), and the top, crown or flower (dominant).

The basis represents the cosmical element of gravitation by powerful masses, simplicity of forms, and dark colouring. This law was especially observed in the excellent decoration of the Roman houses at Pompeii, and is still followed in our wainscoting. We try unconsciously to express the static force from which the dynamic rises.

The middle piece, growing out of the basis, is supported and supporting; it unites the elements of the basis with the top or dominant; it is the connecting link between these two extremes. The basis stands in the same relation to the middle piece, as the latter to the dominant.

The dominant harmoniously reconciles the conflicting forces of striving upwards, and being drawn downwards. Variations in these relations are not only allowable, but form the very element of the artist's creative originality— so long as he clearly marks the purpose of the three elements.

δ. Direction, or motion, in its highest form is only to be found in man. In fishes the axis, or seat of the controlling element, is not fixed as in plants. If fishes pursue some point of attraction, they shoot forward in a straight line, so that a conflict between the static and dynamic forces is never visible in them, because the axes of these two forces are always one and the same. This is entirely different with birds, quadrupeds, and especially with men, who, to a great extent, are masters of their motions; for will, as the force of their conscious intellect, changes their static as well as their dynamic direction.

Man is the symbol of earthly perfection. In him all laws and elements of the universe are united. What is with inanimate nature a static point of attraction, is with man *moral*; the dynamic force of activity, is with him *intellect*. Animals also work, but their works are in general the result of their instinct; whilst with man, though he may also be ruled by unconscious impulses, intellect—self-conscious intellect—is the mainspring of all his actions. These have a reflecting mirror in the glance of his eyes, whilst the changing and changeable effects of scorn, love, wrath, delight, happiness, or despair are pictured in the mysteriously-woven lineaments of his countenance.

ε. Expression, of intellectual and moral impressions, is most concentrated in MAN.

CHAPTER II.

ETHNOLOGY IN ITS BEARING ON ART.

Man is placed on this globe as a radius,—a detached radius. The axis of his body is part of the diameter of the earth, and divides him into symmetrical halves. A line, that passes at an equal distance through the double organs, also divides the single ones into two equally-arranged portions. We possess two eyes, to receive the impression of light; two ears, to be touched simultaneously by the waves of sound; two tubes are opened, to receive the refined, imponderable bodies producing odour; the lips are grouped round a marked central line to the chin. We have two shoulders, two arms, two hands, two legs, two feet; both hands have the same number of fingers, and both feet the same number of toes. On the other hand, the parts, taken by themselves, break through all the laws of symmetrical uniformity. The arms are longer than the trunk; the legs are longer than the arms; hands end in unequally- subdivided fingers; feet in similarly-treated toes. But notwithstanding this want of symmetry there is perfect harmony in the relations of the parts to the whole, so that man may be said to be the very master-piece of creation. In considering the controlling linear elements, in the three grand groups into which humanity may be best divided for a comprehensive study of art, we find that the very fundamental facial lines differ.

I.

We have first the Negro, the fossil, the *black*, or antediluvian man. The eyes, nostrils, and lips are drawn downwards in melancholy lines. He is cross-toothed (*prognathous*), triangular-headed, has flat feet, long heels, an imperfect pelvis, but a very powerful digestive organ, and a correspondingly enormous mouth.

The Oceanic Negro is the best example of this group. He is slow of temperament, unskilled, his mechanical ingenuity being that of a child; he never goes beyond geometrical ornamentation; builds tumuli or triangular wigwams; lives on what he finds by chance, and, at the best, hunts or fishes. His reasoning faculty is very limited, his imagination slow, but his perceptive faculties (the senses) are highly developed. He is altogether incapable of rising from a fact to a principle. He cannot create beauty, for he is indifferent to any ideal conception. He possesses only from 75–83½ cubic inches of brain, his facial angle being about 85½ degrees. This lowest group of mankind branches off into different types. The general features of the group have neither changed nor improved. The Negro is still the woolly-headed, animal-faced being, represented on the tombs of the Pharaohs, because his bodily structure, his facial lines have not altered during thousands of years. In studying the artistic products, the customs and manners of this group, we can picture to ourselves the state in which Asiatics and Europeans must have lived during the oldest stone period. The Negroes use the same kind of flint instruments, manufacture the same crude kind of pottery, adorn their clubs, paddles, and the cross-beams of their huts with the same rope and serpent-like entangled windings and twistings, that are found in various parts of the globe of pre-historic times. The ruling lines of the face and head of the Negro are reflected in his triangular or mound-like architectural constructions.

II.

Next we have the Turanian (from *tura*, 'swiftness of a horse'), the Mongol, the square or short-headed (*brachikephalous*), the traditionary, the *yellow* man. His face is flat, his nose deeply sunken between his prominent cheeks; his reasoning faculty is developed only to a certain degree. He has small, oblique eyes, the lines being turned upwards, expressing cunning and jocularity. His mouth is less powerful than that of the negro. He has broad shoulders, an expansive chest, thin and small bow legs, as if formed to use those of horses instead of his own; he is an excellent rider, but a slow though steady walker. He looks on nature with a nomadic shepherd's eye, and not with that of a settled artist. He excels in technical ability, has great powers of imitation, can produce geometrical ornamentation of the most complicated and ingenious character, and a realistic imitation of flowers, butterflies, and birds, but has no sense for perspective and no talent for shading. He is incapable of drawing the human form. Sculpture of a higher kind is unknown to him, though he can execute perfectly marvellous carvings, which, though quaint in design and composition, are wanting in proportion and expression. Faithful to his nomadic traditions, and the lines of his head and face, his architectural constructions take an according form. Like his facial lines, the roofs of his houses are twisted upwards.

The amount of brain in the Turanian averages 83½ cubic inches, and his facial angle is 87½ degrees.

III.

Finally we have the Aryan, the long or oval-headed man (*dolichokephalous*), the historical, the *white* man, the crowning product of the cosmical forces of nature. His facial lines are composed of the two conflicting elements, the horizontal and the vertical line, and are framed in by an oval. His amount of brain is on an average 92 cubic inches, and his facial angle 90 degrees. His development is not limited. This group of mankind, though divided into many different types (races or nations), which have arisen from an intermixture with the other two groups, or through the influences of climate, food, and the aspect of nature, stands at the highest point of civilisation. As the lines of his face are admirably counterbalanced, and his body is a master-piece of regularity and proportion, he has tried to establish a perfect balance between the conflicting forces in his moral and intellectual nature. To him exclusively we owe art in its highest sense. Once he stood on the same level with the primitive black savage, then he advanced to the ingenuity of the yellow man, and left both far behind him in his gradual but always progressive development. He surpasses the other two groups of humanity, not only in technical skill, but especially in inventive and reasoning power, critical discernment, and purity of artistic taste. The white man alone, has produced idealised master-pieces in sculpture and painting.

The white man in his architecture uses either the horizontal or the vertical line, or both; he takes the triangular building of the negro and places it on the square tent of the yellow man, making his house as perfect as possible; he goes further, and, in accordance with his powerfully-arched brow, over-arches not only rivers and chasms, but builds his magnificent cupolas and pointed arches, the acme of architectural forms.

Ethnology then serves us as a foundation for the study of art in its different phases.

Conforming to the general tendency of modern science, we have tried to express the cause of the artistic development of the three groups of humanity by figures; we have measured the seat and instrument of our intellectual faculty, and have thus tried to leave the sphere of mere conjecture, or unfounded opinion, in order to place the phenomena of art-history on a firm basis. Though art, undoubtedly, belongs 'to the magic circle of the imagination, and the inner powers of the mind,' those powers are dependent on our very bodily construction, the amount of brain and the facial angle. We do not deal in mere hypothesis, but submit to our readers a complete theory borne out by facts.

In considering the frontispiece of our manual, representing the 'TREE OF ART,' we can visibly trace the slow and gradual development of the white man. The negro fixes our attention only as savage; the yellow man has a line of his own, and has remained stationary in his artistic development; the white man has passed through the savage stages, and by his own exertions, undergoing various phases of rise and decline (the real signs of historical vitality), has steadily progressed till he began to attempt, and to succeed in bringing about, 'a harmonious connection between the representation of nature and the expression of awakened emotion, and a mysterious analogy between the emotions of his mind and the phenomena perceived by his senses.'

As all phenomena must take place in *space* and *time* (the two fundamental forms of all existence), the products of art must also have been executed under these two conditions, and can therefore be treated *historically*.

Space is the expansion and extension of the forces of nature into the infinite. Time is the limitation of this activity. Without space no object could arrive at completion. Without time the subject would be eternal. These are the two counteracting elements. The one, space, is positive—the other, time, negative. Time is either relative or absolute. If relative, it can be measured by an ascertained succession of events. If absolute, it becomes measurable by years. In both we can trace a gradual and successive development of artistic forms. In general, time relative, with its succession of products, is more reliable than time labelled with voluntary and more than doubtful dates. For instance, we cannot measure the periods of the formation of the earth's crust by years, and still we are perfectly convinced that the *tertiary* formation could not have taken place before the *primary*; thus we are justified in assuming that the iron period must have succeeded the stone or bronze period; bronze instruments never being found with iron handles, whilst iron blades have ornamented wooden or bronze handles. Man naturally scarcely ever uses the worse material for a practical purpose when he has once found a better one; but he will use the softer material as a means of ornamentation.

That we have plenty of 'survivals' in art, as well as in nature, does not in any way militate against the strict logic of facts. The lowest forms of animals have mostly survived (like the lowest forms of ornamentation), yet no one can doubt or deny the gradual and systematic development of the vegetable and animal kingdoms. If we find no fragments of pottery in Australia, New Zealand, or the Polynesian islands, we cannot assume that a grand and powerful civilisation has perished there, leaving no traces behind. In finding different kinds of pottery, gradually improving even in the quality of the material—the clay being first unwashed, then mixed with grains of quartz and felspar, next carefully washed, then sun-baked, then fire-baked; first hand and then wheel turned, and at last glazed, unornamented or ornamented—we cannot assume that the order was inverted, and that man first ornamented glazed pottery, which he turned out on the wheel, and then went back to unwashed clay and hand-made pottery. The 'degeneration theory' has exploded as entirely as the geocentric and anthropocentric theories have vanished. We know that man, like flowers, trees, rocks and animals, is the product of the combined forces of nature and the influences of climate and food, and that his religious, social, and political conditions are closely reflected in his art. As little as our globe is the centre of the universe, or man the centre of creation, so little did art or science spring at once perfectly armed, provided with spear and shield, from Jupiter's head like blue-eyed Athene. In a certain sense art and science are both of divine origin, but only so far as the originating and creative power is concerned, which, once set in motion, had to grow and to develop according to definite and immutable laws. To trace this development step by step in general outlines, from time relative to the mythical and traditional periods, and thence to the age of history, is the aim of our manual. In generalising thus, and separating the special from the universal, we are enabled to embrace at once with greater clearness a wider range of knowledge, and to give to the treatment of art-history a more elevated and useful character. By a suppression of details, the great periods and features of a common development are rendered more intelligible, and our reasoning faculty is enabled to grasp that which might otherwise escape our limited powers of comprehension.

CHAPTER III.

PRE-HISTORIC AND SAVAGE ART.

Art, like nature, is its own interpreter. A well-finished pattern has not preceded a more simple one; circular ornamentations are of a later date than ornamentations with straight lines. The cave-habitation must have been in use before the construction of independent temples. Art must have had a beginning like language; for it is a language—a language in forms, speaking to our eyes. If what the Arabs say is true, that the best description is that in which the ear is transformed into an eye, the best picture will be one that transforms our eyes into ears. Art speaks through light, as language through sounds. We have tried to discover by means of philology—which in modern times has become a science—a more or less close relationship between idioms and idioms; in the same way we try to trace some general primitive types from which we may deduce the innumerable works of art.

In times long by-gone we find traces of man's inventive and decorative force. The products of that force even in pre-historic ages widely differ in their degrees of workmanship. There are more or less finished hatchets, chisels, knives, arrow-heads, paal-stabs, celts and armlets. The ornamentation, from mere varying straight lines, goes over into spiral forms of different direction and combination. We have therefore no difficulty in classifying the products of pre-historic art in the following way:—

    a. The Palæolithic, or old stone age.

    b. The Neolithic, or new stone age.

    c. The Bronze age, and

    d. The Iron age.

The first two subdivisions belong to savage life, the third to the mythical or traditionary, and the fourth to the historical periods.

During the old stone age we have scarcely any traces of ornamentation; during the new stone age we find some attempts at geometrical lines, and some sketches of animals on ivory blades; during the bronze age we have winding and twisting patterns of excellent geometrical design; and, finally, during the iron age, animals and even human forms are used as means of ornamentation.

During the pre-historic period of man's artistic development we find a peculiar similarity between his dwellings and his tombs. The mountain cavern, and the hut constructed of beams and boughs, covered with skins, were undoubtedly men's first stately palaces. The very oldest traditions bear out this statement. The earliest inhabitants of Greece dwelt in mountain caverns. The people of Siberia, anterior to the Samoyedes, lived, according to Erman, in subterranean caves. The Kyklops of Homer are but nomads, residing in mountain caverns. Of the Hittites, a tribe in Canaan in the times of Abraham, it is recorded that they buried their dead in caves. But it is an incontestable fact that the burial-places resembled the dwellings of the pre- historic man. Crypts, catacombs, and rock-hewn temples may be set down as having originated from man's first mountain home. The tombs of the Tartars in Kasan resemble their houses on a small scale. A Circassian tomb resembles a Circassian cottage. The tombs of the Karaite Jews in the valley of Jehoshaphat, are like their houses. Laplanders live in caves. The aborigines of Germany and France, the contemporaries of the mammoth, rhinoceros, auerochs and elk, dwelt in caves, as their bones are found mingled with those of these now extinct animals, together with various implements, such as adzes, flint arrows, stone knives, and even, as in the cave at Perigord on the borders of the Dordogne, works of art of great artistic power. Jordanes, in his 'De Rebus Geticis,' mentions people in Sweden (Scania) living like wild animals in caves, cut out in the rocks. But the nomad savage could find such dwellings only where there were mountains. If he wandered out of such a district into the plains, and wanted to shelter himself from the inclemency of the weather, he had to collect blocks of stone, and to form with them artificial caves. In this manner cromlechs, Dös, Dyss or dolmens, and gallery chambers arose, in which the long, narrow gallery corresponds to the confined entrance of the mountain-cave, and the chamber to the cavern.

By degrees man began to construct detached houses for himself, and at last temples for his god or gods. No traces of temples are found in pre-historic times, except in the Western hemisphere. The Stiens of Cambodia, in the central parts of Cochin-China, have no temples. From the southern promontory of Africa to far beyond the banks of the Zambesi no temples are found. The pastoral and agricultural people of Madagascar have no temples, though they have huts and houses, ornamented pottery, and are to a certain degree acquainted with textile art. Before man constructs a temple he constructs a house, to protect himself, his herds, and family from wild animals, but above all from his still more dreaded fellow-creature, in whom he sees a dangerous rival. This propensity serves to explain the origin of lake-dwellings—the most ancient proofs of man's constructing capacity, and of his talent to unite for a certain purpose, and to enclose a given space. Herodotus already tells us of a settlement on Lake Prasias, the modern Tachyno (in Rumelia, European Turkey), where men lived on platforms, supported by tall piles. Abulfeda, the Syrian geographer (b. 1273; d. 1313), speaks of Christian fishermen living in wooden huts, built on piles in one of the Apamean lakes on the Orontes (in Asia). The Papuans of New Guinea still live in such pile-dwellings, the floors of which are supported by rudely-carved human figures, an attempt at telamons. These are 'survivals,' but the lake-dwellings in Italy and Switzerland belong to pre-historic times. In tracing their different modes of construction, we find three periods of a progressive architectural development recorded.

We have pile-dwellings of the most primitive construction. Rough piles were used, pointed with the aid of fire or with stone hatchets, later with bronze, and finally with iron tools. They were placed either close together or in pairs, or wide apart—generally in regular order. The heads of the piles were brought to a level above the water to receive the beams of the platform, which were fastened down with wooden pins. Later, as an improvement, mortices were cut in the tops of the vertical piles to receive the cross-beams.

Other constructions, especially those near Nidau (niedere Au, lower meadow), are built on a foundation artificially strengthened with stones, which is, undoubtedly, an improvement on the former method.

Experience taught the pre-historic architects that the piles were not quite safe, and ought to have some support against the turbulent risings of the lake. This produced the still more improved fascine constructions, which certainly gave still greater strength to the dwelling. The platform did not rest on mere piles but on artificial foundations, built up from the bottom with horizontal layers of sticks or small branches of trees, the vertical piles serving as connecting links to the whole construction.

Cranoges, or wooden islands, are chiefly found in Ireland and Scotland. They differ from the fascine constructions in that they frequently were built on natural islands, or on shallows approaching to this character. The huts built upon these pile-constructions were rectangular; some may have been round, like the huts of savages, in imitation of mole-hills, the prototypes of the numerous mounds strewn all over the globe. The huts contained an artificial hearth, made of three or four slabs of stone.

That the inhabitants of the lake-dwellings were acquainted with textile art, is proved by the discovery of an innumerable quantity of clay-weights for weaving purposes, and by pieces of burnt woven flax. The crude pottery, tools and wooden pegs, fibres twisted into ropes, remains of different cereals, fruits, and domestic animals found in these settlements, clearly prove that a certain kind of family life must have existed. At all events, the inhabitants must have reached a higher degree of civilisation than some of the South-Sea Islanders of our century, who, on receiving some iron nails, planted them, in the expectation of reaping a rich crop of this valuable vegetable.

We see that in pre-historic times art was already practised, not only for a merely utilitarian but also for an ornamental and artistic purpose.

This may be said, in a much higher sense, of the pre-historic art-remains in the Western hemisphere. Art had there a threefold development, corresponding to the three groups of humanity. We find the mounds of the Negro; the pottery of the yellow man, with its quaint ornamentation; and the remarkable temples, fortresses, viaducts, and aqueducts of the Aryan group. We possess in our museums abundant specimens of the works of these three groups, as also of their singular hieroglyphic writings, resembling the first attempts of the Chinese and Egyptians to represent ideas in forms. Imagination with savages supplies the form; the mere outlines therefore suffice. The horse drawn in this way (*a*) is a real horse; (*b*) this forms a real goose; (*c*) this is the sun; and (*d*) this a real man. It is a kind of pictorial writing or ideography, to be seen for miles and miles hewn in rocks at Massaya, and practised by humanity at large, as by our own children, in the first stage of awakening consciousness.

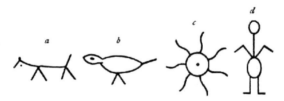

We find not only ethnological, but also philological and artistic traces of the fact, that at an unknown pre-historic period, the Western hemisphere must have been in close connection with the Eastern. The name of the supreme Divinity, Dyaus, Θεός {Theos}, Deus, is in the far West *Teotl*.

Art in the *North* of the Western hemisphere is primitive, kyklopean walls and sepulchral mounds being the principal remains.

In the *Centre* of the Continent, art bears all the traces of a gradually-developed progress. It almost reached the forms of Egypt, but stopped half way. By some means Atalanta was separated from the East, and the pyramids, temples and palaces of central America remained in the same relation to the pyramids, temples and palaces of Egypt as the *tapir* to the elephant; the *alligator* to the crocodile; and the *llama* to the camel.

The West possessed a knowledge of astronomy analogous to that of the Chinese, and their mode of ornamentation in excellent stucco reached a high degree of technical and even pictorial skill. They went so far as to represent scenes of an historical character with some degree of dramatic power; as the stucco of the rock-hewn temple of Mitla in Mexico proves. Their ornamentation is irregular and confused, like their wild vegetation, in which creepers predominate.

Some figures are striking in their resemblance to Egyptian forms.

A sculptured divinity of granite, 3½ feet high, found near a finely-built pyramid not far from Guatusco or Huatusco, is excellently worked and finished in a simple style. Still more curious is a small statue executed in lava, with a head-dress resembling those of Isis, the Sphinx, the capitals of the temple of Denderah, or at a later period those of Antinous. Even the position of the feet reminds us of the sphinx, and proves the absence of a knowledge of proportion.

In South America, in the regions of Lake Titicaca in Peru, lying at an elevation of 13,000 feet above the level of the sea, i.e. about four times as high as Snowdon, we have proofs of a very high civilisation. Artificially-constructed causeways lead over the surrounding marshes to the sacred town of Cuzco, the capital and central spot of the empire of the fabulous yet real Incas. Of those times we have a garden of the Incas, in the warmest and most sheltered part of the island, 'with its baths, and its fountains still flowing with silvery sheen and murmur.' Not far from Titicaca is the island of Coati, sacred to the moon. Here stood the famous palace of the Virgins of the Sun (reminding us of the Vestals instituted by one of the Roman rulers), flanked by two shrines dedicated to the sun and moon. These are the best-preserved specimens of American pre-historic architecture. Round Lake Umayo, on a peninsula, we find a remarkable group of ancient square burial towers, known as the Chulpas of Silustani.

Cuzco was the Rome of the south of the Western hemisphere. The town was traversed by four high-roads in the direction of the four points of the compass. It was divided into an upper (*Hanau*) and a lower (*Hurin*) town. Grouped around the central square in the form of an oval were twelve subdivisions (*Carrios*). Here stood the great palace, one mile in length and a quarter of a mile broad; the *Yachahuasi* (*Huasi*, houses) dedicated to the instruction of the youth; the *Galpones*, edifices in which festivals were held; the convent of the Virgins of the Sun, the *Corichanca* or Palace of Gold, and the temple dedicated to the sun, surrounded by chapels dedicated to the moon, the stars, and to thunder and lightning. Here also stood the eighth wonder of the world—the great fortress *Sacsahuaman*; the entrances with slanting jambs, and a large plinth, constructed like inverted stairs, sometimes in stone, sometimes in excellent stucco, either with or without ornament. The three lines of massive walls round the town, forming the defence, were constructed 'en tenaille,' the entering angles all being ninety degrees; the very best European fortifications, planned by Vauban or Moltke, could not surpass the terrace-like arrangement of these three lines of defence. The polygonal blocks, of which the walls are constructed, are of blue limestone, from eight to ten feet in length, half as much in width and depth, and weigh from fifteen to twenty tons each. The first wall has an average height of about twenty-five feet, the second eighteen feet, and the third fourteen feet. Total elevation of walls, fifty-seven feet.

However cursorily we have touched upon art as it developed in the Western hemisphere, the reader must be impressed by two facts. (1) That there are analogies between East and West which are too striking to be attributed to mere chance; and (2) that those who built the edifices of Uxmal, Palenque, Copan, Chichen, Itza, and Cuzco must have been far beyond a mere nomadic state. They had palaces, temples, and therefore a kind of social organisation and religion. Their religion must have been of a low and cruel character, judging from the representations of their divinities, and from their using detached limbs of the human body as arabesques; though we can trace in their calendar, as in their conceptions of the personified powers of nature, Eastern influences, connecting the pre-historic West with the historic East. Whilst the Eastern world used incense at its religious ceremonies, the West used tobacco smoke. In both hemispheres some mysterious power was attributed to animals. The helmets of all nations took their origin in this common belief. Eagles, vultures, wolves, tigers, lions, dragons and serpents are used to adorn the fighter or to charm his weapons. The custom of wearing masks and helmets or head-dresses of some terrifying form, exaggerating the size of the head, is of purely barbarous origin. In the remains of ancient Mexico, Peru, and the South Sea Islands we find a variety of carved masks; some resembling human faces, adorned with false hair, beards and eyebrows; others representing the heads of birds. They are generally painted, often ornamented with pieces of foliaceous mica to make them glitter, or with turquoises and other precious stones.

That the pre-historic man, whether of the East or the farthest West, had some sort of civilisation may be best studied in his keramic products. Earthenware vessels, pots, jugs, vases, urns, and amphoræ are as interesting to the art-historian as fossil plants and animals to the paleontologist, or the different strata of the earth's crust to the geologist.

Pottery is one of the most reliable historical documents for fixing the degree of civilisation of a nation. Fossil pottery very much resembles antediluvian animals—it is without shape and form. Shells, leaves and fruits suggested it. By degrees gourds and eggs gave man better patterns. At a certain period it must have been the fashion in Egypt, Etruria, Greece, China, Mexico and Peru to use animal and human forms for vases, bottles, jugs and goblets, whilst horns, skulls and boots are found amongst Teutons and some savage tribes. The Teutons hoped to drink sweet honey out of the skulls of their slain enemies in Walhalla. We cannot wonder that so amiable a creed should have engendered quaint drinking vessels. We see in our own times plates and dishes adorned with frogs and lizards, which indisputably prove that there are pre-historic 'survivals.' From Kyprus we have, in the Imperial Cabinet of Antiquities at Vienna, an urn with a human face, which is very much like those found in Mexico, of which the South Kensington Museum and the Christy collection of the British Museum possess excellent specimens.

The wild and fantastic mode of ornamentation in the Western hemisphere, in pre-historic times, is entirely due to the aspect of nature. Man seems to have received patterns from India, Egypt and Greece, and worked them out by reflecting the impressions of an exuberant nature. Flowers, feathers, pearls, trinkets, hieroglyphs, animals, human bodies—all are mingled together in endless confusion. Here and there a symmetrical echo of times long by-gone can be traced. Though, however, the Western artists of pre-historic times sometimes attained symmetry, they continually sin against eurythmy. Of proportion and action they have no conception. They have a style, but a style of their own, devoid of all those requisites which elevate a product to artistic beauty.

CHAPTER IV.

CHINESE ART.

The Chinese undoubtedly reached a high degree of culture earlier than all the historical nations, and still they are in a state of civilised infancy. They possess reliable historical records referring to periods when branches of the Aryan group of humanity were still nomads. They knew that our globe is flattened at the poles, at a time when we thought it to be a square supported by pillars; they were acquainted with the properties of the magnet-needle; worked metal; cultivated the mulberry-tree, systematically fed the silk-worm with its leaves, weaving its product into the very best silk. In pottery they have attained the greatest perfection so far as the material is concerned. In engineering they were not less clever. They have aqueducts, executed with great daring; innumerable bridges span their rivers; they drained and irrigated the land at a time when other people assumed a universal deluge; and yet they remained babies in thoughts and customs, whilst they grew older and older in age. They have all the manners of precocious children with prematurely aged faces. This phenomenon can be explained in figures. There are 400,000,000 of Chinese, nearly all Turanians. Taking an equal number of Aryans, we shall find that they are not less than 3,400,000,000 cubic inches short of brain, of which each inch represents a certain amount of intellectual force. This deficiency in 'brain-force' shows itself in their totally different development, and the stationary character of their institutions. They ingeniously *play* in science, art, politics, and religion. 4,500 years ago they reached a high degree of civilisation, and they remained stationary in their civilised childhood, which they preserve with a pious veneration. To look back, to believe that the past was better than the present, has become the static law of China, and has checked every progress. Their language is agglutinative, only one degree higher than the savage monosyllabic, and forms a link between this and the flexible languages. The 450 monosyllables are used to form 1,230 word- sounds, out of which they compose from 40,000 to 60,000 compounds. They cannot pronounce certain consonants, resembling in this some badly-taught European children. They say: 'Yoo-lo-pa' instead of Europe; 'Ya-me-li-ka' instead of America; 'Ma-li-ya' instead of Maria; 'cu-lu-su' instead of crux; 'Ki-li-tu-su' for Christus. Their mode of writing has developed from pictorial signs. They preserved these; and, although arbitrary characters have supplanted picture-writing, or hieroglyphs, they still retain the clumsiness of this form, and have for every word a special sign.

Notwithstanding these drawbacks they possess an encyclopædia in 5,000 volumes, and a collection of works of fiction amounting to 180,000 volumes. They can boast of a Socrates in Confucius, of a Plato in Mem-tsu, and of a Xenophon in Tsem-tsu.

Five is with them a holy number: they had five emperors during their Golden Age; there are five great principles on which they base the possibility of a regulated social existence, viz. humanity, justice, conformity, uprightness, and sincerity. They have five holy books: the Shoo-King (political precepts); the Y-King (a philosophy of emanations based on figures); the Shi-King (a collection of didactical odes and songs about 3,000 years old); the Li-King (a record of ceremonial customs and social manners); and the Yo-King (a book on music, regulating harmony on the most discordant principles). They have five domestic principles, five elements, five primitive colours, five seasons of the year, five ruling spirits, five planets, five points of the compass, five sorts of earth, five different precious stones, five degrees of punishment, five different kinds of dresses; and their whole principle of ornamentation is based on five points ⫶ • ⫶. By uniting these five points they produce that ingenious system for the conventional treatment of flowers and animals, which has been divided by Owen Jones into—

    a. The continuous stem system;

    b. The united fragmentary system; and

    c. The interspersed fragmentary system.

In these three systems they observe the natural laws of radiation and tangential curvature.

But in all their works of art appears the spectre of childishness, with wrinkles in its withered face. Their patterns in textile art are such as some people delight in for the sake of their quaint originality. They altogether neglect the laws of ornamentation; and we never know whether in ornamenting a vase they did not intend to dress a Chinese lady for a tea party, or whether in dressing a high-standing mandarin, or a lady in stiff brocade, they did not intend to ornament one of their peculiarly-shaped tea-pots. In fact their vases are ladies in brocade dresses, whilst their gentlemen and ladies look like ambulatory vases. We often see on a lady, 'doves as big as bustards, cooing; flowers and trees growing on plates and vases upside down, and inside out.' We see a mandarin strutting about, adorned with an embroidered tree with fifty different foliages. One screen is decorated with fishes with feathers, another with birds with fins, or monstrous dragons creep on the ground or fly in the air. Everything in art is done as it ought not to be done. It is as if some merry and mischievous hobgoblin had instructed the Chinese to make up a kind of artistic patchwork out of all the odds and ends of ornamental fancies, distorted figures, and incomprehensible combinations.

Their towns look like large encampments of nomad hordes, ready at a moment's notice to take up their tents and run away. Though they have constructed a huge wall, which is 25 feet thick at the base, diminishing to 15 at the platform, provided at distances of 100 yards with towers about 40 feet square at the base, diminishing to 30 at the top, and about 37–48 feet in height; though they have carried this over the ridges of lofty hills (one of them 5,000 feet above the level of the sea), and led it through the deepest valleys, or upon arches over rivers—their architecture is still in its very infancy. It is a kind of toy-architecture. The walls of their houses may be pulled down, and the houses still remain standing. For architecture with the Chinese is in no way an organic total; it is not even a chemically-united composition; but a mechanically-joined something, without any ruling and connecting idea. Contrary to all rules of good architecture, they express in their constructions the principle of the separation and independence of the active elements of the building, instead of their union and harmony. It is variety without unity. Their walls are mere screens in bricks or wood, mere frameworks for tapestry. The wall with them does not support; it appears movable and totally distinct from the roof. The scaffolding which supports the horizontal, as also the vertical enclosures, belongs more to textile than to tectonic art The Turanian is still addicted to fascine work, like the pre-historic lake-dweller, or our contemporary aboriginal New Zealander. The divisions in the interior of the house are movable; either consisting of real carpets, lattice- work, wooden-jointed leaves, or boards, ornamented to imitate carpets or movable screens. Imitations of flowered woven-stuffs, lacquered panels with impossible perspectives, bamboo tress-work, with protruding knobs, carved and turned into gaping and grinning fantastic monsters, are also among the principal characteristics of Chinese architectural ornamentation. Chinese trellis-work has a fairy-like appearance. The patterns are infinitely varied, either closely fitting or perforated, dividing and enclosing spaces, surrounding terraces as railings, running up the staircases, or forming large borders between column and column.

The trellis-work of the Chinese may be divided into three classes:—

1. The bamboo *wicker*-work, a close imitation of textile fabrics; in fact, woven wood-work.

2. The *lattice*-work, a kind of transition or metamorphic work between

trellis and cross-barred work. The patterns are of a grosser kind.

3. The *mixed*-work, a combination of the two classes.

The first is generally used in ornamenting the interior of the basements of the houses. The natural bright yellow tint of the bamboo is either left, or it is lacquered in variegated colours to heighten the effect of the patterns.

The lattice-work is used for door and window-frames. In the latter case the holes are filled up with transparent shells, coloured paper, or painted glass, which has been in use since 3000 B.C.

The mixed-work runs along the walls, forming a frieze of gilt metal or alabaster. The last-named material is employed in summer-houses as a finish to the outer space, connecting bright red or light blue columns. When thus used the effect is undoubtedly charming. The roofs are tinted dark green, an unconscious reminiscence of by-gone times, when they were made of the leafy branches of trees or the broad foliage of plants. The dark azure of heaven shining through the perforated trellis-work, contrasting with the white marble of the substructure and the red columns, forms a combination both striking and agreeable. The upper parts of a building appear to swim in the air.

The brick walls of the Chinese are bare of stucco; the void predominating. They use the walls either as enclosures for court-yards, as isolated protecting walls before the entrances of houses—reminding us of the gates of India or the propylæa of Egypt—as substructures, or as enclosures and partitions for dwelling-places. All these walls are constructed of air-dried, fire-baked, or glazed tiles and bricks. The latter are only used for temples or imperial buildings. Whilst we possess a Board of Public Works that unfortunately has no administrative power, and cannot prevent our thoroughfares from being constructed according to the principles of a most inveterate symmetrophobia (hatred of all order, shape, style, and homo- geneousness), the law in China goes so far as to regulate even the use of building material, not according to any esthetical rule, but pandering merely to rank and class interest. White marble may only be used for imperial substructures, the enclosure of imperial courts, and in the construction of imperial bridges, and must never be used as wall-decoration. Their cement for coating walls is like ours; the stucco flat coloured, and the colours mixed with the plaster before laying on. According to his station in the State, the owner of a house may surround it with a wall of clay or lime, or with one of air-dried or fire-baked bricks. Only the walls of princes may have stone plinths. The encircling walls of imperial palaces have a roof of bright yellow, and light- green glazed tiles. The Tshao-Pings, or protecting walls, placed before the entrance doors of houses, like screens before our fire-places, have large protruding plinths. They differ in colour according to the rank of the owner.

Generally they are white, with painted ornamentation. Before the houses or palaces of princes the colours are red with gold, and the covering green or yellow. Before *Miaos*, temples of honour, they are nearly always of bright yellow. The outer walls are mostly white, decorated with incrusted landscapes or other conventional decorations. The inner walls are red and richly ornamented with gold; they have a kind of frieze ornamented with trellis-work, so as apparently to detach the support from the supported roof. In the houses of the higher classes the walls are decorated with damask, and in those of the commoners with paper-hangings, which latter we have adopted. Drapery is also freely used, hanging down and serving to divide the interior spaces of the houses. Doors and windows are still formed of curtains, as in the primitive times of civilisation in Assyria, India, and Babylon.

We are all acquainted with the excellence of Chinese silk-weaving, interspersed with golden threads, as also with the brightness and originality of some of their patterns, whenever they keep to an imitation of nature in their floral forms. They are generally, however, too realistic, the material not unfrequently appearing like a botanist's herbarium, or like a collection of butterflies or stuffed birds. Their embroidery is not less old than their silk-weaving. As early as 2205 B.C. in their statistical records (numbering about 4,768 volumes) gold, silver, copper, ivory, precious stones—*five sorts of pigments* of mineral extraction—silk, hemp, cotton, weavings of these materials, and the feathers of all sorts of birds are mentioned. The woven stuffs are of one colour. Silk is either red, black, white, or yellowish, weaving in colours not being known. The frequent mention made of birds' feathers may serve as a proof that they were used for embroidery, which in primitive times was more an 'opus plumarium' than embroidery proper, which is the forerunner of the art of painting. Feather crowns, kilts, and dresses are still in use amongst the savages of our own times. The colours are given by nature, and suit the grotesque taste of the undisciplined mind by their bright variegations and incongruities.

The oldest Chinese embroidery in colours was perfectly plastic. The plants, flowers, animals, and even figures, formed a polychromatic relief on the flat surface of the stuff. This style is still fashionable in China, though, instead of feathers, artificially coloured threads are used, always so as to make the objects appear raised from the surface. Even at present life-size figures in relief, or whole scenes, are executed with the needle in brightly-coloured silk threads. We are here involuntarily reminded of the reliefs of Nineveh, and we may assume that they are nothing but a transformation of embroidery into stone or alabaster.

The dresses, furniture, saddles, tea-pots, shoes and boots, jackets, covers, weapons, doors, and windows of the Chinese are all ornamented with patterns which have had their origin in this kind of relief-embroidery, traces of which are found even in their lacquered and keramic products.

The roofs of their houses are curved and drawn up like their features; they are copies of lids of baskets, tea-caddies, urns, or of caps and hats. The protruding parts are richly ornamented with dragons. The dragon with the Chinese is the prototype out of which man developed; the dragon is therefore the symbol of the imperial power.

Whilst the Chinese are altogether deficient in painting, because they have no idea of perspective or shading, they certainly excel in the technical treatment of keramic works of art, especially in the paste, which they make of kaolin, a decomposed feldspathic granite. The forms of their genuine pottery are most primitive in outline; dishes, cups, plates, and bowls are cylindrically shaped, as are their bottles and jars. Our South Kensington Museum abounds in specimens illustrating this.

Sharp naturalism and an exact reproduction of the forms of nature, without any skill in the conventional treatment of flowers, creepers, leaves, stems, fruits, and animals, prevail in all Chinese and Japanese works. The artist, if he intends to work in the Chinese style, must divest himself of all considerations for the higher esthetical principles of art; he must stoop to the tastes and delights of children, must study thoroughly their every-day customs and manners, enter into their mode of thinking, try to make the quaint quainter, and the grotesque still more grotesque. A big sun with thick rays in a corner to the right; some sharply-drawn trees in the middle; a bridge up in the clouds with a dog running over it; some children with large heads playing to the left; a bright stream marked with rough waves, through which fishes are peeping; the whole excellently finished so far as the lacquered work goes— and a Chinese tray is complete. The coloured enamel on keramic works, and their lacquered or varnished ware, notwithstanding their unimaginative naturalism and monstrously fantastic delineation, surpass anything we are capable of producing in the West of Europe. Their magnificent folding- screens, trays, tubs, wash-hand basins, toilet-cases, work-tables, perfume- cases, frames for looking-glasses; their jewel-tables—full of little drawers, secret nooks and corners, puzzling openings, and hidden shuttings—are so many additional proofs of their childish nature. They use the fret, which they have in common with the Mexicans, Peruvians, and Greeks. Whilst, however, the latter arrived at a continuous system of fret ornamentation, the Chinese still use it mostly fragmentarily, either one link after the other, or one above the other, without forming a continuous ornament.

We see in the Chinese one of the most interesting phenomena in the history of mankind, whether we look upon them from a social, religious, or artistic point of view. They govern their State on paternal principle, and on the grand rule, 'Do to another what you would he should do unto you, and do not unto another what you would not should be done unto you. Thou only needest this law alone; it is the foundation of all the rest' (Confucius in the sixth century B.C.), and yet they have made no progress in sciences and arts. The paternal government and home-rule check every thought. A moral principle of the very highest meaning has, as with many of us, worked badly. They have done unto others what others have done unto them. They cheated because they were cheated; they told falsehoods because they were deceived by others; they were hypocritical because others were so too; and they robbed and plundered others, because they were robbed and plundered themselves. In this moral chaos they forgot to cultivate the intellectual force of reasoning; they thus further disturbed the already deranged equilibrium between morals and intellect. And though they had gunpowder before the West of Europe, it remained in the far East of Asia a mere toy to amuse young and old at festivals, whilst in the possession of Western Europe it became, next to the art of printing, the most powerful agent of civilisation. They had paper before the West of Europe; they knew how to print at least five centuries before Europe thought of re-inventing this Chinese invention. They are as polite, if not politer, than the most civilised Frenchman, and are witty and good-humoured. They have no fear of death; trade with the same skill and perseverance as we; cultivate the soil with even greater industry and ability than we; so that their territory, about equal in extent to the whole of Europe, looks like one great well-drained and irrigated garden, in which no spot which can yield some return for assiduous labour is left uncultivated. There is amongst the 400,000,000 of subjects of one single emperor not one who cannot read and write. All places in the administration are assigned after a severe competitive examination, and still they lack the capacity of self-conscious, independent reasoning both in science and art. They can paint a tiger-skin with such truthfulness that it appears a real skin, framed under glass; but in the conception and reproduction of the head of the ferocious brute, with its bloodthirsty jaws and its merciless cruelty, they altogether fail. They have an aversion to a proportionate division of space; they never attempt to counterbalance their artistic ideas, and to arrange them according to a law. They abhor spiritual, imaginary, and all higher intellectual culture to such a degree, that they concentrate all their powers on mere technicalities. Therefore they have remained stationary, whilst others, who began their self-conscious national existence thousands of years later, have left them far behind. The Chinese sacrifice everything to preconceived ideas of custom—in morals, science, and art. As our forefathers did, let us do also. The result of this principle has been that curious, grotesque, and ingenious, but above all childish art, which we must study as the link between savage and Aryan art. Whilst the Negro scarcely went beyond geometrical figures, we find the Turanian already capable of using plants and the lower kinds of animals in ornamentation, in addition to geometrical figures. As soon, however, as he approaches beings, in whom proportion, action, and expression, as the higher elements of form, prevail, he loses his power of reproduction altogether.

Matter-of-fact prose is the element of the Turanian; he is without every higher artistic feeling, because his mode of writing, speaking, and thinking, his religious, social, and political organisation, has till lately checked all expansion of the imagination, and the use of the intellectual faculties. Art with him has remained undeveloped, and however interesting his products may be, they form only a subject for our curiosity and perhaps momentary fashion, showing what humanity at large did when in its *infancy*.

CHAPTER V.

INDIA, PERSIA, ASSYRIA, AND BABYLON.

Our tree of art, with its manifold branches, flowers, and fruits, rooted in the unknown origin of the three great groups of humanity, shows that the Negro, or black branch, had a very short growth. It still lives on in savage art, but is crippled, and has no vitality. Next we have seen the long line of Turanian art, represented by the Chinese; it originates in the geological age, passes through the mythical, traditional, and historical periods, and continues uninterruptedly to modern times. We have up to this point treated of the artistic productions of the Negro and Turanian groups, both of which stand without the pale of real history.

We now take up the art-history of the Aryan, the historical group. The birth-place of this group undoubtedly was Central Asia. Thence the pure Aryan group took two divergent roads. One division crossed over the Himâlâya Mountain chain, and settled round the Brahmapootra, the Indus and Ganges rivers, and the other remained on this side of the mountains. The Aryans may, therefore, be best divided into Trans-Himâlâyans and Cis- Himâlâyans. In these two groups we find the oldest traces of a power slowly awakening to full consciousness. We can perceive in remote ages, only measurable by means of analogy and deduction, an endeavour to solve the greatest problems of our existence.

To find answers to these *three* questions: Where from? What for? Where to? To measure the *three* dimensions of space and time; to trace the cause of which the *three*, ever stable and still ever varying, phenomena are the effect; and to know what creation, preservation and annihilation, or rather only transformation, are, has been the chief aim of the Aryan mind; and, as history teaches us, they have found more or less distinct answers to these questions. We are not only capable of philologically tracing the development of the different languages of the Aryan group step by step to one common parent-language—the Sanskrit, but the art-historian may trace every mysterious conception of the powers of nature, every form of personification or incarnation, and every religious tenet or mystery, symbol or myth, to these same Indians, who with the words *Pitâ, Matâ, Brahtâ, Duihtâ*, have taught us the holiest relations of our family life. For words, like pictures, are only representatives of outward impressions. To the Trans-and Cis-Himâlâyan

Aryans we can trace all theogonies, cosmogonies, systems of esoteric pathology and mythic anthropology. They first saw in geometrical forms the phenomena of the material as well as the spiritual world; gave meaning and interpretation to these mystic types; peopled heaven and earth with visible and invisible, good and evil, gods, goddesses, and spirits. They first acknowledged the 'noumenal,' or invisible, divine nature with its creative force; and recognised the 'phenomenal,' or visible, nature of the world as an emanation, evolution, development, outgrowth, or mere work of the invisible Creator. All the gods of the Persians, Assyrians, Babylonians, Egyptians, Greeks, and Romans, and a great number of the customs of Hebrews and Christians, may be traced back to Indian conceptions, forms, and modes of worship.

Not historical events only, but the whole life of humanity centres round religion. For science and art were in olden times the direct offsprings of religion. Neither science nor art can be understood, unless we have a clear insight into the mythologies and religious conceptions of the ancient peoples. Our great mistake has been, that till very lately we detached one of the different branches of the tree of knowledge. We criticised its bark, leaves, blossoms, and fruits separately, never concerning ourselves about the ramifications of the root, the soil in which it first spread, the chemical substances on which it fed, the conditions of climate under which it flourished or withered, never enquiring whether it brought forth only flowers and never fruits, or for what purposes its fruits and flowers were used by those who gathered both. Now without such understanding artists are mere unconscious machines, groping in the dark of ignorance, never capable of a clear reproduction of forms. Education and a higher conception flow like invisible magnetic streams through the hand, whether it hold pencil, paint-brush, chisel, or engraver's needle, and endow the work of art with a vitality which forms its real charm. It is never the technical correctness that appeals to us most strongly when contemplating even the smallest work of art, but the thought which animated the artist when constructing his forms.

Whilst the savage scarcely ever acquires a correct notion of time and space, and the Turanian only a limited one, the Aryan gathers from them the first dim recognition of the Infinite. In time and space perceptible changes take place, through the influence of an invisible power which creates all visible things. In time and space all created things are preserved, and in time and space all either perish or assume different forms. The Aryans endeavoured to express these abstract, yet concrete phenomena by signs. A triangle with three equal sides appeared best to express the mystery of the three equally powerful forces—creation, preservation, and transformation.

In the very earliest dawn of civilisation, therefore, the triangle became the hallowed symbol of the Divinity. After the *Symbolic* and *Dialectic* period had given place to the *Mythological*, time and space were looked upon as the origin of all things, out of which Brahmā, Vishnu, and S'iva had sprung. These three incomprehensible forces were expressed by geometrical figures, or, so to speak, crystallised, before they became incarnate persons. The creator had the sign of a double triangle ⟨⟨triangle figure⟩⟩ which formed three triangles symbolically representing the three forces in ONE, the CREATOR. Vishnu was designated by an equilateral triangle with the apex pointing downwards, ⟨⟨inverted triangle figure⟩⟩ meaning the preserver; whilst S'iva had for his symbol a triangle with the apex upwards, ⟨⟨triangle figure⟩⟩ denoting the transformer.

The divinities were placed in the following order: S'iva first, then Vishnu, and Brahmā last, to whom no temples were built. This was the case with nearly all the races of the Aryan group; there are scarcely any temples to Amn, Brahmā, Zeruane-Akerene, Uranos, Wodan, &c.

The order of the symbols, as given below, with their five significations—

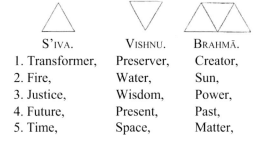

S'IVA.	VISHNU.	BRAHMĀ.
1. Transformer,	Preserver,	Creator,
2. Fire,	Water,	Sun,
3. Justice,	Wisdom,	Power,
4. Future,	Present,	Past,
5. Time,	Space,	Matter,

produced the most sacred word—

ΛVM or ÔM,

expressed by this triangular combination—

This was the mysterious TRIMURTY of the Indians, from which in time, according to the influences of nature, the degree of intellectual development, and the social and political condition of the different groups of the Aryan races, grew the different mystic conceptions of the *triune* power in *one*, working in nature.

Whilst the Trans-Himâlâyans, influenced by a gorgeous nature, allowed their imagination to run wild, and to distort the primitive mystic simplicity of these religious conceptions, the Cis-Himâlâyans remained more faithful to the first impressions of nature, and worshipped Light and Fire as the symbols of intellect, righteousness, and virtue, in opposition to Night, as the symbol of

ignorance, injustice, and sin. To the triangular forms, the circle, the serpent, was added, the form without beginning and end; no wonder that, encircling the equilateral triangle and joined to the square, it became the symbol of the mysterious, incomprehensible forces of nature. The triangle, square, and the circle

united, intersected, combined, isolated, and crossed, formed the fundamental lines of temples and their decorations. It was only at a later period that animal and monstrous human forms were conceived to personify abstract divine powers. The attributes of Ether, Water (Indra), and Fire (Agni), were transformed into acting persons. The three equal sides of the triangle, influenced by the imagination of the expounders of matters divine, were changed into an individual with three heads, so as to give a more comprehensible form to the incomprehensible divine power.

The Trans-Himâlâyans, once settled on the gigantic triangular peninsula stretching into the Indian Ocean, had leisure to work out a vast theogony, which has served the Aryans down to our own days as a store-house for different mythologies and religious systems.

The *Divespiter* of India (Deus pater, Jupiter) became the Lord of the sky, the Lord of hosts; his weapon was the thunderbolt. He possessed a splendid garden, the paradise, *nandana*.

Gânesa is Janus, the god with two heads. He was the guardian of ways; he had a *rod* or *sceptre* in his hand (the shepherd's crook or crosier) and a *key* —symbolic of his power to enter upon all the important undertakings of mankind.

S'rî or *S'rîs* (Seris—Ceres), also *Lakshmî*, *Padmâ*, and *Camalâ*, was the goddess of abundance, sprung from the sacred Lotus.

S'iva, the Greek *Zeus*, the Egyptian *Jao*, the Hebrew *Javeh*, the Roman *Jovis*, with their analogous attributes of revenge, jealousy, indomitable caprices, terror, and irreconciliation, all point to one and the same origin. Of S'iva (as of Zeus, Jovis, or Javeh elsewhere) it is recorded in Indian mythology that he had to fight with Daityas (Titans, or fallen angels), the children of Dity. Indra, on this occasion, provided the God of Fire, Justice, and Transformation with fiery shafts. Again, Jove overthrew the Titans and giants, whom Typhon, Bisareus, and Tityus led against the ruler of Olympus. The same is done by Javeh or Jehovah, who hurled the legions of proud and overbearing angels under Satan's rule into the infernal regions. The analogy is too striking to require any further comment.

Paulastya (the Greek and Roman *Pluto*), or *Kuvêra*, the Egyptian *Typhon*, the Hebrew *Satan*, bears a general family resemblance to the conceptions of the chiefs of the lower regions.

Garuda, the beautiful bird with a lovely human face attending on Vishnu, is the prototype of the youthful, blooming *Ganymede* attending on Zeus, not only in similarity of name, but especially in similarity of function.

Durga, who takes her name from brandishing a lance, is, like *Pallas* or *Minerva*, the Indian representative of heroic valour and reflecting wisdom. Both *Durga* and *Pallas* slew demons and giants with their own hands; both protected the wise and virtuous who paid them due respect and adoration. *Seraswati* and Minerva have also much in common. The Minerva of Italy invented the flute, and Seraswati presided over melody.

Is'wara and *Is'i* of India are undoubtedly the originals of Osiris and Isis.

Dypuc read backwards gives us *Cupid*. The Indian name is derived from *De'paka*, the inflamer. The mischief-maker of India and Greece had one and the same name. We find his name and character in Shakespeare's masterly delineation of *Puck*.

These analogies go much farther and deeper than is at first sight apparent.

S'iva is said to have had three eyes, symbolic of the three dimensions of time. A serpent, denoting the measurement of time by years, formed his necklace. A second necklace of human skulls marked the lapse and revolution of ages, and the extinction and succession of the generations of mankind. He holds a trident in one hand, signifying that the attributes of the other gods are united in him. S'iva is also called *Trilôchana* (three looks—*lôchan*, the eye, the look). Pausanias tells us that Zeus was honoured with the name of *Triophthalmos* (three-eyed), and that a statue of Jupiter had been found at the taking of Troy exhibiting the father of the gods with a third eye in his forehead.

Vishnu appeared on earth in several incarnations. The Indians look upon the planets as habitable. The sun was set down as the motor, directing the movements of these planets, furnishing them with light, and endowing them with the genial heat of vitality. *Krishna* (the black or blue one) was, like the Greek Apollo, the symbol of the sun, of light, of purity, and of love. He is represented as the promised Saviour, the eighth incarnation of Vishnu. According to the Vedas, the Earth complained to Vishnu, and demanded redress. It then received the promise of a Comforter and of a total renovation. Time is then said to have hastened to the birth of *Krishna*, 'that bright offspring of the gods, who sets forward on his way to signal honours. The world with its globular, ponderous frame, nodding signs of congratulation, when the *sweet babe* will distinguish his mother by her smiles!' Krishna, whom the Samaritans believed to have been Joshua, the long hoped-for Messiah, at last appeared on earth, where he passed a life of a most extraordinary and incomprehensible nature. He is said to have been the son of *Devaki*, a virgin, by King *Vasudévas*, but his birth was concealed for fear of the tyrant *Kansa*, his uncle, to whom it had been predicted that a child, born of that mother, would destroy him, and put an end to his dominion. Krishna had to hide, and was brought up in *Mal'hurâ* by honest herdsmen. He performed most amazing miracles, saved multitudes by his supernatural powers, raised the dead, and descended into the infernal regions of *Pátàla*, where the king of serpents, *Séshánàga* (suggestive of the name of Satana), ruled, that he might reanimate the six sons of a pious Brahman, who had been killed in battle. Krishna obtained a glorious victory on the banks of the *Yamuná* over the great serpent *Kaliya Nága*, which poisoned the air, destroying the herds of that region. *Apollo* also destroyed with his arrows the serpent Python. The whole legend, in both instances, took its origin in the action of the rays of the sun, purifying the air, and dispersing the noxious vapours of the atmosphere, which bred loathsome animals. Krishna and Apollo are thus identical in their actions. Krishna is disappointed by Tulasi, Apollo by Daphne; both conceptions liked the companionship of shepherds and shepherdesses. The *Tulasi* (or lotus) was sacred to Krishna, as the *Laurus* (laurel) to Apollo.

These and similar legends ought to be studied by artists to enable them not only to understand Indian art from a higher point of view, but to learn that many a monstrous form had a sacred symbolic meaning, that outward signs may be hallowed by hidden conceptions; and that, wherever this is the case, art will not succeed in reaching the bright spheres of beauty. The finest sculptured Durga without her necklace of human skulls, the protruding red tongue, the four arms with outstretched fingers balancing severed human heads, &c., would no longer convey to the mind of an Indian worshipper the idea of the goddess of valour and wisdom. Thus we may understand how a baked clay Indian idol, in spite of its revolting form, may be the symbol of some grand idea, through which it obtains value in the eyes of the credulous believer. In considering the causes that produced the peculiar development of Indian art, we must not omit to refer to the continually increasing power of the Brahmans.

Symbolism and mysticism were used by the priests of all ancient nations for thousands of years in preparing intoxicating draughts of superstition for the people, and proving the necessity for making sacrifices. At first depraved passions only were to be sacrificed, but by degrees they tried to typify those passions by animals, with analogous propensities. Goats became the representatives of licentiousness; bulls, types of indomitable fury and insubordination; and these animal types were offered to the gods. As soon as the priests had convinced the people that the blood of animals, the smoke from their burning bodies, the odour of roasting sheep, might appease the anger of S'iva, fanaticism went a step further, and drew human beings into the awful vortex of prejudice, and thousands of men and women were crushed, joyfully screaming, under the heavy wheels of Jugurnaut's, S'iva's, or Harris's cars. Men and women were burned alive; intellectual progress stopped, asceticism and blind submission to priestly despotism were enforced, and the possibility of a progressive art was crushed for thousands of years.

This desolate state of society required reform, and *Manû* stepped forward. He divided society into four distinct layers: the Brahmans, Kshattryas, Vaisyas, and S'udras, of which the two first were Aryans, the third caste Turanians, and the fourth Negroes; consequently, in spite of the excellence of his laws, which were assumed to have been dictated by Brahma himself, no real art was possible.

The Indians have two great national epic poems, containing nearly the whole substance of all the epic poems of the other Aryan races, and the many scenes from the Ramâyâna and Mahâbhârata in carvings and sculptures stand in the same relation to Greek art, as these poems to the Iliad and Odyssee. In both, scenes of heroism are displayed; but, whilst symmetry and proportion rule in the Greek poems, fantastic irregularity, wild incongruities, exaggerations and impossibilities are heaped up in the Indian. The beauty of some thought is effaced by overburdened metaphors, gushing forth in an endless stream like the waters of the Ganges. There are passages in the 28,000 double verses of the Ramâyâna surpassing anything written.

As an indisputable proof I will quote a few lines from the opening passages of the Ramâyâna. The gods are assembled before the first, incomprehensible cause, and address it in the following words:—

> O Thou, whom *three*fold might and splendour veil,
> *Maker*, *Preserver*, and *Transformer*, hail!
> Thy gaze surveys this world from clime to clime,
> Thyself immeasurable in space and time:
> To no corrupt desires, no passions prone:
> Unconquered conqueror, infinite, unknown;
> Though in one form Thou veil'st Thy might divine,
> Still, at thy pleasure, every form is Thine.
> Pure crystals thus prismatic hues assume,
> As varying lights and varying tints illume;
> Men think Thee absent, Thou art ever near;
> Pitying those sorrows which Thou ne'er canst fear.
> Unsordid penance Thou alone canst pay;
> Unchanged, unchanging—old without decay:
> Thou knowest all things—who Thy praise can state?
> Createdst all things—Thyself uncreate!

The endeavour to give forms to such sublime abstractions made the Indians lose their regulating power in pictorial and plastic art. A god was to be made powerful, and he was provided with four or twenty arms, and three heads. The miraculous and symbolic were the greatest enemies of Indian art.

In the Mahâbhârata, exceeding Homer's combined poems seven times in quantity, having not less than 110,000 double verses, we read of sentiments, feelings, and deeds which are our own—but nothing is within the pale of the credible. The birth of all the heroes is miraculous. Their deeds surpass the standard of human acts. They constantly associate with the gods, talk, argue, and dispute with them; their palaces are of immeasurable grandeur and splendour: ivory gates inlaid with jewels, golden pillars, diamond thrones, glittering with the splendour of a thousand suns; their armies are reckoned by millions; their heroes uproot trees, and kill hundreds of thousands at one blow; time and space have no meaning with them. Kings reign 27,000 years; Prathama-Raja reigned 6,300,000 and lived 8,400,000 years.[1] How could art in a higher sense exist under such conditions?

[1] By striking off the zeros, which are put on by the Brahmans *out of respect*, the figures may be reduced to some natural compass of possibility.

Art in a more comprehensible form appeared in India only when Buddha came to attempt a second regeneration of the people. He abolished castes, preached equality and freedom, and succeeded in awakening a high force of artistic activity in the dreamy Indians. But their art was altogether confined to the construction of rock-hewn temples, of stupas, topes, and religious buildings—architectural constructions in comparison with which even our greatest cathedrals dwindle into mere child's play. Their works of art are tinged with the same exaggerations as their great heroic poems, and when Buddhism was stamped out in its birth-place about the seventh century A.D., the Brahmans constructed their temples, vying with those of the Buddhist artists in architectural grandeur. They went back to their monstrosities, but they could no longer check the artistic power of the Aryan spirit.

The rock-hewn and isolated temples of India have details in stucco, of ornamentation, foliage, and general decoration, which, like their mythology, their heroic poems, and their abstruse philosophy, went through all the artistic metamorphoses of pliable, plastic, elastic and solid substances. In all we observe an unbounded play of imagination, uncontrolled by any law of symmetry. The walls are decorated with the most exquisite shawl and lace patterns, either in stucco or hewn in stone; a proof that before the application of those delicate forms to wall decorations they must have existed as textile fabrics of high finish. The rock-hewn temples exhibit clear imitations of rafters and cross-beams; wood had, therefore, been long in use before they attempted to imitate it in stone. Their sculptures are wood-carvings, terra- cotta or plaster-of-Paris works, turned into stone. The pliability of the softer materials visibly predominates. The gateways before the Sanchi Tope (see the masterly cast of one of these in the South Kensington Museum), though hewn in stone, are a close imitation of wooden posts and cross-beams joined together. This imitation is so faithful that even the rough and crooked outlines of the badly-cut posts and beams are preserved. The richness and variety of their decorative patterns, as also the minuteness of the details, prove that such patterns must have been carved in wood or fashioned in clay long before they were executed in the harder material—stone. Stucco must have served as a means of transition from wood-carving to sculpture. In the Ramâyâna the town of Agodhyá, built by *Manû* (the father and lawgiver of *man*kind), is thus described: 'It was adorned with beautiful palaces, high as mountains, and with houses of many stories; everything shining as in Indra's heaven. Its aspect had a charming effect. The town was enlivened by ever-changing colours; regular bowers and sweetly-blooming trees delighted the eyes. It was full of precious stones. Its walls were covered with variegated-coloured fields resembling a chess board,' &c.; the latter allusion giving a description of tesselated or mosaic work with which the walls must have been decorated. In a description of a palace in the Sakuntalâ, by Kalidâsa, who lived a century B.C., we read: 'Over the gate rises an arch of ivory; above it float flags of a deep yellow hue, the tassels of which appear to beckon and to call to you: Step in—step in. The *panels* of the door are of gold and stucco, glittering like the diamond breast of a god. Look here! there is a row of palaces shining like the moon, like shells, like the stem of a water-lily. *The stucco is laid on as thick as a hand.* Golden steps adorned with different stones lead to the higher rooms, from which *crystal* windows surrounded with pearls look down, glittering like the bright eyes of a beautiful maiden.' The passage that the stucco was laid on as thick as a hand can only mean that the ornament was worked in relief. Richly-painted ornamentation in stucco with mosaic and other patterns must therefore have existed. These undoubtedly originated, like the Persian, Assyrian, and Babylonian wall-decorations, in textile fabrics, which, having been found to perish too quickly, were made of a stronger, more durable material, preserving, however, all the character of the original patterns and material.

The Indians are distinguished by a keen observation of nature, and, so far as the conventional treatment of flowers, fruits, creepers, trees, and animals is concerned, we may learn much from them; but we have carefully to avoid their over-ornamentation. In their treatment of architecture, want of subordination of the single parts to a well-proportioned total is the greatest fault; in their sculptures of the human figure, the soft and waving lines predominate, creating a kind of voluptuous sensuality which is entirely opposed to good sculpture. Their naturalism is objectionable, and leads to a wild, fantastic coarseness which can never be pardoned in art. Measure and harmony are wanting. Gorgeous and mean, powerful and petty, sublime and ugly, are their products. Indian art, religion, and poetry are so closely united that it is impossible to understand the one without a diligent study of the other two. We have in Indian art the first attempts of humanity to step out of childhood. To children, wisdom is best communicated in symbols, mystic signs, fables, legends, and fairy-tales, and therefore Indian art is distinguished by these characteristics. The *tupo, sutupo* or *sutheouphu*, from the Sanskrit *stûpa*, a heap (our word *top*) or a pile of earth, corresponding to a tumulus, was at the same time a symbol of the religious principles of the Hindoos. It is said of Buddha that he once preached to his disciples, on the shores of the Ganges, on the instability of all things, the frailty of human life, on the grief and sorrows of our existence, comparing life to a water-bubble, consisting of the four elements and still perishing so quickly. The water-bubble thus lent its form to the tope and *daghopa*, which latter, according to W. v. Humboldt, means 'hider of the body,' destined for the reception of Buddha's relics. The tower which rises inside the tope is symbolic of the nine incarnations of Vishnu. We have in the Indian temple, as in our Gothic churches, a homily in stone. The arched dome has to remind us of the perishableness of life; the daghopa, with its seven or nine divisions, tells us that there is hope for the immortal soul to reach heaven through seven or nine degrees of purification. The protecting canopies (umbrellas) are symbolic of Buddha's intercession, which he is sure to accord, if we only recognise the *nihilism* (nothingness) of our earthly existence.

The religious construction was also extended to every-day utensils, a tendency which was universal with all the people of the Aryan group. To these typical ornamentations belong the lotus flower and the tree and serpent ornament. The religious conception is everything with the Indian. It is not the form itself that he cares for, but the religious thought which is expressed emblematically, allegorically, or symbolically. This is the reason why he clings to his fourteen-armed divinities. It is God and His powers that he wishes to represent; but, whenever man attempts to express the incomprehensible or the abstract in visible and concrete forms, he errs. The soul of the Indian is absorbed in God: in Him is everything; the world is *without* Him and still *within* Him. All beings take their origin in Him and return to Him. An everlasting *emanation* and *absorption* is continually proceeding before the eyes of the Indian, and, looking for a type of this wonderful process, he found it in the 'Aswatha' tree, the Indian fig-tree (*Ficus Indica*). The banyan takes root, so to speak, in the air, grows downwards, grasps the earth with its branches, shoots upwards again, and repeats this process 'ad infinitum.' Everything coming near its feelers is embraced, covered over, and in this mystic encircling, annihilated. From time immemorial this sacred tree has been the *tree of life*, the symbolic tree of the petrifaction, vivification, and incarnation of God's spirit in minerals, plants, animals and man. This pantheistic conception is not favourable to art: it crushes the powers of the artist, who has to deal with too great an ideal weight in forms.

There is another species of fig-tree (*Ficus religiosa*) which does not take root again, but the leaves of which appear eternally to tremble; it became the symbol of the ever-moving and oscillating spheres filling the universe. The tree combines two working cosmical forces, it partly remains the same and still continually changes and varies; it is now covered only with leaves, by degrees with leaves and blossoms, and at last with leaves and fruits; then its vitality apparently dying away, leaves, blossoms, and fruits vanish, to be renewed again with the same regularity and abundance. The mind, not yet accustomed to account for every phenomenon by simple or compound gases, globules, or atoms, set in motion by affinities, is altogether absorbed by the miraculous phenomena of nature, and, having been kept for thousands of years in this absorption, is incapable of seeing objects in their proper light. It sees in every form a metaphysical cause, which leads in ornamental art to those entwined, confused, monstrous, and bizarre combinations, which mar *symmetry*, mock *eurythmy*, distort *proportion*, have no *direction*, and, trying to express the inexpressible, have no *expression* at all.

The artist, if he wishes to work in the Indian style, must make himself acquainted with the feelings that animate the Indian mind. He will do best by generally using their arabesques, and arranging them after a careful study of the antique into symmetrical forms. The Indian conventional treatment of plants in surface-decorations is unsurpassed, and in this we may learn from them; but we have to beware of their monotonous excellence, and their everlasting repetitions. We may, here and there, use their forms, but we must bring order and measure into the wild and unintelligible chaos. If we want to produce entirely Indian patterns we must not alter them, or else we destroy their effect; but we may be original in merely using the form, and endowing it with a spirit of our own; this being the great advantage of the historical study of art.

Indian architecture has been well systematised by Mr. Fergusson. We have in the north the Bengallee, in the south the Dravidian, and in the west the Chalúkyan style; besides these we have three distinct religious styles—the Brahmanic, the Buddhistic, and, at a later period, the Mahomedan.

Turning to the Cis-Himâlâyans, who appear under numberless names of tribes, nations, and races, and by degrees peopled Assyria, Babylon, Persia, Greece, Northern Europe, Italy, Spain, France, and England, and carried religion and civilisation into Egypt; we begin to tread, for the first time, on really *historical* ground, for we shall be able to place events in time absolute.

Persia—the Hebrew Elam, the Indian Paraça, from Pars, or Fars, or Fardistan—differs entirely in geographical position, climate, and natural products from China or India. Hekatæos, Artemidoros, Eratosthenes, and Strabo describe the climate and soil of Persia as cold and sterile in the north, temperate and fertile in the central or valley regions, and hot and enervating in the south. We have, therefore, enterprising activity, energetic courage from the north, and a counteracting regulating element in the centre, tinged with the dreamy idleness of the south. The aspect of nature is less oppressive. Instead of gigantic creepers, the vine, with its juicy grapes, clings to tall and fruitful trees; bright-eyed gazelles abound; lions and tigers excite to daring hunts; exquisitely-coloured and fragrant roses perfume the air, and open the mind to the gentler impressions of a tender beauty. The Persians, Assyrians, and Babylonians rose to power, declined, and passed away with all their grandeur; but in these very changes there were activity and life. The Persians were the first to proclaim a governing universal *unity*, which endowed men with forces, enabling them to become virtuous and intellectual *by their own exertions*. They remained faithful to the first impressions of nature, in which the Eternal Spirit revealed himself.

The Persians, like the Indians, expressed the cosmical elements of creation symbolically by means of geometrical signs, which are given below.

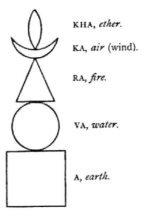

KHA, *ether.*

KA, *air* (wind).

RA, *fire.*

VA, *water.*

A, *earth.*

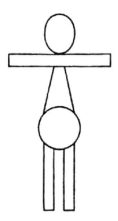

This *five* in *one* comprised the creation; it was the work of Chudâ (Khuda), Choda from the Sanskrit Svadâtta (self-given, God-given). From the Zend word Chuda, or Choda, we have the words G<small>OTT</small> and G<small>OD</small>. At a later period man's imagination soon perceived in these abstract signs a concrete form; it turned *Cha* into the head of a being, *Ka* into the arms, *Ra* into the chest, *Wa* into the lower parts of the body, and *A* into the feet, and thus the first embryonic, ill-shapen incarnation, or embodiment, of the creative power of nature was formed. This embryo, by degrees, developed into the master- pieces of Greek sculpture.

In Persia, the pure and exalted consciousness of a first, incomprehensible cause leaving its products, the special manifestations of its creative power, *free* in themselves, was fostered and developed. To the Persians we owe the first clear conception of a God independent of nature. Spirit and matter are not *one* with them, as with the Indians. With the Persians God is separated from His creation—the universe. God, as the ruling Spirit, acquires subjective reality; man, His creature, whether good or bad, whether poor or rich, whether righteous or unrighteous, whether high or low, is, as His creature, equal and free. Man thus obtained a free position face to face, if we may say so, with the Supreme Being—the Creator. What a totally different mode of thinking to that in China or India! In China man is a mere machine, regulated by stereotyped moral maxims. In India duties and rights depend on the chance of birth; the Brahman is a born priest, whether he has talent or not for his vocation; the Kshattriya, a born soldier, though he may be the greatest coward; the Vaisya, a born merchant or artisan, in spite of his utter incapacity for business; and the S'udra, a born slave, though he may be gifted with greater wisdom than the Brahman, more heroic virtues than the Kshattriya, and more talent for commerce, trade, or art than the Vaisya.

In Persia the Aryans acquired, for the first time, a kind of collective freedom, but not yet an individual consciousness as free agents. The Indian language and Indian metaphysics, in the garb of mythology, were undoubtedly components of Egyptian, Persian, Assyrian, Chaldæan, and Babylonian art, and the forms thus produced, in their turn, became the direct elements out of which Grecian art in its infancy developed itself.

The Persians are direct descendants of the Zend people. Their language is nearly the same as Sanskrit. Out of ten Zend words, seven or eight are Sanskrit.

Persian history may be traced back into time relative; for, when it passes into time absolute, the advanced state of the people in science, especially in astronomy, their social condition, and their architecture and ornamental art, prove that they must have existed in a social bond for thousands of years, in order to develop and to attain that progress which excites our astonishment even after the lapse of more than 6,000 years.

Their history may be divided into the following periods:—

1. The mythic period, from an unknown time down to the foundation of the vast, well-organised, and powerful Persian empire by Kai-Khorus, or Kyrus, in the sixth century B.C.

2. The second period affords reliable accounts of the existence of the empire down to Alexander the Great, from 560 B.C.-330 B.C.

3. The history of the Persians, as members of the Greek-Makedonian empire, ending with the conquest of Persia by the Arabs from 330 B.C.-137 B.C.

4. The empire of Central Persia, under the Arabs, down to its extinction by the Mahomedans in 651 A.D.

5. The dominion of the Kaliphs down to its destruction in 1258 A.D.

6. The last period continuing to our own time.

The mythic and historical periods of Persia resemble two diverging lines, of which the undoubted fact of the reign of Kai-Khorus forms the connecting point. Whilst the historical line grows more and more distinct as it proceeds, the mythic line retreats farther and farther into the dim region of the unknown. Passing from the known to the unknown, we must assign to the development of Zend thoughts, institutions, mode of writing, and mode of building, a greater antiquity than to the Assyrian and Babylonian monuments. Of Persian remains we possess nothing but skeleton buildings, which, from the entire absence of connecting walls, lead us to infer that they were still mere tents, and that the textile fabric had not yet undergone the further process of incrustation in stucco or stone sculpture.

This is not the case with Nineveh and Babylon, the great towns, or, as we should say, the great empires, on the Tigris and Euphrates. Through the indefatigable exertions of the Right Hon. Mr. Layard, M. Botta, Lord Loftus, and Mr. Rassam, we possess now, in London and Paris, tablets with records more than 3,000 years old. The boundary stones prove that some fixed laws regulated territorial property, even at these remote periods. The personal ornaments, consisting of mother-of-pearl studs, silver rings, bracelets, gold and pearl earrings, beads, and shell-bosses with bronze pins, testify to a high civilisation. The mode of writing in Nineveh and Babylon was borrowed from the Zend people; and the religious conceptions of the Persians are undoubtedly older than the already-complicated idolatry based on the astronomical notions of the Assyrians and Babylonians.

The Zend-Avesta (meaning the living word) may be said to be like an Egyptian Nile-meter, erected on the primeval soil of history, measuring the yearly deposits and alluvial sediments of by-gone ages. Through the pure crystals of myth and poetry we may see the inner formation of society, whilst from without the vast construction of history is mysteriously going on. We wander through endless lines of Memnon statues, all resounding with the legends of past ages, in perusing the Zend-Avesta, and are suddenly led before the fountain of all matter, at which the high-priest stands, commanding in the harmony of the seven planets the birth of the world, and the origin of all things.

Our first parents, according to the Zend-Avesta, dwelt in *Eriene Veedjo*, or *Iran Veji*, or Aria, Aturia, Asshuria, meaning the *fiery* or *bright* land, figuratively the blessed land, in a happy garden, the paradise, assigned to them by *Ormuzd*—contraction of *Ahura-Mazda* (the divine Being or the Great Lord). From this they were driven by Agrômainyus, *Ahriman*, the murderer from the beginning, who changed the seasons, transforming the *seven* beautiful summer months into *ten* cold and dreary winter months, leaving only *two* tolerably warm months. The division of the year into *twelve* months is clearly proved by this mythic statement. Can anyone count the ages, and describe the means by which Persians, Chaldæans, Medes, Egyptians, and Indians arrived at a systematic arrangement of time, dividing the year into twelve months? After the reign of the Abads (fathers, *abbas*) *Azer-Abad* ruled; then *Dshey-Afram, Kedor-la-Omer* (Cadam, Adam) followed; he ruled 560 years, and attained the venerable age of one thousand years. We find here, as in all old records, the tendency to ascribe to man a longevity which he has long lost. Like shadows which are more gigantic in the rising and setting sun than in the broad mid-day, historical facts in the first dawn of consciousness are exaggerated and turned into fables, which again vanish in the bright light of scientific criticism. *Cadam* was followed by *Siamek*, who was succeeded by *Tahamur*, who conquered the Devas, or evil spirits. He learned from them the art of writing and reading, constructed aqueducts and viaducts, and taught his people music and the use of iron. The Aryans on this side of the Himâlâyas had passed the savage state (the *palæolithic* period of art), entered into the nomadic (the neolithic period), settled down and used bronze instruments, and then were taught, *no longer* as with the Indians, Egyptians, and Greeks *by a divinity*, but by one of their rulers, to extract iron from the ore and to work it. With Tahamur we step into the iron or historical age.

Dshemshid, the Greek *Achæmenes*, the Biblical *Nimrod*, the mighty hunter before the Lord, *pierced the earth with a golden dagger*—allegorically meaning that he improved agriculture. Dshemshid ruled 616½ years; he built Persepolis, or Takt-i-Dshemshid (the throne of Dshemshid). He was, however, conquered by *Zahok* and *sawn into two pieces*, meaning that the empire of Dshemshid had been divided by *Zahok*, who was a descendant of the cursed race of Aad. He is said to have been the *Sesostris*, or *Sesoosis*, of the third dynasty of the Egyptians, the 332nd king after Menes the builder of Memphis, a great conqueror who went to India, took possession of Thracia and Skythia, and united Æthiopia, Libya, and Egypt into one mighty empire in the fortieth century B.C. He is also said to have been *Ninus*, who with Semiramis, the night-born queen of doves, and the daughter of the water-sprung *Derceto*, is set down as the builder of Nineveh, and the founder of the empire of Babel. Takt-i-Dshemshid existed before either Nineveh or Babylon; its priority is borne out not only by these records, but, as we have said, by the very ruins left of the Persian metropolis. The name *Parsagad*, or *Passagarda*, means 'camp of the Persians,' and points to an early, unsettled state of society; as also do the ruins, which may be divided into two classes:—

1. The ancient Persian monuments of Dshemshid.

2. The monuments of the reign of the Sassanides.

The name Persepolis was first used by the Greek historiographers who accompanied Alexander the Great, to denote that part only of the vast town in which the tomb of Kyrus was situated, and this gave rise to much confusion.

Passagarda, Isthakr, or Estakar, was situated on the border of one of the richest and most beautiful plains of Central Asia, watered by the Bendemir (the Araxes of the ancients), and surrounded by lofty mountains, 'whose rugged masses rise from the verdant plain like islands from the ocean.'

The *oldest* monuments are:—

1. The ruins of the palace now called by the Arabs *Tshil-Minar* (the forty

columns), and two great tombs close by.

2. Four other tombs, about four and a half English miles to the north- west, and in the plains of Murghab the ruins of Passagarda, built by Kyrus to commemorate his victory over Astyages, who came from Hamadan (Ecbatana). Here is situated the pyramidically-constructed tomb of Kyrus, made of white marble blocks. Farther north are the ruins of *Bisutun*.

Passing to the monuments under the reign of the *Sassanides*; they consist of reliefs and inscriptions hewn in rock at a distance of about four and a half miles from the ruins of Persepolis. They are called *Naksh-i-Rustam* (the image of Rustam), because it was assumed that the exploits of this hero were here glorified. De Sacy, in his 'Mémoires sur diverses Antiquités de la Perse,' has explained the inscriptions as referring to the kings of the Sassanide dynasty. The reliefs are portraits of these kings, recognisable by their head- dresses.

The distance from Passagarda to Tshil-Minar is about forty-nine English miles, and this space is crowded with Persian monuments. It is most probable that the more recently-made subdivisions did not exist, but that the capital of the ancient Persian empire extended from Passagarda to Tshil-Minar, including Isthakr, Naksh-i-Rustam, and the king's palace, called by the Greeks Persepolis. The palace was cut out of the beautiful grey marble rock towering over it, and stood on three well-defined, gradually-rising platforms. The arrangement was like that of the Indian, Egyptian, and later Greek temples; the first terrace corresponding to the Pronaos, where the people paid their homage to the king; the second to the Naos, where the ambassadors of the different nations assembled; and the third to the Adytum, where the king had his special temple and private abode. The whole foundation was constructed of bold Kyklopean masonry.

At the gates stood colossal fabulous animals, fantastic representations combined of the lion, the bull, the horse, the wild ass, the rhinoceros, the ostrich, the eagle, the scorpion, and the unicorn. Besides these there were winged and horned animals, and others having the winged body of a lion, the feet of a horse, and the head of a man, with well-curled, long beard and crowned with the tiara—the symbol of the king's power, endowed with intellect, force, and swiftness. The bull with the Persians was, like Nundi with the Indians, Apis with the Egyptians, and Taurus with the Greeks, a sign of strength and power.

The capitals of Persian columns were not yet made to support a heavy stone weight, but only a light wooden beam. The foundation walls were, like those of Nineveh and Babylon, covered with sculptures, the designs of which were all of textile origin. But in these sculptures, as in those of Kouyunjik and the Palace of Nimrod, the theological, or religious, and symbolical element is entirely left in the background. We have the friends, relations, and servants of the king; tributaries submitting to kings; officers holding fly-flaps of feathers; horses crossing rivers; kings hunting and slaying lions; armies before besieged towns; warriors returning from battle; battering rams; chains to destroy the action of rams; soldiers mining ramparts; infantry with bows and shields; removals of cattle and spoil from captured cities; boats floating on rivers; galleys going to sea; damsels and children with musical instruments; and mathematical tablets with calculations of square roots. We have man active, warring, scientific, and only here and there some scenes of a religious character, and these more frequently in Nineveh and Babylon.

The cause of this phenomenon was the religion of the Zend people. Its founder was Zarathustra, Zerdusht, Σοροάθεος {Soroatheos}, Zoroaster—partly a mythical, partly a real person. His name appears to have been derived from the Sanskrit Sûrya-dêvas, meaning 'the Sun-god.' According to Aristotle Zoroaster lived 6,000 years before Plato. The Biblical Abram, Sesostris the Egyptian king, and Moses, were all honoured by this name. Svedius mentions a Zoroaster 500 years before the Trojan war. The historical Zoroaster, the compiler of the religious tenets of the Zend people in the Zend-Avesta, lived about 589 B.C.; he was therefore a contemporary of Confucius, Pythagoras, Jeremiah, and Ezra. He received the holy books from Ormuzd on Mount Elbruz.

The Zend-Avesta assumes *one* Universal Being, clothed in an outward form, but this form is *Light*. Light is neither a serpent, nor a stone, nor a four-handed monster, nor a three-headed Brahmā, nor a bull, owl, or hawk; it is a simple manifestation, it has no particular existence, it perceptibly pervades universality. It admits of a highly symbolical interpretation; it is virtue, it is truth, proficiency, knowledge, and directing will. Light involves an opposite —darkness, just as virtue has an antithesis—evil. Both light and darkness took their origin in the unlimited All (Zeruane-Akerene). We have here clearly a purer Trinitarian conception. We have (1) the Infinite All, producing (2) light or good (Ormuzd), and (3) darkness or evil (Ahriman). With the Indians *Brahmā* is ether; *Vishnu*, water; and *S'iva*, fire; and in spite of all spiritualisation we have *matter* before us. The Persians, in becoming conscious of light and darkness, destroyed the innocence of mankind, but proclaimed to the world *moral* consciousness. Without a knowledge of evil there is no knowledge of good; to be virtuous is to know the evil and to do the good.

This led the Cis-Himâlâyans a step further. The two opposing phenomena, light and darkness, were placed, like good and evil, purity and impurity, right and wrong, truth and falsehood, knowledge and ignorance, in eternal conflict. Creation was thus considered as in everlasting strife. This strife was life-activity in honour of Ormuzd or Ahriman. This activity was carried beyond this world; for the followers of Ormuzd, there was a heaven, and for the followers of Ahriman, a hell in the future. Ormuzd had *Fervers* as attendants; Ahriman, *Dews* or *Devas* (in Keltic *Dusii*, devils). On the Persian and Assyrian slabs we see, floating over the heads of the kings, their winged portraits; these represent their protecting Fervers, one of whom continually watched over each good man, and protected him from the influences of Ahriman's servants.

The worship of Ormuzd, in whose sight all creatures were *equal*, but equally dependent, was threefold:—

(a) *Pure thoughts*, through which alone we may approach the beginning of all things, wisdom and light—God.

(b) *Pure words*, the word of God (the Logos), which is no longer personified as some visible form, but is the mere vibration of the spirit of God, embodied in abstract signs in the Zend-Avesta.

(c) *Pure deeds*, accomplished by one's own efforts, as we are endowed with perfect individual freedom.

This religion was the cause why the Persians had no special temples, but only small altars. The vaulted azure heavens were the glorious temple of Ormuzd, which he was compelled to share with Ahriman. Neither light nor darkness, however, could be carved or painted; the dynamic force of the artists was therefore directed to matter-of-fact scenes, to ornamentations, showing a better balance between forms and ideas. The rosette, the palmette, the sun with its disc, the moon, the pine-cone, the pomegranate, intermixed with clearly-defined, and not much entwined, geometrical patterns, were the principal means of ornamentation.

At a later period a tendency to allegorical and emblematic figures appeared. The artists composed cherubim, chimeras, basilisks, griphons, kentaurs, and sphinxes; undoubtedly influenced by Indian and Egyptian ideas, for Nineveh and Babylon were the ancient Venice and Genoa of the far East, situated as they were on the commercial high-roads, the twin-rivers, the Tigris and the Euphrates. The Babylonian textile fabrics were highly appreciated from time immemorial. Serpents and trees, winged witches and flying-fish, were first spell-bound in Babylonian tapestry, and then carved in stone on the walls of Nineveh. The immense riches which we possess in the British Museum, enable every student of art-history to see before him the active life of the Cis-Himâlâyans, whether as Assyrians, Persians, Medes, or

Babylonians, in clear and distinct outlines. Their knowledge of embossing gold and silver was considerable. Their household furniture, drinking cups, tables, candelabra, bracelets, and rings are of strictly *architectural construction*. We miss that overburdening confusion in ornamentation which distinguishes the Indian products; and the more correct treatment of ornamental outlines, especially to be seen in their mosaics and tesselated pavements, approaches Greek forms.

The commercial spirit, which swayed this portion of the river-valley of the Tigris and Euphrates, engendered a powerful activity in a practical direction. Whilst we build railways—the Babylonians dug canals, connected the two rivers, and constructed aqueducts. They built palaces at Nineveh, castles (El Kassr) at Babylon, and an immense nekropolis at Vurka, about 180 English miles from Bagdad, and about 8 miles to the east of the Euphrates. At every step in the interior of these ruins we find clay-coffins piled up to a height of from 15–20 feet. All these ruins are now covered with saltpetre, small shells and broken pottery. The remains of the walls are from 12–22 feet thick, partly of unbaked and partly of baked bricks. The construction everywhere closely imitates wood-work, and the decoration reproduces textile fabrics such as carpets and striped tent covers. There are capitals in stucco of the Ionic and even of the Corinthian type; though the leaves are those of the palm-tree instead of the Acanthus. The volute of the Ionic capital is rather in the form of two serpents drinking from a cup, than in the form of rams' horns. We might call this old Babylonian stucco capital, the proto-Ionic type.

On the two shores of the Euphrates, as far as Babylon, coffins of green glazed clay and small terra-cotta tablets with cuneiform inscriptions have been found by thousands. These coffins were imitations of dead bodies, swathed in cloths and tied with cords. In addition to this reproduction of textile fabrics in clay, we find with the Cis-Himâlâyans a tendency to overlay wood-carvings with metal coatings. When they advanced more in metallotechnic they still held to patterns which clearly had their origin in wood-carvings. The plant-like forms predominate; then we have the quilloche, palm-leaves, or feathers arranged in the form of palm-leaves, and the pine-cone, which is often used in eurythmical variation with the conventionally-treated open or closed tulips, and open or closed lotus flowers.

The pictorial art of the Assyrians and Babylonians shows us two distinct periods—an older and a more recent one. The older works had a bluish-green ground; the later a light, either whitish or yellowish, ground. In both styles the outlines are marked strongly in black or dark red. In the older, the sinews are more rope-like and less correct in their anatomy. In the more recent style a finer treatment, and a more correct knowledge of the human frame, may be traced. Wild animals are reproduced with a keen eye of observation, and a strong tendency to naturalism.

Polychromy was known to them, but it is very difficult to decide whether they coloured in tempera or in fresco, with wax or by some other means—perhaps even in oil. The incrustation of clay walls with baked and painted, and even glazed, tiles it is difficult to explain. In many instances, as at Vurka, each cone has its own colour, and, by a proper arrangement, squares, imbrications, diapers, and networks were produced; but at Babylon and Nineveh the tiles show clear marks of painting. Diodorus (probably after Ktesias) gives us a description of the interior circular wall of the royal palace at Babylon, and says: 'It was decorated with all sorts of coloured human and animal forms baked in clay, much resembling nature. The whole represented a hunt. The figures were more than four yards high. Semiramis was to be seen by the side of her husband Ninus, she killing a panther, he piercing with his dart a lion.' The principles of decoration with the Assyrians far surpass mere ornamentations in geometrical patterns. Dramatic life of a higher kind is introduced, showing greater artistic power than the reliefs in stone. The outlines are neither black nor red, the treatment is tasteful, the colours a tender blue, brown, white or yellow, and the ground a lightish green. These paintings are not mosaics, as at Vurka.

The baking and glazing must have taken place in the following manner. The unbaked tiles were arranged and numbered in a horizontal position on the ground, then they were painted and placed vertically on the wall as a tapestry decoration. When the wall was finished it must have been heated, so as to change the light and fluid colours into a kind of enamel, giving the clay-wall a thin terra-cotta coating.

The utilitarian purpose was everything with the Persians, Assyrians, and Babylonians. This is evident in their furniture, especially in their tables, chairs, and footstools. The construction of the frame was taken from plants and trees, whilst wild animals were used as silent and obedient domestic creatures. In supporting their furniture with the legs of the lion, tiger, or leopard, they used these animals for an excellent ornamental purpose. The legs of the brute were made to support, the body was turned into a seat, and the head was conventionally used as a side-ornament for the backs or arms of the throne or chair. We see in the Cis-Himâlâyans, in accordance with their greater activity in life, a further progress in art. Merely geometrical figures do not suffice; not monstrous divinities, but animals and men, are the most important subjects of sculpture. Their architecture was without symmetry and proportion, the material of their buildings in no accordance with the monumental tendencies of their construction, and their efforts did not carry them further than the vague attempts of half-settled nomads. Their walls, which once consisted of textile hangings, retained this character, stretching for thousands of feet without any interruption, except that the doorways had their colossal symbolic guards, which to a certain extent relieved the monotony of the construction. The art of Persia and Assyria is in every sense the transition-link between nomadic and monumental art.

CHAPTER VI.

EGYPTIAN ART.

'Anything capable of uniting many souls—is *sacred*,' says Goethe. The sacredness of religious tenets or monumental buildings is at once explained by this. To unite humanity into one great brotherhood was first attempted by the Babylonians with their huge tower of Belus, Baal, or Babel. Men for the first time left patriarchal particularism, and tried to build a beacon reaching up to the stars, calling humanity together to one spot, by a work produced by their united labour as a visible sign of their union. This first attempt at a really monumental building was made in the plains of the Euphrates. Whilst the people of Asia still struggled to settle down, and changed their habitations and with them their forms of art, we see monuments emerge from the dim past, which reflect man for the first time in his grandeur as wielder of matter.

The sphinx in its incomprehensible, mysterious form, half brute, half human being, may be looked upon as the very emblem of Egyptian art.

It is written in one of the Hermetic books, 'O Egypt, fables alone will be thy future history, wholly incredible to later generations, and nought but the letter of thy stone-engraved monuments will survive.' Our knowledge of Egypt is scarcely half a century old. It originated in a black basalt stone, the so-called Rosetta-stone, deposited, at the beginning of the century, in the British Museum. Approached by Dr. Young, of Cambridge, with the wand of investigation, this stone poured forth a little spring, which has now swollen into a mighty river, carrying off with irresistible force all those little souls who, on their small boats of prejudice, with tiny chronological ladles, try to stop the sweeping power of historical truth. We know something at least of Egypt; we have *monumental* evidence, which surpasses all *written documents*, which may be voluntarily or involuntarily falsified. Egyptologists may be divided into two parties:—the *long* and the *short* chronologists. The *short* chronologists, in the face of our advanced knowledge of geology, of the vast accumulation of pre-historic relics, consisting of flint instruments, pottery, weavings, and architectural remains (lake and pile-dwellings), deserve no consideration. They follow the chronological dislocation of Rabbi *Hillel*, of the first half of the fourth century A.D., with childish ignorance. This view is the most charitable, as otherwise we should be driven to accuse them of interested knavery. After the exertions of a Champollion-Figeac, Böckh,

68

Barucchi, Bunsen, Brugsch, Henry, Lesueur, Lepsius, Hincks, Kenrick, Uhleman, &c.—who all belong to the *long* chronologists, to turn to the short chronology is impossible.

Lepsius succeeded in tracing Egyptian history, king by king, event by event, to Alexander the Great, and hence through the XXXIst, XXXth, XXIXth, XXVIIIth, XXVIIth, XXVIth, XXVth, XXIVth, and XXIIIrd consecutive Egyptian dynasties, back to Sheshonk Shishak, founder of the XXIInd dynasty, who conquered Jerusalem 'in the Vth year of King Rehoboam,' as is hieroglyphically recorded in Karnac. This furnishes us with a perfect synchronism between Egyptian and Hebrew history up to 971–3 B.C. From this point we have innumerable Egyptian tablets, papyri, and genealogical lists, carrying us upward through the XXIst, XXth, XIXth, and XVIIIth dynasties to Ramses I. (Ramesu) 15th-16th century B.C. Here we have a short period of anarchy, represented in the *Disk heresy*, and find sundry royal claimants, at the head of whom stands Atenra-Bakhan, or Bexen-aten, called by Lepsius 'Amenophis IV.' From the reign of his father Amenophis III. every king is known, by means of hieroglyphical inscriptions on stone and papyri, back to the beginning of the XVIIth Theban dynasty, in the reign of AAHMES I. (Amosis), about 1671 B.C. Here again we have the mysterious period of the *Hyksos* or Shepherd kings, who, according to Manetho, ruled 511 years. Three dynasties may be put down for this period—the XVIth, XVth, and XIVth. But we again step into the broad daylight of monumental facts when we reach the XIIIth dynasty, and with it the 'Old Empire' in the land of K$_{HAM}$, Ham, the venerable *Chemnus*, the Sebakhetps and Hepherhetps of the XIIIth dynasty; whilst the glories of the XIIth blaze forth effulgently, thanks to the critical investigations of the *Turin Papyrus* by the immortal Lepsius.

The XIIth dynasty ends about 2124 B.C.

Though little is known of the XIth, Xth, IXth, VIIIth, and VIIth dynasties, the VIth and Vth dynasties stand solid as rocks on the *Turin* papyrus, and are thoroughly known in consequence of the recovery of all the kings, but one, from the tombs opened at Memphis. The remains of the IVth dynasty surpass belief; those who doubt can refer to the folio plates, the 'Denkmäler,' by Lepsius, copies of which are in nearly all our libraries.

Of the IIIrd, IInd, and Ist dynasties we have no monuments, but even this unknown age must have been preceded by a long period of development, till at last M$_{ENES}$ is set down as the first Pharaoh of Egypt about 3892 B.C. according to Lepsius, or 5702 B.C. according to Böckh; 5613 B.C. according to Unger; Brugsch puts him 4455 B.C.; Lauth 4157 B.C., and Bunsen 3623 B.C. But before Menes constructed Memphis; Teni, This, or Thinis, was already a once flourishing and then decaying town. Menes erected at Memphis a green sanctuary, ornamented with the figures of men and animals. Memphis (Men-ofer) means 'the good station.' The king in the times of Menes had already several titles. He was called the great house—*Per-āo*, Pharaoh; as we speak of the 'sublime Porte.' The king was to his subjects *nuter* (divine), or *neb* (master). He was addressed by the title of *hon-f*, corresponding to our 'Your Majesty'; or only by *on*, which would be our 'Sire.' The Egyptians under Menes had already rewards in the form of decorations, in *nub*, the golden collar, corresponding to our 'order of the garter.' The court consisted of nobles and attendants. The nobles were *Sez*, and had to distinguish themselves by wisdom and learning. The house of the king's children was under a governor, who was responsible for their health and education. Those belonging to the highest classes had the title of *erpa*, illustrious, *ha*, chief, or *set*, your excellency. The affairs of the court were entrusted to intendants, the *hir-sesta*, the secretary and numerous scribes. The king 3000 or 5000 years B.C. had a quartermaster-general; a director of vocal music; a director of amusements; a chief of the chamber of the robes; a chief hair-dresser; a master of trimming the nails of H.M., and a superintendent of the baths. Inferior court-officials were intrusted with the supervision of the granaries, the fruit and oil-chambers; there were royal purveyors of meat, royal bakers, and equerries. Architects, who were held in the very highest honour, because they could marry the daughters of the king, had to inspect the public works. Judges administered the law, already divided into a civil and criminal section. The title *hir-sesta* meant 'he who is above a secret,' There was a hir-sesta of heaven (the royal astronomer), one of 'secret words,' a kind of private secretary, who had to compose important political or social essays; another of grammar. The scribes again were divided into different classes. They had to transmit orders from their superiors; to register dry facts; to keep accounts. The very titles of these court-officials are enough to convince us that at the time of Menes, Egypt must have already possessed a highly-complicated and civilised State-organisation.

The successor of Menes, Atos or Akotus, is recorded to have written 'books on Anatomy,' and constructed the royal palace of Memphis.

This was the state of Egypt under *Menes*. His name suggests a more than merely accidental analogy with *Manû*, *Minos*, or *Man*, and has reference to the time when *man* became conscious of law, and assembled into a social bondship. The Egyptians, before a Menes could have ruled over them, must have gone through the savage and nomadic, or pastoral stages, and have passed from the palæolithic, neolithic, and bronze ages of art into that of iron. When did they invent their *hieroglyphs*, which must first have been *ideographic* before they became *phonetic*? From the first-recorded meeting between the Hebrews, then still nomads, and the Egyptians, it appears that the latter already then formed a well-organised State-body. As regards their monuments, we see them enter the mythical age with their grand stone-constructions, their pyramids, colosses, temples, palaces, sphinxes, catacombs and obelisks, as a developed artistic nation. All these stupendous works are constructed for eternity; there is nothing nomadic in them, though this element here and there shows itself in colossal petrifactions. Wood- constructions and textile fabrics form the bases of their ornamentation, but this influence must have taken effect in antediluvian, nay, even pre-Adamitic, times, when humanity everywhere else was sunk in a state of unconscious inactivity. The mound, constructed with geometrical accuracy as a huge pyramid, must have had an origin somewhere. The construction itself has a purpose. The crystal form surrounds an inner kernel, around which the stone shell is laid; it not only serves to point upwards, but also downwards. Thus mortality and immortality are already blended into one in these hoary monuments.

To proclaim the grandeur of the silent inhabitant, once a mighty ruler, to the four quarters of the globe, was the purpose of these pyramids.

Natural caves must have suggested their tombs and catacombs. The sacred Nile with its majestic flow is reflected in the endless horizontal lines of their temples. The rising peaks of mountains seem to have suggested their huge pylons. The rays of the sun were transformed by them into stones, recording, as gigantic obelisks, the deeds of their kings. When did these obelisks shake off the rough shape of mere huge monoliths, placed in plains to commemorate some grand event? To point upwards in isolated forms was the secret tendency of these half-sculptured, half-architectural marvels. Trees and forests were turned by the Egyptian artists into hypostyle halls, with innumerable columns, spreading a mysterious gloom about them.

The Chinese were practical; the Trans-Himâlâyans metaphysical; the Cis-Himâlâyans agricultural, commercial and warlike; and the Egyptians pre-eminently architectural and *monumental*.

Their whole historical life may be divided into the following art-periods.

> *(a)* The Ante-monumental.
> *(b)* The Pyramidal.
> *(c)* The Hieratic.
> *(d)* The Ptolemaic.

A. These four epochs of art-development resemble layers in the earth's crust. Whilst with other nations the remnants of art are mere skeletons, colourless frames of an extinct social organism, with the Egyptians we have art in all its different phases, with the dried flesh and the scarcely-faded colours, embalmed like a mummy. Life and death were with them so closely allied, that we may say, their life was a continual death, and their death was everlasting life.

The spiritual conceptions of the Egyptians, which might have served to enable us to understand their art thoroughly, were lost with their sacred books, of which, with one exception, we have merely the titles. Plato considered them 10,000 years old in his time. They consisted of:—

1. The *two* books of the Chanter—like the Vedas and the Zend-Avesta containing hymns in honour of the gods, and a code of laws like those of Manû.

2. The *four* astronomical books of the Horoskopus; treating of fixed stars, and of solar and lunar conjunctions, making the sun the centre, round which we revolve.

3. The *ten* books of the Hierogrammatist, or the Sacred Scribe, treating of the art of writing, which was: hieroglyphic (sacred), hieratic (a kind of hieroglyphic tachygraphy—short-hand writing, used by priests only), and enchorial or demotic, used by the people. These books contained, further, the elements of cosmography and geography; tablets, on which the high-roads of the earth were marked; astronomical records, mentioning, according to Diogenes Laertius, 373 solar and 832 lunar eclipses, referring thus to a period of 48,863 years; a chorography of Egypt, and the delineation of the course of the sacred Nile; an inventory of each temple, of the landed property of the priests, and a treatise on weights and measures.

4. The *ten* ceremonial books of the Stolists, which were entirely devoted to religious worship, containing the ordinances as to '*the first-fruits, and the sacrificial stamp, sacrifices, prayers, processions,*' and the like. No human sacrifices were offered up from at least 3000 years B.C.

5. The *ten* books of the prophets, consisting of thirty-six sections, called the hieratic writings, with which the prophets, the first order of the priests, were entrusted. A description of the deities, regulations for the education of the priests, and general laws formed their contents.

The oldest books of law, were attributed to *Hermes* (Toth), implying, that the first germ of an hierarchical organisation of society sprung from the sacred songs, and that law was entirely based upon the religious conceptions of the secret forces of nature by which man had been impressed. Like the Code of Manû, which took its origin in the Vedas, or the Laws of Zoroaster based on the Zend-Avesta, or the injunctions of Confucius founded on the holy records and songs of by-gone ages, the Egyptian laws took their origin in the first poetical feelings of awakened humanity, excited by the mysteries of nature under the rule of an incomprehensible first cause.

6. The *six* books of the Dead. The only books still extant, written in hieroglyphs, and divided by Lepsius into 165 sections. The first fifteen chapters form a distinct and connected whole, with the superscription: 'Here begin the Sections of the glorification in the Light of Osiris.'

It concludes with a book entitled 'The Book of Deliverance in the Hall of the *twofold* Justice (Reward and Punishment), and the Book of Redemption.'

With such a deep and mystic literature, encompassing the gods, nature, and man, in life and death, it is no wonder that a mystic and symbolic art should have succeeded in Egypt.

Their mythology was not less profound than that of the Trans-Himâlâyans; there was more of symmetry, at least architectural symmetry, in their conceptions and representations than in those of the Brahmans, though Egyptian priests and Brahmans have apparently taken their conceptions from one and the same source. The Egyptian had eight gods of the first order, twelve gods of the second, and seven gods of the third order, pointing by these very numbers to an astronomical basis, thus:—

1. The cosmical forces of creative nature.

2. The twelve months of the year.

3. The seven days of the week.

Astronomy is the first powerful divisor of time and the supreme lord of agriculture. Only when the 'Sacred Nile' deposited its fructifying alluvium on the barren limestone of the valleys, formed by the Libyan and Arabian mountain ranges, man could exist and develop in that region. The regular inundation appeared to have taken place under the influence of the sun, moon, and stars. The sun (Osiris) was, therefore, believed to call forth the Nile (Isis) from regions *unknown down to our own days*, and sun and water became, as with the Indians (*Indra and Agni*), the first visible, creative forces of nature.

The eight gods of the first order were:—

I. A$_{MN}$ (Brahm), Am-Ra, Ammon, the Greek Zeus (the son of Kronos and Rhea), the Roman Jupiter; the 'Concealed God,' the 'Lord of Heaven,' the 'Lord of Thrones'; the first creative, incomprehensible, invisible force of the universe. The Brahmă of the Indians, the Zeruane-Akerene of the Persians.

II. K$_{HEM}$ (Kama), the generative God of Nature, Brahmā. He was worshipped, under the *second Thinite Dynasty*, under the symbol of the goat.

73

The primitive, *active*, or male element of nature.

III. M_{UT} (μαῖα {maîa}, matter, Demeter, Leto, Latona, Bhavani), the primitive, *passive*, or female element of nature.

IV. N_{UM} (Nu, Kneph, ChNUbis, the Indian VischNU, Noah, Neptun). In Arabic *nef* means to breathe. The breath of the universe when condensed —'water;' the creative spirit, the Ἀγαθοδαίμων {Agathodaímôn}; the πνεῦμα {pneûma} (the wind, the air) of the Greeks.

V. S_{ETI} (in Koptic Sate), the ray, the arrow; at a later period the frog-headed goddess, the consort of Kneph; the sun-beam, the fructifying heat in union with water (cosmical moisture), producing the inner force of creation.

VI. P_{HTAH} (Ptah, Phthah, S'iva, Vulcan), the creator of the world, which sprang from the mouth of Kneph, meaning at his bidding. His symbol became at a later period the scarabæus. The more numerous this animal was in the Nile valley after the subsidence of the inundation, the more fruitful was the year. Phtah was in reality telluric heat.

VII. N_{ET} (Neith, Athene, Pallas, Minerva, Doorga), the bright goddess of intellectual power, wisdom, knowledge, virtue, passionless happiness. Isis was her substitute. Her temple at Saïs had no roof, but was vaulted over by the sunny or starry canopy of heaven, and bore the mysterious inscription: 'I am all that was, and is, and is to be; no mortal has lifted up my veil, and the fruit I bore is Helios.' Past, present, and future, are mysteriously entwined in the conception of intellect, pervading and ruling the universe.

VIII. R_A (Helios, Apollo, Adonis, Adonaïs, the Lord, Baal, Mithras, Moloch, Teotl, Toth, Hermes, Odin, Thor, Atys, Janus, Kekrops, Endymion, &c.), the sun, the reflected light (with the Cabalists *Hachoser*, in opposition to the expanding light, *Hajashor*).

The representations of these divinities were not monstrous, like those of the Indians; the human form predominates, but the *symbolic* is still the most important element. The outward form has an inward, secret meaning. 'Meaning' and 'meant' are still in wild conflict. The sublime forces of the deity were to be hewn in stone, or given in outlines, or painted; the result was a grotesque product of art, and as such a complete failure.

The twelve gods of the second order were the children of four of the gods of the first order.

I. A_{MN} had only one son, Khunsu (Chous, Chaos, the prototype of Herkules).

II. K_{NEPH} had also only one son, Teth (Toth, Thoth, Hermes), who taught men to write and to read.

III. Pₕₜₐₕ had two children, Atumu (Atum, Atmu), and Pecht, the cat-headed goddess of Bubastis (the Greek Artemis or Diana).

IV. Rₐ had eight children, Hat-her (Athyr, Athor, Aphrodite); Mau (Jao); Ma (Truth); Tefun (the lion-headed goddess); Muntu (Mant); Sebak (Sebek), the crocodile-headed god; Seb (Kronos), and Nutpe (Rhea).

The seven gods of the third order, emanations from those of the second, as these were emanations from those of the first, were:—

1. Set, Nubi, or Typhon, celebrated for his struggle with Horus, the son of Osiris, in the infernal regions. (See what is said of Krishna, p. 70.)

2. Hesiri, Osiris (also the solar year), HSR.

3. Hes or Isis, HS, the Nile, the moon (the lunar year).

4. Nebt-hi or Nephthys, the sister of Isis; sister and wife of Typhon.

5. Her-Her (Aroëris, Arueris).

6. Her (Horus, the child of Osiris and Isis, Harpokrates), who, with Isis and Osiris, formed the great, incomprehensible, mystic trinity of the Egyptians, of which we have the following record:—

Osɪʀɪs was the father, husband, brother, and son of Isɪs.

Isɪs was the mother, wife, sister, and daughter of Osɪʀɪs.

Hoʀᴜs was the brother and son of Osiris and Isis, and was Osɪʀɪs himself.

7. Anubis (Anupo) the dog-star.

Who does not understand at once that, out of these half-astronomical, half-cosmogonical conceptions, a religion and art full of mysticism, blending into one *Fetishism, Astrology,* and *Anthropomorphism,* must have grown? Only through a careful study of Egyptian mythology are we enabled to comprehend that gigantic power which urged the people to construct those temples and palaces, those labyrinths and catacombs, as mystic in themselves, as the hidden powers of nature. The masses in Egypt were kept in a degraded state of passive obedience; they were overawed by metaphysical subtleties, and by huge stone monsters, which filled them with horror, and made them subservient to the dictates of a gloomy priesthood. Religion and art, both supported by a vast store of natural science, were the exclusive property of the priests, of whom the Pharaoh was the merely *tolerated* head, a kind of stone idol in the flesh. Egyptian art was an echo of priestly caprices, which, wrapt in symbolism, had a powerful hold on the untutored minds of the people. Careful investigations have proved that these priests were of a different race to the aborigines; their mythological analogies point to immigrated Brahmans, who brought some religious notions with them from the Ganges, and transferred them to the Nile.

Egyptian art reflects in every form the gorgeous influences of religion. The whole life of every Egyptian was placed, in seven phases, under the protection of seven divinities. The *first* period of man's life was under the influence of *Isis*, the moon (Luna, Selene). The *second* was devoted to *Hermes*; during this period man had to learn to read and to write, to play the harp, to dance, to develop the body in the gymnasium, and to make himself well versed in knowledge according to his station in life; but the only station that granted man an insight into knowledge was that of the *priest*. During the *third* period man was under the care of *Hat-her* (Athyr), or Venus. Love was to rule the youth; the world was to appear to him in the rosy hue of a mystic foam of incomprehensible longing. The *fourth* period was under the dominion of *Ra* (Helios); when love had ceased to disturb the mind, and to fill this world with illusions, the light of truth and earnest activity was to ripen man, and to prepare him for the *fifth* period, under the protection of *Man* or Mars, the God of War; man was to learn either to conquer others, or to conquer his own passions, and to work in the State as a useful member. Few only reached the *sixth* period, guided by *Amn*, the supreme representative of abstract wisdom; during this period man was admitted to act as a judge, to sit at the board of a hierarchical council, or to teach priests as high-priest. At last man became, during the *seventh* period, vapour—breath—air—under the dominion of *Num* (Kneph), and was detached from reality; if good, transferred into a state of ideality; if not, doomed to begin life anew as a loathsome animal, till he atoned for his evil deeds, and, purified, reached the bright abode of Osiris.

B. The *pyramidal period*, the most ancient of Egyptian art, is the outgrowth of these mystic religious conceptions. Nature was to be reproduced, and surpassed in her sublime grandeur. The mountain was brought into a geometrical shape.

The three principal pyramids were built during the reign of the fourth dynasty, 3426 B.C.-3220 B.C.; the first, by Shufu (Cheops), was, in extent, 13 acres 1 rood and 22 perches, more than twice the area of St. Peter's at Rome. The original quantity of masonry was 89,028,000 cubic feet. Total height 480 feet; 16 feet higher than St. Peter's, and 120 feet higher than St. Paul's (London); 360,000 human beings worked at it for twenty years. The stones are from 9 to 12 feet in length, and 6½ to 8 feet in breadth. The second pyramid was smaller, built by Shafra (Chephren), only 454 feet high; and the third by Menkare (Mykerinus), 218 feet high. The mode of fitting the polished stones together is a perfect master-piece of architectural construction.

Osiris was to be worshipped in all halls of festival, in all creation, in all places. Temples were erected in honour of the gods, which were approached through avenues of sphinxes. These sphinxes were of six different kinds. 1. The pure lion (symbol of Amn). 2. The lion with the ram's head (Krio-sphinx —symbol of Khem or Amn). 3. The lion with hawk's head (symbol of Ra). 4. The lion with a male human head (the symbol of Osiris or Horus). 5. The lion with a female human head (the symbol of Mut or Isis). 6. The lion's half-body and legs, with female human head and arms, as in the reliefs of Karnack, and on the Campesian obelisk (probably the symbol of Net).

The tombs were, more or less deeply, hewn into rocks. They generally begin with a small sanctuary, from which an inclined passage leads down into the sepulchral chamber. The decoration is an imitation of wooden trellis-work in very gay colours. The threshold also distinctly bears the traces of a primitive wood construction; a round, trunk-like beam generally unites the two door-posts, and even the ceilings of the apartments are repeatedly made in imitation of wooden boards fastened together. The pillars are square, and united either by a rectangular architrave or by circular beams.

The temples point, by their forms, to a civilisation which took its course from south to north. This bears out the theory that Meroe was once the seat of a colony of priests, who spread religion, and with it science and art, from Upper into Lower Egypt. Thebes appears to have been the most ancient seat of the Egyptian Pharaohs, one of the first of whom was perhaps Osiris, though he has been placed amongst the gods, and was said to have been, like Krishna, an incarnation of the Supreme Being, who revealed himself in love and kindness, and was to put an end to the dominion of Typhon, the Eternal Evil. Might not this myth conceal some historical fact—the advent of a wise hero, who conquers a wild and reckless tyrant? For Osiris had to go through all the sufferings of humanity, and even to suffer death, so as to become the saviour, the deliverer of his people; and then only was he able to turn the earth into a powerful kingdom. By *Earth*, we may assume, Upper Egypt was meant, where the god-man Osiris presided, who, in spite of his having become man, and belonging to the third order of the gods, was placed on an equality with the gods of the first order. The temple or tomb of Ipsambul may be considered the very oldest rock-hewn construction; it has a figure of Osiris twenty feet high over the entrance door. We pass over the remains of Philæ, Elephantine, and Edfou, and come to those of Karnac and Luxor, the venerable Thebes, which, in the fifth century B.C., during the times of Herodotus, were already in a state of dilapidation.

Upon extensive brick terraces, raised high above the flat banks of the

Nile, the Egyptian temple stood, a strictly secluded building. Strong walls, rising in pyramidal form, crowned with an overhanging fluted cornice, gave the mural enclosure a mysterious and stern character. No opening for windows, no colonnade interrupted the monotonous flatness, which is covered, as by one long tapestry, with hieroglyphs, and representations of gods and Pharaohs. The entrance to these buildings, like that of the temple of Edfou, was placed between two tower-like structures called propylæa, the walls of which were decorated with sculptured figures—in three or more rows. Then followed a court, surrounded by pillars, placed at a distance from the walls on both sides, roofed over with stone, and forming a gallery. Thence we reach the pronaos or portico, after which we enter the cell, divided into the naos and adytum. The naos was generally a kind of hypostyle hall, with a flat roof raised in the middle. The pillars and columns had a variety of capitals, but these were generally of one pattern throughout the temple. The quadrilateral Isis-headed capital, as at Denderah, was often used. The monuments of the 'hundred-gated' Thebes are the best school for the study of genuine Egyptian art. The temples on the eastern side of the river are symbolical of the dawn of life; on the western side we find tombs, catacombs, and Memnoniums. At Karnac we have one of the grandest constructions of the world in the ruins of the hypostyle hall, with its gigantic stone ceiling supported by 134 columns, of which the twelve middle ones, about 65 feet high and 11 feet in diameter, are larger and taller than the others, supporting a loftier central nave. The width of this hall is 338 feet, the depth 170½ feet, and the area 57,629 feet, or about five times as large as the church of St. Martin-in-the-Fields in London. Columns and walls are completely covered with sculptured forms of deities; Osiris predominates. Pylons, propylæa, obelisks, colossal statues of red, grey, and black granite cover the courts; chapel-like apartments, connected and unconnected, are strangely intermingled.

Next to the temples we must mention one of the most gorgeous buildings, the *Labyrinth*, containing between three and four thousand chambers in rows, facing inwards the winding alleys, which ascended in a spiral line to the middle, and descended from it in the same way. It has been minutely described by Herodotus, Pomponius Mela, Pliny, and Ezekiel. The building was to be a strict architectural imitation of the planetary system. The inner 1,500 chambers were divided into twelve courtyards, corresponding to the twelve signs of the zodiac, six of which were towards the north, and six towards the south.

The Memnons were monolith statues of imposing size, symbolic of the rising sun—of Horus or Osiris. Homer mentions Memnon, for his remarkable beauty, as the son of the east. Diodorus speaks of him as Tithonus, a general, sent out to aid Priamus of Troy against the besieging Greeks.

The walls of temples, palaces, tombs, and catacombs were partly decorated with reliefs *en creux*, and partly with tapestry-like patterns, using geometrical figures, sometimes, though rarely, intermixed with plants, or plants treated with conventional stiffness. The walls with the Egyptians had a different purpose than merely to encircle or to enclose; they served as huge blackboards of stone, on which the priests wrote their mystic records. The superfluous thickness of the walls suggests that they were once made of brick, like those of Nineveh or Babylon, and, further, the overlaying of these immense granite blocks with stucco, serves to bear out this supposition. The walls of the enclosures of temples and the sarcophagi were covered with hieroglyphs or scenes from life, both on the inside and outside; tombs and catacombs were decorated on the inside only. These scenes are framed in with borders, reminding us of the broad seams in woven stuffs. In temples the scenes refer to burial rituals, or the judgment of the dead; in palaces to hunts and conquests of the kings. We see the Asian and African conquests of Ramses II. represented on the walls of Ipsambul (Aboosimbal in Nubia) in bright-coloured pictures. The king brandishes a pole-axe over the heads of Negroes, Hebrews, and Aryans, that is, over one mixed and two pure groups of mankind. Above his head runs the hieroglyphic scroll: 'The beneficent living God, guardian of glory, smites the South; puts to flight the East; rules by victory, and drags to his country all the earth, and all foreign lands.' High officials and private persons ornamented the walls of their houses and tombs with scenes of every-day occurrences. We may study in these their whole domestic and public life, their customs and manners, their amusements and toils. The ceilings of the chambers are not covered with *symbolic* pictures, but generally with patterns of conventional wall-decorations. In temples they are sometimes decorated with zodiacs, as at Denderah—the best-preserved Egyptian temple, of which, however, the date is doubtful.

C. The *hieratic style* of the Pharaohs substituted a greater amount of very tasteful symbolic ornamentation.

The Hathor-masks, the names of kings in cartouches, the viper as a symbol of divine or royal power; serpents, scarabæi, winged globes, either symbolic of the sun, the moon, or the earth, formed the principal elements of the innumerable variety of severe ornamentation. In addition to these the following were used:—

1. The papyrus, as the symbol of bodily and intellectual food.

2. The lotus, as a symbol of the creative mysteries of the universe.

3. The palm-tree, with its graceful and simple form, served as the

prototype of their columns, the capitals of which were either open or closed lotus-buds or flowers.

4. Lastly, the feather ornament, as the emblem of sovereignty.

The columns during the *pyramidal*, or old style expressed with distinct clearness their purpose to serve as a support; in the *hieratic*, or new style this purpose is detached from the outer form of the column, which no longer has to support, but merely to serve as an ornament, or to proclaim some mysterious tenet in symbolic types. The face of Isis is to look to the four quarters of the globe; the closed or open lotus to symbolise the mystery of creation, the fountain of life, the cup of plenty, and the fount of all blessings. In this treatment they went so far as to imitate the very dew-drops on the lotus, in granite. A strict naturalism was the foundation of all Egyptian conventionalism, and in many instances they succeeded in producing perfectly astonishing effects. In their columns we recognise the very plant which must have suggested the forms. When made circular and of granite, these columns still retained the triangular shape of the papyrus by means of three raised lines on the round surface. At a later period they were fluted, and apparently tied together under the capital with a strap, cord, or band of a broad fibrous substance; the capital above rose in four divisions in the form of a closed lotus. In the hieratic style the fluting of the columns disappears— they are smooth, round, and covered with hieroglyphs, but the base still discloses the plant origin, disguised in an ornament of palm or reed leaves. Characteristic in these columns is the expression of tension in the swelling shaft, which was probably an unconscious imitation of wood-construction; the heavy cross-beams pressing on the thin posts produced this effect, which has been slavishly copied in stone. With the Greeks this swelling of the column became one of the elements of its beauty, because with them it was an abstraction of symmetrical proportion, consciously done, to express the conflicting powers of pressure and resistance. With a proud obstinacy the Egyptians, during their hieratic period, insisted on separating the ornamental from the architectural part of the building, so that no organic connection existed between sculpture and architecture. This is most striking in those colossal sitting figures which are placed in the front and at the back of propylæa, or before the walls of pylons. It is a clear separation of matter and spirit, of purpose and form, which is altogether contrary to the fundamental principles of good architecture.

Art with the Egyptians was thoroughly *polychromatic*; they tinted granite, of whatever colour, with a red pigment, so that the stone might have its proper divine colour, hallowed by the priests. They coloured in flat tints, and used no shading or shadow; they had, however, no difficulty in conveying to the mind the original forms which they intended to copy. *Priestly canons* regulated the size, form, colour, and expression of every statue, and every attribute had its prescribed form, the meaning of which was concealed from the artist, turning him into a mere unconscious machine, a tool in priestly hands. This is the reason why their works of art look monotonous, and everything with them is impressed by the crushing influence of over-regulation. The Typhonic blast of uniformity killed every higher aspiration in the artist. The human figure had to consist of nineteen units; the *second finger was that unit*. Squares of this unit were drawn on the flat, and according to these measurements the human figure was constructed with geometrical accuracy, looking as flat as possible. Dreary deserts of religious prejudices, gloomy superstitions, and childish formalities hindered all progress, and marked their sculpture and ornamentation with fixed, stereotyped stiffness, until the last period of their art.

D. The *Ptolemaic* style began to develop a little more life and taste. The statues did not look as if cast in a general mould; the gods were allowed to have their feet asunder, the one in advance of the other, which gave them some appearance of motion. How taste may be degraded by prejudice and custom, can be seen in the fact, that when this innovation in Egyptian art was settled by a general law of the Pharaoh, with the connivance of the high ceremonial courts, the masses, on seeing their gods with legs apart, as if ready to walk, rushed from all sides with strong ropes, and tied the divinities to their pedestals, horrified at the possibility of their leaving the country altogether. And the gods did leave the country. Anything based on superstition or prejudice, anything having for its vivifying element symbolism or mysticism, must die away in time.

What we said of Indian art holds good of Egyptian forms. Take away from the Uræus, the lotus, papyrus, palm, crocodile, cat, and bull their symbolic meaning, and these elements of ornamentation lose their vitality. The Greeks, and more especially the Romans, have shown us how we may use some of their patterns to advantage: how an entrance hall may be decorated with silent and mournful-looking sphinxes, and what an unsurpassed charm there is in the obelisk, directing the thought upwards. A pyramid still remains one of the finest monuments for one who has filled the four quarters of the globe with his fame.

In their every-day ornaments, rings, bracelets, necklaces, head-dresses and furniture, the architectural straight lines prevail; variety is not much required, the forms as well as the patterns must be the same. Just as we reproduce horse-shoe upon horse-shoe because they bring 'luck,' the Egyptian jeweller reproduced the scarabæus, and the Turin Museum has not less than

180 different kinds of scarabæi. In their architecture they suffered from one great evil—from a horror of symmetry. Their grand palaces or temples have no ruling element; everything is out of proportion, and though in their detailed ornamentation they were symmetrical, and even eurythmical—the harmony of purpose is often wanting. The thought of building for eternity, however, is always present, whilst no one can deny that in our buildings the ninety years' lease is to be traced in every corner. The Egyptians tried to represent the forms of monumental architecture, and they certainly succeeded in reaching the sublime, but they did this in neglecting the beautiful. Their symmetrophobia, which many of our architects imitate only too successfully, spoilt everything. Their weavings were excellent; their wood-constructions, as far as furniture was concerned, faultless; music was known to them; they worked gold, and ornamented it in the so-called 'champ-levé' manner, and were acquainted with enamel 'cloisonné.' They also fixed thin layers of gold thread on metal, and filled the remaining spaces with enamel of different colours, which method the ancients called 'encaustum.' Notwithstanding all these advantages Egyptian art never reached the ideal of beauty; it has only the charm of the *mysterious* for us. To keep this sentiment alive is the duty of any modern artist who wishes to work in the Egyptian style. He must try to convey some mystic cosmogonical or incomprehensible religious thought in diapers, and floral ornament, or in the use of animals or the human frame in outlines, he must place his ideas and forms under a strict linear canon. He may then succeed in reproducing the artistic forms of a nation, during a period, in which humanity did not go beyond the hierarchical in religion, and the practical in art; during which mankind struggled to find forms, but was prevented from the freer exercise of its innate artistic force by the dictates of a despotic priesthood, and was tied with merciless tyranny to monotonous canons, crushing under the weight of symbolism and mysticism every higher artistic aspiration.

CHAPTER VII.

HEBREW ART.

Little, or rather nothing, can properly be said of Hebrew art, for it is a non-entity. The Hebrews are a mixed race. They assert themselves to be of the Semitic group of mankind, but ethnologically they are a composition of black, yellow, and white men, and are closely related to the Arabs and Phœnicians. They were generally slaves. For 450 years they were in bondage in Egypt, whence they first emerged into a national existence. From Moses to Saul, for 450 years, they lived under a kind of theocratic democracy: God, the supreme ruler in heaven, and the Jews on earth his *chosen* people. For another 450 years they had a kind of theocratic monarchy: God ruled in heaven, as the king ruled on earth. This period lasted from Saul to Zedekiah, and gives us—

(α) A period of 100 years under the first three kings, when the twelve tribes were yet united; and

(β) Another period during which they formed two separate kingdoms. Of these

(a) Israel, in this condition, lasted 220 years under twenty kings, who ruled at Samaria, and was destroyed by the Assyrians.

(b) Judæa, as a separate State, existed 350 years under twenty-one kings, and was annihilated by the Babylonians.

Not less than 650 years intervened between the destruction of Jerusalem and its second destruction by the Romans. During this period the chosen people were

1. 200 years under Persian sway.

2. 170 years under the dominion of Alexander the Great and his successors.

3. 130 years they enjoyed a certain independence under the Maccabees.

4. 100 years they were ruled by the Herodes and Romans. After the second destruction of Jerusalem the Jews ceased to have an independent State of their own, and were scattered all over the earth. They in reality enjoyed only 550 years of freedom, as a grand and united nation, out of a period of not less than 6,000 historically-known years.

Intellect came to absolute consciousness for the first time amongst the Jews, and in this their historical importance and weight lie. Man, created in the image of God, lost his state of innocence, absolute contentment and immortality, by eating of the tree of knowledge. The Jews were the first to recognise in a higher sense the double nature of man—his godhead and his animal nature. The country in which they developed is a perfect geological marvel. The region in which they settled was divided by a river and a sea. This sea is 1,400 feet below the level of the Mediterranean. The river flows downwards, like the Stygian river, far beneath the level of the ocean. The banks of the Jordan and the lake Asphaltites are the lowest regions of the habitable globe. In the west the Jews found some fertile plains, but they never could obtain full and peaceful possession of them, nor of the sea-coast. They were shut out from the world in a mountainous region as in a gloomy Puritan chapel, and had ample leisure for self-contemplation, and for attempting to solve the riddle of man's destiny with the help of Egyptian wisdom, Persian, Assyrian and Babylonian theories. Rocks and sand formed the foreground of their earthly existence; the background was made up by a gloomy river and a still gloomier sea—the sea of death, the Acherusian, the Plutonian lake. A sea too low, too mephitic and poisonous for art to exist round it. A region of sorrow, sinfulness, and abject wretchedness cannot be the abode of art and science. The fine art of the Jews was like a migratory bird in its passage over the sea of death.

Not only with the Jews, but also with the Egyptians, Persians, and early Greeks, to represent a god in the likeness of man was considered sinful. The Persians abhorred idols in any shape. The Egyptians gave their gods shape and form, but a merely symbolic form, expressing in concrete signs some higher abstract conception. The human head, the body of a beast or fish, the horns of a ram, or the ears of a cow; the human leg with the foot of a goat, or the human arm with the claws of a bird of prey, were sacred, because symbolical. They had a metaphysical theology written in hieroglyphs. All this was prohibited with the Jews. They allowed some exceptions, and borrowed the figures of the cherubim from the Assyrians, the oxen of the temple from the Egyptians, and the sculptured lions of Solomon's palace from the Persians; their artists were foreigners, and the imitation of these works was ever after forbidden.

'All those things,' says Rabbi Manasseh Ben Israel, one of their most learned commentators, 'which are esteemed holy in the presence of God, or idea of man, may not be imitated in any known form or shape, although made without the intention of adoring them, so as to preclude the possibility of their being worshipped or deified hereafter. Thus the figure of the divine chariot, which Ezekiel saw, may not be made, nor the likeness of angels of any degree, nor of man, for these creatures are all superior from being made in the image of God.' ... The prohibition is further applied by him to everything appertaining to the holy temple, and no house or palace could be built of its size or proportions.

Poetry and music were exempt from this enactment. The importance and influence of the social and religious condition on the development of art may best be studied in the Jews. They had no great architects, sculptors or painters, no inventors, no philosophers in natural science, but many excellent poets, theologians, cabalists, necromancers, philologists and composers. In our times, however, influenced by the vivifying spirit of Christianity, they count amongst themselves, in addition to an inordinate number of picture-dealers, some creditable painters.

They possessed legitimately only *one* temple. Their first temple was a portable tent. The second was almost entirely of cedar-wood, richly provided with metallic ornaments, made by artists from Tyre and Sidon. They possessed one palace, that of Solomon. Babylonian or Assyrian architecture was probably reflected in this, and we may thus form a dim idea of what Solomon's palace must have been. First the temple, then the palace was constructed.

The fact that the first temple was a mere tent, shows at once the nomadic character of the Jews, at a period when the Egyptians had possessed their architectural marvels for thousands of years. To the student of history, architecture is a sure measure of the degree of artistic and social development of a nation. We may boldly say, show us the plans of the houses, palaces, and temples of any nation, and we can determine the degree of its civilisation; we can do even more, we can read its character and religious fervour in these wood, brick, or stone records. That the Jews, having been compelled to witness all the misery and superstitious dulness which the Egyptian hierarchy and theocracy produced, should have detested architecture, and looked upon sculpture or any stone and brick as a curse to humanity, was quite natural; and that, once escaped from the bondage of Egypt, they should have hated any monumental, architectural, or artistic sculptural attempt, is equally obvious.

The egotistical character of the nomadic trader may be traced in the architectural constructions of the Jews. Any nation that loves its god or gods with zeal and self-denial will be sure to build grand temples to his or their glorification. The Persians had no temples, because they spiritualised the divine conception to such a degree, that they thought the first cause present everywhere like light. The Jews borrowed the same idea, and yet to fix the Eternal Spirit visibly amongst themselves, they assigned him a permanent abode, where he was exclusively to dwell; to be near them and to watch over them. Religious egotism was the mainspring of their national existence, and this general egotism made every individual Jew an egotist; and egotists are always bad supporters of anything by which the masses generally may benefit. Such people look only to the satisfaction of their momentary wants; they will collect trinkets, earrings, bracelets, armlets, goblets, gold and silver vessels, but the divine art of architecture, which binds masses together, will be neglected. We see them at first contented with a mere tent, and, when they undertook to construct a lasting building, it was done with all the pomp and gaudiness of a *parvenu*; they borrowed from all the surrounding rich people anything they could lay hands upon, merely to be able to say, without reason or taste—'Look, my special God has also his special house.' In the most powerful period of their national existence, which was a very short one, the Jews roused themselves to the construction of at least *one* temple to their Javeh. They wished at last to possess an Akropolis like the Egyptians, who had so many, or the Greeks, Persians, Assyrians and Babylonians. Their God was at last to be housed, like the gods of the despised Gentiles.

The temple of Solomon has been much written upon. Prejudice, religious fanaticism, blind faith, and unconscious or *voluntary* ignorance, dictated the descriptions and guided the reconstructions. Michaelis, one of the greatest Jewish authorities on Scriptural matters, tells us that 'all the representations which we possess of the temple of Solomon are ornamented with arbitrary forms, and if we ask for authority or proof of this or that ornamental form, we invariably receive the answer: It must have been so, for I would have built in this way.' It is naturally very difficult to obtain a correct description of the temple of Solomon, for with regard to its construction we must rely on the records of the Jews themselves. Unfortunately the Books of the Kings, Chronicles, Ezekiel, and the writings of Josephus, the varying descriptions of the translators, and the host of commentators, who generally obscure the simplicity of the simplest subject, are all at variance.

We may divide Jewish history into the eight following periods.

During the *first* period we find them as nomads on the shores of the Euphrates and Tigris.

During the *second* period they were received as shepherds in Egypt Here they learnt for the first time the arts of a settled people. They found a mighty hierarchy already established; astronomy, chemistry, architecture, and sculpture were practised by priests, who were well-versed theologians, lawyers, physicians, and philosophers. Not only the Jews, who lived amongst the Egyptians, but also the wisest and most learned men of Greece, owed much to the land of hidden wisdom, which was undoubtedly the cradle of the Jewish faith and of Greek philosophy. Moses, Lykurgus, and Solon sat piously listening to the oracular instructions of the Egyptian priests, who taught in mystic symbols. Thales, Pythagoras and Plato borrowed their philosophical theories and systems largely from the Egyptians. The Egyptians worked out the incarnation theory with mystic refinement. Osiris, the concealed Lord of heaven, had to become flesh, to conquer evil. He condescended to become a redeemer—had to suffer a cruel death in order to paralyse the influences of Typhon. The Greeks and Jews never could grasp the mystery of a god changing his almighty subjectivity into an objective human form, in order to attain, through suffering and death, what he could have fulfilled in a thousand other ways. Osiris was not only the supreme ruler in heaven, but he was also the supremely just and inexorable judge in hell. The division of the universe into an abode of bliss for the departed just, and of eternal darkness and fire for the unjust, was an Indian, Persian, and Egyptian dogma. To the blessed it was promised that they should pluck the sweetest fruits in heaven, 'for they have given food to the hungry, and water to the thirsty; they clothed the naked, and lived in truth; for their heart was with God and God was with them, and they will enjoy eternal life in his presence,' Of the wicked, on the contrary, it was said: 'that they could not see the countenance of the Lord of heaven, nor ever hear his voice; they would go about without heads, drag after them their hearts, be boiled for ever in a cauldron, be hanged for ever by their legs.'

From these metaphysical and mystic Egyptians, the immortal Jewish lawgiver borrowed the division of his nation into twelve tribes, in imitation of the twelve zodiacal signs, and the division of Egypt into twelve nomes. In Egypt he learnt to distinguish between clean and unclean animals; to practise circumcision, which was with the Egyptians confined to their priests; but Moses promised to make his compatriots 'a nation of priests.' He established the tribe of the Levites, in imitation of the Egyptian priest-caste; and regulated their income, mode of living, and duties according to the ten books of the prophets (see p. 112); he divided the priests into four different classes, which at a later period were called *Peshat*, exegists, *Remes*, expounders of dubious points, *Derush*, composers of homilies, and *Sod*, the hierophants, or those versed in the real mysteries. The initials of the four names are taken from the Persian word PRDS (paradise) which may be adduced to prove that what Moses originally instituted was worked out, and systematised, at a later period, under Persian influence. The whole arrangement of the tabernacle was Egyptian; the serpent-worship was Egyptian, and so was the idolatrous predilection for the golden calf. Moses in his wise gratitude forbade the Jews ever to be hostile to the Egyptians.

During the *third* period they left Egypt, and though they were acquainted with all the smaller arts of their Egyptian task-masters, and knew how to weave, to cut stones, to model, to cast, and to found gold and silver, they had to seek and to gain by hard fighting a new home to settle in. During this period they forgot everything; their accomplishments were gone when they settled in the Holy Land. For during times of war the growth of sciences and arts was never fostered.

During the *fourth* period they reached the very climax of their national glory. David became master of a large empire which extended from the shores of the Euphrates to the frontiers of Egypt; this expansion was accomplished by the force of arms. His successor Solomon administered and consolidated the empire, founded on blood and iron, by wisdom and the culture of the arts of peace. After a Cæsar, the Jews had an Augustus. Solomon lived in friendship and peace with the surrounding mighty kingdoms, especially with Hiram, King of Tyre. It was Solomon who began to build Tadmor (afterwards Palmyra, the queen of the East), to establish in the desert a common emporium for Phœnician wares, and to enable the Jews to trade with them.

During the *fifth* period the vast empire was divided into two parts, the one of which was altogether annihilated, and the other fell into the hands of the Babylonians, and the temple of Solomon was destroyed. Slaves and captives are rarely good artists.

During the *sixth* period, after Kyrus had freed the Jews and permitted them to return to their native country, their national position improved. Under Darius, Zorobabel received permission to reconstruct the temple of Solomon on the foundations of the one erected by that wise king, and it was accordingly rebuilt, but this could only be done in accordance with the impoverished condition of freed captives.

During the *seventh* period, under Alexander the Great and his followers, the Jews, attacked by Persians, Egyptians, and Syrians, showed that they could rise to the very highest deeds of heroism and self-sacrifice.

Finally, during the *eighth* period, under the Romans, they gave up all hope of maintaining their position as a chosen people; they revolted sometimes, but more for theological than political reasons. Pompey treated them with great kindness and consideration after the capture of Jerusalem. During the reign of Augustus the town attained a grandeur and extension which it had never possessed, even in its brightest days under the sway of Solomon. But stubborn and arrogant as the Jews always were in times of prosperity, though enjoying a certain amount of freedom, they revolted, and the town and temple were destroyed. Nothing was left but the candlestick with seven branches, symbolic with the Egyptians of the seven planets, and with the Jews of seven archangels, or of the seven days of the week, sculptured in marble on the Arch of Titus, together with a facsimile of the holy ark, and some of the trumpets, used in religious ceremonies. It would be most interesting if the original relics, which it is assumed are buried in the Tiber, could be recovered; and, as so many venerable relics of by-gone ages have been brought to light, we do not despair of once seeing these remains.

The tabernacle, or earliest temple of the Jews, was entirely constructed on the plan of an Egyptian temple. To convince ourselves of this truth we need only compare its plan with that of the temple at Edfou. The triple division into a Pronaos, Naos, and Adytum, or the Holy of Holies, was strictly observed in both. The Adytum was a cube 10 cubits, or 15 feet each way; an outer temple, as Naos, consisted of two such cubes, 15 feet broad by 30 feet long. Adytum and Naos were covered by a sloping roof, which projected 5 cubits (7½ feet) in every direction beyond the temple itself, making the whole 40 cubits, or 60 feet, in length, by 20 cubits, or 30 feet, in width. Adytum and Naos stood in an enclosure—the Pronaos, 100 cubits (150 feet) long, by 50 cubits (75 feet) broad. From Moses to Solomon, for 600 years, this tabernacle was the only temple of the Jews. When Solomon began to construct the temple, he adhered strictly to the above arrangement, only doubling all the dimensions. The temple partook more of the character of a square shrine, or a store-house intended to contain precious works in metal; a kind of opisthodomos. The principal ornaments were two brazen pillars, Jachin and Boaz (sun and moon), by the skilful Hiram of Tyre. They were said to have been marvels of metal-work. The pillars of Susan or Persepolis, which had capitals of the same relative proportions, may give us some idea of these. In Egyptian temples it was also usual to place propyleæ at the porch of a temple, and the same custom prevailed with the Phœnicians, as in the case of the celebrated Venus (Astarte or Astharote) shrine at Paphos. After the construction of the temple by Solomon, Jerusalem became the holy and exclusive central point of Judaism. There only, and nowhere else, did they allow their God to be present. Zorobabel erected on the very spot another altar and temple in the same spirit, and this is the reason why the erection of a second temple at Heliopolis by Onias, under the Ptolemæians, caused such animosity and jealousy amongst Egyptian and Judaic Jews. It is said that the necessary marble, wood, and stone, and also the gold, silver, and brass vessels had already been weighed and prepared for the construction of the temple during the reign of King David, who gave his son the plan of the whole architectural construction. According to Chronicles, however, it appears that David made little or no preparation, and that Solomon only found some of the brass-work ready for use. This latter assertion is clearly verified by the correspondence between Solomon and Hiram. Solomon asks for wood for building in general, as also cedars and cypress trees from Mount Lebanon; adding that he wishes that Sidonians, as experienced carpenters, should help his own workmen, whom he designates as less able. This does not say very much in favour of the artistic skill of the Jews, who at the period of Solomon's reign had not yet attained the same degree of proficiency as the pre-historic constructors of pile-dwellings. The request of Solomon was granted by the King of Tyre, and Adoniram was sent as foreman of the Sidonian carpenters, of whom 30,000 were appointed by Solomon; 10,000 of these worked alternately from month to month. Besides the 30,000 carpenters, there were 80,000 sculptors, or rather stone-cutters and masons, and 70,000 journeymen, making altogether 180,000 working men, under 3,300 overseers, employed in the construction of the temple, all tributary *strangers* whom David had conquered. The construction began 592 years after Exodus, about 975 years B.C. Mount Moreah, or Moriah, was the site chosen, and the temple was completed in *seven* years. The inner temple was 60 cubits (90 feet) long, 20 cubits (30 feet) broad, and 30 cubits (45 feet) high. Josephus says it was 120 cubits (180 feet) high; this would make the edifice resemble a square tower. The Pronaos may have been 120 cubits high. The space, 60 cubits long and 20 broad, was separated into two divisions. Of these the rear was 20 cubits square, forming the Holy of Holies, the 'sekos' of the Egyptian temples. The other division, 40 by 10, formed the Naos, the holy place, which was preceded by a hall, the Pronaos. The division: One God, one priesthood, and one people, was thus expressed. Rooms were constructed round the temple three stories high, corresponding to the rooms in the Egyptian Labyrinth, and the Brahmanic and Buddhistic choultries, or cloisters. There were thirty rooms on each floor. The height of the temple having been 30 cubits, this would give 15 feet for each story, walls included. Josephus doubles all these dimensions, and adopts inconceivable measurements. The ninety rooms were used as receptacles for the sacred vessels, and the temple was thus literally a holy treasury. The Holy of Holies having been only 20 cubits high, a space of 10 cubits, or 15 feet, would have been left above it; of this room no intelligible mention is made. In the Septuagint there is an allusion, which differs from the Vulgate and the different translations. In Chronicles we have upper chambers mentioned, which were overlaid with gold; this might have been the rooms or chambers above the Holy of Holies. No special staircase led to this room. It was undoubtedly a mysterious apartment, and, like all mysteries, excited some writers to very varied speculations on its possible nature. Amongst others the learned Ben David, in a letter to Lichtenberg in the Berlin 'Archive der Zeit,' asserted that this chamber must have contained an electric battery, for golden chains connected the room with the pillars of Jachin and Boaz, which were hollow, and could be placed in communication with the altar of brass. The points of the temple were golden. At the consecration of the temple, clouds, produced by incense, suddenly filled the interior of the temple, and a flash of lightning ignited the sacrifice. Michaelis tells us that the temple was never struck by lightning—the lightning, therefore, setting fire to the sacrifice must have been produced within the temple.

No stone roofs or vaults are mentioned in connection with the temple or palace built by the Jews; architecture was, therefore, in its most primitive stage. The inner temple and the Holy of Holies were entered through folding- doors. The Holy of Holies was entirely empty, symbolic of the incomprehensibility of the nature of the Deity. This was also the case in Egypt with the 'sekos,' which was, in fact, a shrine either quite empty, or containing a scroll, on which were written the words: 'I am that was, that is, and that shall be.' Two courts surrounded the temple, an inner and an outer court. The outer court was open to every Jew, but the inner court to the priests only. The former was surrounded by a double row of pillars overlaid with cedar-wood. It is said that Solomon had valleys filled up in order to make the concrete subconstruction of the length even. Each side of the outer wall surrounding the whole temple was 4 stadia or 1 stadium (606 feet 9 inches English) in length, giving 2,427 feet all round. The pillars Jachin and Boaz stood on the staircase of the inner court; each was 36 feet in circumference, 54 feet in height without the capital, which was 15 feet high. The shafts were hollow and the brass 4 inches thick. On the south-eastern side stood the round brass basin, called the sea, 30 feet in diameter, in which the priests used to wash their hands. Besides the 'sea,' there stood on pedestals on either side of the temple five cups, 12 feet in diameter and 9 feet high. The altar of the burning sacrifice, in the middle of this space, was 60 feet broad and as many feet long; all these secondary necessaries of the temple stood in the east. The surrounding courts rose in terraces like those of the palace of Persepolis. The temple, whatever its magnificence might have been in precious stones, gold, silver, carved cherubim, brass and silver vessels, washing-basins and candlesticks, was architecturally an utter failure, whether compared with the monumental temples of Egypt, the grand and splendid palaces of Assyria, Babylon, or Persepolis, or the temple of Diana at Ephesus. The latter, which was built on a marsh, that it might not be endangered by earthquakes, was 425 feet in length and 220 in width, and had 127 columns 60 feet high, each the gift of a king. This is the account given by Pliny, who, however, describes either the seventh or eighth temple. Stable as was everything in religious matters with the Jews, they did not venture in rebuilding their temple to make any alterations; a stone displaced, an ornament improved, might have driven their God from his chosen abode. With such ideas art is impossible. The additions made to the temple under the Romans, in order to render the building more in harmony with their street architecture, were only outer courts with rich colonnades of Corinthian columns, and had nothing to do with the temple itself. These formed the Stoa-Basilica, with the court of the Gentiles, which is spoken of as imposing and forming a mighty group, and must not be confounded with the temple itself, which was certainly no specimen of architecture, either in dimension, in plan, or in decoration, if we except some stiff vine foliage on capitals, which was exceptionally characteristic of the Jewish style.

The numerous tombs in the neighbourhood of Jerusalem are rock-hewn, clearly betraying their Egyptian origin; they are provided with numerous hollows for the reception of the bodies. These sepulchres are without any artistic stamp; on some façades we can see the Egyptian fluted corona. The façades of the so-called royal tombs of Jacob or the judges are decorated in a Greek style, as are the tombs of Zacharias and Absalom; the latter stand out from the rock as independent structures, ornamented with Ionic pillars, and above the Egyptian corona rises a pyramidal or conical structure; a combination of the pre-historic tumulus with Egyptian and classic elements. Something is borrowed from everyone to make up a chosen national element.

In books or in conversation this may avail, but in art, where the outer impression is to create a corresponding sensation, assertions must be borne out by visible productions, and to falsify architectural records is much more difficult than to interpolate passages, alter dates, or make assertions in utter defiance of probability and possibility. The Hebrews, whether as Jews or Israelites, had no art, and never pretended to have one; they were contented with the art-products which other nations made for them, in perfect accordance with the clearly-expressed promise of the God of Abraham, Isaac, and Jacob: 'That He would give them great and goodly cities, which they would not build; and houses full of good things, which they would not fill; and wells digged, which they would not dig; and vineyards and olive trees, which they would not plant.' With such principles neither architecture, sculpture, nor ornamentation could flourish. Art in Asia never became master of matter from an esthetical point of view, for, in all these works, matter sways the mind; it is either an exhibition of precious stones on walls, or lace- work in marble, or endless heaps of huge granite blocks and columns without purpose, or decorations in wild, fantastic, and endless combinations. The Eastern mind could not free itself from the influence of a mighty hierarchy. In the East it was the eternal *Hermes*, the *Logos*, the *priest*, who read truth in the stars, manufactured gods and goddesses, wrote the language of heaven, drew up plans for temples, squared out the proportions of the human body, and gave laws to sculptors and painters, to stone-cutters and masons, to joiners and carpenters, weavers and dyers. Hermes, with his followers, was the physician, the lawgiver, and the judge of the masses; he prayed, he sacrificed for them, he prophesied, circumcised, married, embalmed, and buried them. The priest in the East, whether as Brahman, Buddhist, Hierophant, Magi, or Levite, generally placed the idea, the spirit, the word, the λόγος {logos} above the form, which, in itself, crippled the form the more effectually, because the form, however revolting, was the mere symbol of some sacred mystery. The creative genius of art was thus almost extinguished under the stifling and petrifying influence of hierarchical formalism, and, until it had been freed from this, could neither develop nor prosper. The process of freeing humanity from this formalism was first begun and accomplished by the Greeks.

CHAPTER VIII.

GREEK ART.

Art has appeared to us till now under peculiar circumstances. We have seen it in Asia and Africa, and in both parts of the world it represented the uninterrupted struggle of humanity for self-consciousness. Humanity was too much under the influence of the marvellous and incomprehensible, and neither the marvellous nor the incomprehensible can be brought into shape. The Indians tried to give forms to the metaphysical phenomena of nature; the Persians were bent on the glorification of the power of one visible earthly despot; the Egyptians tried to copy the realistic phenomena of nature, and inscribed them with mystic signs, uniting Indian abstractions with the real phenomena of nature. When a thought was fixed into a form; the thought, being at the same time a religious conception, could no more be changed; it became in art what a technical name for a natural phenomenon is in science. Oxygen is oxygen, and designates only that element; so when once a form was settled, as that of Vishnu or Amn, S'iva or Osiris—or the serpent fixed as a symbol of eternity, or the hawk as a symbol of light—the inner or spiritual life of the artist was fettered down to outward forms with special inward meanings. Thus the constraining sway of misunderstood nature on one side, and the stationary precepts of an omnipotent hierarchy on the other, entangled the artist's imagination and paralysed every effort of his subjective power of production. The different nations began to be wrapped up in their different artistic forms, which became by degrees hard and impenetrable *national* and religious incrustations; the masses, held in abeyance, led by theocratical art, had only to glorify one visible or invisible tyrant, with whom the universe was blessed. Eastern art was to a certain degree plastic, only too plastic as in India; but it was too penetrated with an incomprehensible spiritualism to find the right objects for its plastic tendencies. Even where geometrical figures, flowers, or trees were used, the effect of their simple combination was marred by a want of harmony between thought and form, or idea and body. This harmony between outward form and inner spirit, wherein real beauty consists, this balance between the dynamic and static cosmogonical elements, was wanting in Eastern art. The East rent nature asunder, and looked upon *matter* as *evil*; and yet matter was to be used, to bring spirit into form. The element of S'iva, Ahriman, or Typhon was to give visible form to the conceptions of Brahmă, Ormuzd, or Osiris, and could not do this, because the connecting link to blend the apparently-opposed powers into one, was wanting. A uniting force for this mysterious antagonism, a mediator between heaven and earth, divinity and humanity, was sought for, but not found. The Persian unconsciously set Meshiah (man, *mensch*) down as that element, but Meshiah was not yet allowed to come to any free development, and he sank into the pitiful and degraded position of a slave to despotic oligarchs, or still more intolerant spiritual hierarchs. Meshiah (humanity) was first freed by the *Greeks* in *form* and by *Christ* in *spirit*.

There can be no doubt that the Greeks were, for a short time at least, the ancient representatives of the well-balanced static and dynamic forces in humanity. Of all the geographical districts of the world, whether in the Eastern or Western hemisphere, none are so admirably adapted for the cultivation of social intercourse as the Grecian isles, and the Grecian peninsula, the classical region of the Ægean Sea. Nowhere is so large a coast- line found, surrounding so small a territorial surface; nowhere such a variety of creeks, capes, promontories, inlets, and harbours as round the Peloponnesus, and the islands uniting Asia Minor with Greece and Italy. No streams like the Ganges, or the Hoang-ho; no mountains like the Belur Tag or Himâlâya. Gorgeous uniformity is the characteristic of China and India; variety and change the very element of the Greek world. Mountains, plains, valleys, streams, are all of a limited size; there rules a sweet, eternal harmony between spirit and form; nothing is exaggerated, nothing overawes man; he feels at home; the dark-blue sky over-arches his verdant, hilly, amiable earth, adorned with brooks and hills, boskets and flowers. Valley chases valley; rivulet pursues rivulet; clouds follow clouds; the morning dawn flies before the bright noon, and the noon dies away, in the cool sighs of the evening breezes, into the embrace of dark night. The self-conscious spirit of *youthful* humanity came into life for the first time in Greece. Everything with the Greeks was *feeling*, but a feeling, conscious of a real purpose in religion, the State, the family, and in art. We shall see that intuitive feeling grow by degrees into *critical reflection*, but in the first instance everything with the Greeks was ingenuous, or, as the French call it, 'naïve.' This classical 'naïveté,' this unconscious, unaffected simplicity, enabled them to become masters of intuitive productions, and to look upon this world with an unbiassed eye, prone only to see what was harmonious and beautiful. The whole life of the Greeks was thus one long *ideal* dream of poetical and artistic *reality*. They took an interest, however, in objective individuality only; the beauties of nature as one great total did not yet affect their subjective comprehension. They could not grasp the pantheistic notion of the Indians, who saw in every detailed phenomenon of the universe the working of ONE indivisible and incomprehensible first cause. They shuddered at the Egyptian monsters, which were to serve as symbols of that sublime conception which lost on the Nile all its primitive grandeur. They found the Persian absorption of the universe into a conflict between light and darkness too dreary, and ascribed to it the loss of all individual freedom. They worked out a system of their own, based on Indian grandeur, Egyptian symbolism, and Persian abstractions. To be thoroughly acquainted with this combination of influences is the very first step towards an understanding of Greek art.

The Greeks were Aryans in language, and in mode of thinking; Aryans who had detached themselves very early from their Cis-Himâlâyan brethren, and peopled Asia Minor and the surrounding islands. They were strengthened by Egyptian and Phœnician immigrations, and invigorated by Thracia's warlike spirit.

Like a plant that only lives and grows by means of the antithetic activity of air, light, and water, the Greek State-body had air supplied by Orpheus from Thracia, light by Kekrops from Egypt, and water by Kadmus from Phœnicia. Independent freedom and love of the arts were the gifts of the North; the South furnished them with deep knowledge, and Phœnicia gave them the vivifying spirit of commerce. Their language is an offshoot of the Sanskrit, but stands in a more distant relation to it than the Zend—to which it is closely allied. They are principally distinguished from the Asiatic nations by their decided hatred of everything arbitrary and chaotic. From their love for individuality and diversity of customs, manners and modes of thinking, sprang the national unity of the Greeks in the fairy realms of Poetry and Art. When they began to feel themselves a people, they assumed the name of Hellenes; and their first historical deed was the admirable completion of a language which, for simplicity, power, and beauty, has remained up to our own days a model for all other languages, for it alike possesses eurythmy and power of expression. The overwhelming metaphysical subtleties of the Sanskrit are simplified; the variety of consonants and vowels reduced, and the mode of writing corrected; everything proving a deep sense for order, clearness, and moderation.

They had three dialects: the Doric, distinguished by a broader pronunciation; the Ionic, possessed of softness and a melodious richness; and the Æolic, a kind of mixture without a special character. The Dorians came southwards from the hoary mountains of Thessaly, and gained step by step an influence and dominion over the other tribes of Greece. The Ionians occupied the east, and were considered the connecting link between Hellas and Asia; but whatever the Hellenes took from Byblos, Sidon, Tyros or the Libanon, assumed a really Hellenic form, after it had passed through the purifying element of Doric correctness. The south gave *ideas*, and the north brought them into *form*.

Whatever the Hellenes touched they beautified. The powerful giant Bhîma of the Mahâbhârata is the prototype of Herakles; but in the myths concerning Herakles we recognise the mere personification of commercial daring and enterprise. Accompanied by his dog, he finds the cochineal; the goblet in which he sails to Erytheia is but the Phœnician merchantman; the Phœnicians are referred to, when it is recorded of him that he had broken the devastating horn of the mountain-streams. Moloch, to whom Assyrians, Indians and Hebrews sacrificed, without ever being capable of investing the fire-spitting monster with anything like poetry, was destroyed by Herakles. The gods of Asia became with the Hellenes demons, from whom they learned some useful trades. Poseidon, the god of the sea, is, like the element over which he rules and in which he dwells, of a sinister, implacable character; he requires human sacrifices, annihilates horses (meaning ships), in fact does, as incarnate divinity, what the sea does in our own times. The Titans are acquainted with astronomy, and are personifications of a certain knowledge in maritime matters. Proteus, the Egyptian Pharaoh, is with them the keeper of the seas, and Atlas the father of nautical astronomy, and both were companions of the Tyrean Herkules. In all the myths and legends of the Greeks we can trace some facts. The divinity they could only comprehend in the well-proportioned form of a human being, and a hero or benefactor of humanity became with them a divinity. This blending into one of the divine and human is the most important feature in Greek thought. Vishnu and Osiris also became incarnate—but their deeds were supernatural; the principal feature of their 'man-godhead,' or 'divine manhood,' is an incomprehensible mysticism. Their anthropomorphism had in it something gloomy. When the divine Apollo uttered the memorable words: '*Man, know thyself,*' the Greeks became suddenly conscious of the inborn spark of the divine intellect in man; the gods were intelligible to them, and the Asiatic world of abstractions emerged in a thousand different human forms of divine conceptions.

Uranos (*Varuna* in Sanskrit) is heaven, or rather space—*Kronos*, time, and *Gæa*, earth. *Uranos* as well as *Kronos* and *Pontos* were offsprings of the Earth. So far we have to deal with the same mystical elements which engendered all the Asiatic cosmogonies. But Uranos and Gæa are set down as male and female, and are endowed with powerful children—the Titans and Titanides, the Hekatoncheires (or Kentimanos, hundred-handed, powerful giants with fifty heads), and the Kyklopes, who were very clever, and invented many useful arts.

The most important gods were Okeanos, Japetós, and Kronos. The human character of Greek mythology begins even before the birth of Zeus. Uranos was afraid of his own children, and had them confined in eternal darkness in Tartaros; their mother, Gæa, had pity on them, and armed the youngest, Kronos, with a sickle, with which he attacked Uranos, and deprived him of his creative power. From that moment Uranos was idle, could produce no new forms, and was neither worshipped by gods nor men. The fact which underlies this dramatic scene, in which gods are the actors, is a cosmical phenomenon. In time all things were created, and in time the creative force, as far as our earth was concerned, ceased with the creation of man, to be productive of new forms. Kronos had five children—Hestia, Demeter, Here, Pluton, and Poseidon, and these he devoured. In this cruel image we see represented the revolving movements of time, in which the present is everlastingly the prey of the past, engendering the future. The sixth son of Kronos, Zeus (creative ether), was saved by his mother's cunning, for she gave the inhuman god a stone instead of her child; Metis, however (Maya, Matter), afterwards the wife of Zeus; rescues the children that Kronos had swallowed, and he is obliged to give them back again in an eternal circle. These children of Kronos are years, months, weeks, days and hours. We have here an instance of the manner in which phenomena were turned by the Hellenes into living beings. Kronos was an old man with a long flowing beard, and held a sickle or scythe in his hands, with which he cut down everything. And as symbol of eternity a serpent lay by his side.

Zeus serves us even more as a specimen of the anthropomorphic tendency of the Greeks. He was the *father* of the gods, and had to *fight* with the Titans. He led the immortal gods, who assembled on Mount Olympus against these terrible Titans, who mustered in great strength on Mount Othrys. For ten years the battle raged without result; heaven, earth, and sea resounded with the frightful struggle. Gæa advised the gods to call in the Kyklopes and Hekatoncheires. These presented Poseidon with the trident, Pluton with the helmet that had the power to make the wearer invisible, and Zeus received from the depths of the earth the flaming thunderbolts. Then only the Titans had to yield to storms and lightnings, and were chained down at last in Tartaros. We read a chapter of geology when we peruse Hesiod's description of this struggle. In the Titans, Kyklopes, and the hundred-handed giants we recognise the antediluvian monsters—the mastodons, megatheriums, and saurians, petrified for ever in the strata of the earth's crust. Zeus, after his conquest, began to rule the Olympian gods and mankind. He himself was full of passion and wrath, of human failings and shortcomings; but, after all, he was kind, dignified—even in his weakness, just and grand. He smiled, and love and joy pervaded the universe; he frowned, and the universe shook to its very foundations. He indulged in freaks, and still was afraid of his haughty and jealous wife, who acted in many instances as a well-bred lady would, who had the misfortune to be wedded to an amorous husband. Zeus was frequently so troubled by his riotous gods and goddesses, that he had a bad headache, and was once obliged to call in Hephaistos to cure him with a heavy blow, and on this occasion Minerva (wisdom) sprang forth armed with spear, helmet, and shield. The truth that intellect and reason are of divine origin was proclaimed in this myth. In the Greek legends the poet's imagination has turned the forces of nature into beautiful men, women, or children. How much the gods, with them, were the creatures of man's fancy, may be seen in the fear of the opinions of their earth-born children with which the gods were endowed. The Almighty Thunderer, when his heavenly subjects made too much noise, often cried: 'What will my earthly sons say?' and for fear that they might find fault with him he yielded, and made concessions, and heaven and earth, sun, moon and stars were again at peace.

It is true that in Indian lore the same characters are drawn, but, like their supernatural gods, they are gigantic and monstrous. Men and women in the Indian fables, behave like unwieldy spectres, that frighten us during an uneasy dream; we must first divest them of their inhuman forms in order to comprehend them. The conceptions are too marvellous to impress us with moral lessons; we are lost in allegories, metaphors, symbols and double meanings. This occurs less in Greek mythology. *Atlas* was the representative of patience; he had for ever to carry the world on his shoulders, and was turned at last into a rocky mountain range. *Epimetheus* was the prototype of senseless carelessness, and was destroyed by his own folly. *Prometheus* at last was the embodiment of considerate prudence; he was devoured by the *vulture* of 'care and sorrow for the morrow.' Prometheus may be said to be the best, most intelligible emblem of classic humanity, as Faust may be considered as the incarnation of romantic mankind. Prometheus wanted to bring matter into form; Faust to *know* what held spirit and matter together. Prometheus stole fire from heaven, made man of clay, and vivified him. Faust knew that this heavenly fire was a force over which he had no control, and he called in a spirit to teach him 'how all one whole harmonious weaves, each in the other works and lives.' The *'formal'* is the longing of the Greek Faust, and the *'spiritual'* the aspiration of the Teuton Prometheus. All the Greek eîdola embodied some power of nature. Philomela was a pining woman. The Laurel was formed out of the lovely Daphne (from the Sanskrit Dahanah, our word 'dawn'). In every tree a Dryad dwelt, in every wave a Naiad sported. Demeter's tears for her lost daughter Persephone nourished rivulets. On the bright heights of Mount Olympus, on Helikon, or Parnassus, or Pindus, above the petty cares of every-day life, sat the earnest *Klio* with an open scroll and a stylum, recording with lovely patience the events of the past. *Euterpe*, with her two flutes, brought harmony into the discordant sounds of the earthly spheres, and filled the world with songs and tunes; *Melpomene*, armed with gloomy mask and dagger, presided over the fictitious sufferings of humanity struggling with the inexorable fates, reflecting in an artificial mirror—reality. *Thalia*, with a shepherd's staff and a Silenus' mask, endowed with an eternal smile, comforted man with more cheerful views. *Terpsichore*, with a lyre of seven chords, taught him to express joy, happiness, and pious veneration by the rhythmical movements of his body. *Erato*, on her Kythera with nine chords, warbled love-songs, and inspired and aided young poets to pour out in measured language the immeasurable feelings of their souls. *Polyhymnia*, or Polymnia, protected orators, philosophers, and stage-players, and enabled them to keep within the boundaries of moderation, for she placed the first finger of her right hand on her lips, impressing them with the necessity for caution. *Urania*, with her eyes lifted to the starry heavens, tried to draw man's attention to the well-regulated courses of the heavenly bodies, proclaiming in eternal silence with fiery tongues the glories of the universe. *Kalliope* finally taught man to record heroic deeds in epic poetry. These *nine* muses, presided over by the manly and wise, valorous and glorious Apollo, nursed, taught, and accompanied the Hellenes through life; they met them as lovely charmers in a thousand different forms, in temples, on friezes, metopes, goblets, pateras, amphoræ, and urns; nothing possessed a meaning for them that had not a poetical, artistic, and scientific aim.

Life with the Greeks was one continual festivity. They worshipped their gods in singing joyous songs, in running, playing, and wrestling. They thought it a duty to develop both body and intellect, the gifts of the immortal gods. They deeply loved poetry, wrote it if they could, or recited it, or listened to it and imbibed it with their whole souls. They rejoiced in athletic sports; influenced by Terpsichore, they showed the wondrous beauty of their harmoniously-constructed bodies. Joy and delight swelled their muscles when they wrestled, and throbbed through all their veins when they moved in rhythmical simplicity, like the stars in heaven. They prayed when they composed epic poems; they worshipped when they wrote tragedies or comedies; they honoured the gods when they built temples; they humbly beseeched their blessing when they sculptured. The whole life of the Greeks was one grateful act of artistic devotion. Their temples were so many hymns in stone and marble; their ornamentations in reliefs, sculptures, winding frets and meanders, are epic poems, dramatic representations, and lyric effusions of the very highest intellectual refinement. Art with the Greeks was cherished, cultivated, and loved for its own divine sake. Rich and poor, old and young, men and women, boys and girls, used art and poetry, science and philosophy, as the plastic language of their ever-praying lips, hands and minds. Whenever the life of a nation is thus inspired; when the comprehensive culture of intellect, the harmonious development of the body, and the mysterious feelings of existence are guided by the mighty and productive energy of an awakened and excited imagination, and regulated by a consciousness of order; art must attain that expansive, noble, and beautiful form which we admire in the Greeks.

Greek poetry and philosophy had the same basis of reality as their mythology. That which was asserted by the Asiatic and African law-givers to have been directly dictated by the gods, was gradually acquired by the Greeks through deductive and inductive reasoning. Soon the mythological conceptions of the poets were turned into eîdola. Aphrodite was set down as the representative of matter, out of which all things were formed. Pallas-Athene lost her individuality, and became intellect pervading humanity. Apollo was no more the 'god-man' or the living sun, but cosmical heat. The forms of fearful monsters that originated in Asia, with ferocious jaws, with three heads, spreading fear and awe, looking as if nothing but human flesh could satisfy their voracity, also terrified the Greeks during the mythic period of their national existence, and human flesh was accordingly sacrificed. Such sacrifices were prevalent wherever monster-gods, without human shape, without legs or arms, with fishes' tails, dog's or cat's heads, with round and glaring eyes, and many arms, inspired the masses with fear and trembling. This was the case in Greece when monsters and pirates peopled the sea-coasts; when *Geryon*, the giant with three bodies, three heads, six hands, six legs, and two wings; *Echidna*, the wife of Typhon; the *Lernean* serpent, with nine or with fifty heads; the *Chimera*, with a lion's or goat's head; the *Sphinx*, with a woman's head and bust, the body of a lion, and the wings and tail of a dragon; and the fearfully howling *Skylla*, with six heads and six long necks, formed part of their pantheon. As soon, however, as poetry threw a glittering veil of beauty over the forces and phenomena of nature, no one thought of sacrificing human flesh to the gods. Who could have slaughtered a human being in the sight of the Olympian Zeus or the Pallas-Athene of Pheidias, the Venus of Alkemenes, or the Apollo of Praxiteles?

The Greek mind, once on the road to progress through a correct appreciation of beauty, developed with incredible rapidity.

The elements of art as well as of science are threefold. We have:—

α. The reign of *imagination* through the emotional element, more or less regulated;

β. That of *intellect*, the reflective element, more or less influenced by imagination; and

γ. That of *reason*, the speculative element, discerning between imagination and intellect, and binding the two into one.

The first element is the province of the unconscious artist. He trusts his own subjective imagination, and sees things only from his individual point of view.

The second tries to compare the different products of art, to draw analogies between them, and to assign causes for certain forms. This is the province of the chronicler, the antiquary, and the art-historian.

The third reaches the sphere of philosophical consciousness. In it the esthetical writer combines a correct appreciation of art as a grand total, with all its essential details. He sees distinctly its inner element based on immutable general laws, and comprehends the necessary organism, without which an artistic work cannot exist.

Poetry and philosophy, like art, passed through these developments in Greece. First we have the epic and lyric poets: Homer, Hesiod, Sappho, Alkæus, and Pindar; next the dramatic poets: Æschylus, Sophokles, and Euripides. At last the philosophers and historians: Plato, Aristotle, Herodotus, Thukydides, and Xenophon.

In analogy with these purely mental phases we have in art: the architect, who constructs a small world of organic coherence out of inorganic matter by means of his imagination; the sculptor, who reproduces with discernment the organic world around him in inorganic matter, but endows it with individual expression and feeling; the painter at last, who creates with his colours a union of spirit and matter, of idea and form.

Beauty was in all Greek products the vital element. 'True beauty, the companion of the gods, must be sought for,' says Pausanias, and makes no advances; it is too elevated to communicate itself,' And Plato propounds: 'The Supreme has no image; he converses only with the wise; with the vulgar he shows himself proud and forbidding; always equal, he expresses the emotion of the souls, he wraps himself in the delicious calm of that divine nature of which the great masters in the arts, according to ancient writers, endeavoured to seize the type.' This delicious calm may be traced everywhere in Greek art, and forms its essential element.

The temples of the Greeks were national and public buildings. They were not mere shrines destined as exclusive dwelling-places for some visible or invisible, concrete or abstract, theocratic monster. They were the central spots for their national assemblies, their gatherings, and for the celebration of their public festivities.

The Olympian, Pythian, Nemæan, and Isthmian games attracted visitors to these temples. These games did not consist of mere exhibitions of athletic prowess; but poets like Pindar—tragedians like Æschylus and Sophokles—historians like Herodotus—read to enraptured audiences the masterly products of their intellectual powers. Wrestlers and runners, sculptors and poets, and tragic and comic writers vied with one another to be crowned with a laurel wreath, or to receive a palm-twig, some a crown, or a tripod. No sordid feeling of gain mingled with their yet unalloyed pleasure in being distinguished for mere distinction's sake; the commercial question was unregarded. The prizes, given away in the sight of the delighted masses, were for everything—for bodily as well as for intellectual excellence—even for proficiency in the art of kissing. At the festival of the Philesian Apollo a prize for the most exquisite kiss was conferred upon a young lady. At Sparta and at Lesbos, in the temple of Here, and also among the citizens of Parrhasia, women contended for the prizes with men. How much we try to imitate Greek customs may be judged from the fact, that we also give prizes for exquisite dogs, cats out of proportion, and fat babies; but we are sorry to say, that this is done with a keen eye to business—to advertise a baby-food or a dog-or cat- fancier. That art is not altogether Greek with us need astonish no one. We are trained for practical purposes, but the Greeks were trained to appreciate beauty, symmetry, and harmony, not in verses only, but also in the human frame and in every product of art. Architecture with them was thoroughly plastic; it was never subservient to some metaphysical subtlety; it was finished in itself; a total of which every part formed, as in the human body, a completing element—without which the whole conception of a temple would be as incomplete as a man without arms, legs, or toes. The Greek temple entirely differed from the gloomy buildings of Egypt or India, which were constructed as symbols of hell, earth, and heaven; hell was for the sinners, the outcasts and the poor; earth for the respectable middle-classes; and heaven for the priests, the kings and their high officials. The constructions never made any attempt at symmetrical beauty, but aimed only at gorgeous pomp, in order to overawe the credulous mob—mystery was their essence. Sudden turnings placed the terrified worshipper, unawares, face to face with some colossal idol, looking to the excited and surprised imagination twice as large as it was, and ascending and descending staircases visibly divided the temple into abodes of splendour and horror. With the ancient Greeks in constructing a temple, the first question was the aim of the building; to whom was it to be dedicated—to Zeus, Apollo, Poseidon, Minerva or Venus? This question once decided, the most convenient spot, in accordance with the character of the god to whose worship the temple was to be dedicated, was chosen. The building to be erected was always to be in harmony with the surrounding scenery.

The temple with the Greeks generally stood on a terrace-like base of several steps.

The Doric, Ionic, and Korinthian orders, as architectural subdivisions, are most usual. So far as the different styles are concerned, a fourth must be added, which modern art-historians call the Attic. The Greeks were undoubtedly the first people who succeeded in producing architectural works of art; they were also the first:—

(a) To distinguish the material;

(b) To bring about symmetry and proportion; and

(c) To construct with a clear consciousness of purpose.

Marble was most profusely made use of; wood also, but the latter by degrees disappeared altogether. The Athenians completed even the roofs of their temples in stone.

The Greeks availed themselves of soft materials, such as clay, chalk, gypsum, and marble dust, for stucco (κονίασις {koniasis}), in which they excelled all other nations.

Metal too formed an important element in their decorations. It is asserted by many authorities that the Korinthian capital was not the latest development of Greek architecture; but that on the contrary it was older than the simplified and more correct Doric capital, which, showing no traces of wood-construction, is altogether of a pure 'stone-feeling,' whilst the forms of the Korinthian capital bear undoubted traces of wood-carving and metallotechnic.

We see that the Greeks employed pliable, plastic, elastic and solid materials; the great secret of their success lay in the fact that they made use of these elements appropriately.

The vertical and horizontal were the principal lines used by the Greeks. The curved line was not altogether excluded. The uprising straight lines in columns were cylindrical or conical. The relation of the lines to one another, and to the whole of the building, was regulated by a strict observation of the laws of proportion.

The diameter or half-diameter of the column (the module) served as the unit for the whole building. As in the human body the general law of proportion does not exclude an infinite diversity of forms, so in the Greek temples regulation did not preclude variety. In man the height is limited, and, to a certain extent, determined by his bones. This was the case in the Greek temple. The height was limited by the diameter of the column. Taking two columns of the same height, the one thin and the other thick, the thin column will appear high and the other short, but both will have a certain proportion, taken from their own body; the one will be, say, nine times the diameter of its body, and the other only seven times. Proportion in no way fetters the artist; it allows him perfect freedom, but *freedom in order*, without which no good building is possible. All architectural elements are of geometrical origin. These elements are to be divided into those that support, and those that are supported. The column is the most perfect supporting body; surrounding a vertical axis in a slightly conical form. Through the '*contractura*,' the swelling or tapering, it assumes the most perfect expression of the dynamic force in the striving upwards. Through the square plinth (Abacus) a harmonious union is effected between column, as supporter, and architrave, as the supported, or static, element of the building.

The Greek temple was pre-eminently the house of the man-like god. The god in the most exquisite idealised human form was visibly present. A forecourt (pronaos) led to the cella (naos); there was a rear-court (posticum), and occasionally a special court (the opisthodome) was added. Architecture and sculpture were closely allied in Greece; and still so clear and rational a separation between these two art-sisters, as existed there, has nowhere been observed. Through this apparent contradiction, architecture gained an independent soul, full of emotion and life, whilst sculpture obtained a well-proportioned body, the closely united artistic product being thus endowed with solidity and firmness.

The general architectural arrangement of a Greek temple was invariably the same. The cella, the abode of the divinity, was of smaller or larger dimensions. Two rows of columns adorned the interior, supporting an upper gallery. If the central space was left roofless, to supply the temple with light, it was called *hypæthral*. A temple, surrounded by one row of columns, was designated a *Peripteros*; if two rows of columns ornamented it, a *Dipteros*. With a front portico it was *Prostyle*; provided with a court, both front and back, *Amphiprostyle*. The pillars projecting on the side walls were *antæ*; and a temple having this decorative element was styled an *Antætemple*. The colonnade surrounding the temple at smaller or greater distances, represented a combined power of support. The base marked the independent existence of the separate columns. The shaft was covered with channelled flutings, and rose vertically with a convex extension of its circumference (called *entasis*). It then strongly contracted, thus expressing in the most perfect manner not merely passive sustaining, but an active and lively support. Above the capitals the mighty beams of the architrave (epistyle) were held together by a broad band, on which rested the frieze, sometimes adorned with triglyphs and metopes, or with reliefs; above it projected the overhanging plinth of the principal cornice. On the narrow sides of the oblong building, bordered by a cornice (the corona, geison) and the roof-gutter, rose the pediment with its groups and statues. On the front edge of the roof, both at the corners and in the middle, there stood smaller sculptures or marble palm-trees; whilst at the sides the rain-water was ejected through lions' heads; the finishing horizontal lines were eurythmically crowned with palm-shaped tiles (antifixæ). The roof and the rest of the building, in the noblest works, were of marble, the architectural product being thus transformed into an elegant chiselled work of sculpture.

The Greeks had in their mythology:

1. Powerful gods and goddesses, as Zeus, Pallas, Poseidon, and Mars.

2. Charming and lovely divinities, as Aphrodite, Eros, and Persephone.

3. Mixtures of sublime power and beauty, of manly dignity and womanly grace, as Here, Diana, Bacchus, and Apollo. In studying the characteristics of these three groups of divinities we become acquainted with the principal features of the three orders of their architecture.

I. The *Doric* order is full of power and monumental dignity. Force is its most prominent characteristic.

II. The *Ionic* order mingles southern imagination with northern severity; this order, with its voluted capital instead of the simple abacus, is of a more complicated character and livelier expression.

III. The *Korinthian* order exhibits, instead of the tapering Doric, a slender column—ending in a richly-decorated, upward-striving capital. There is something of the Doric style in the Ionic, and something of the Ionic in the Korinthian. The Doric was, however, the basis of Greek architecture.

A. The *Doric* order had six distinct developments of style.

a. The *proto-Doric*, compressed and heavy.

b. The *lax Archaic-Doric*, slender, with more distinctly-tapering columns.

c. The *stern Archaic-Doric*, more finished and graceful in its proportions.

d. The *pure Doric*, most correct in all its details.

e. The *Attic-Doric*, during the rule of Perikles, combining utmost severity with the very highest refinement in execution.

f. The *Makedonian-Doric* style; not correctly proportioned, the columns becoming elongated, and the distances narrowed. Gorgeousness and vanity predominate.

B. The *Ionic* order had three distinct phases of development in style.

a. The first *simple* in form, with the strongly-pronounced volute.

b. The *richly ornamented* style, as in the temple of Minerva Polias.

c. The *compound* style; half Doric and half Ionic.

C. The *Korinthian* order passed through four phases of style:

a. The *undecided* style; half Ionic and half Korinthian.

b. The *finished* style; graceful and rich.

c. The *over-decorated* style, with strong Ionic forms.

d. The *variegated* style, with decorative additions of trophies, winged-horses, dolphins, and eagles; half northern and half southern—combining Asiatic with Greek forms.

D. The Doric intermingled with Ionic forms produced in Attica a peculiar order, or rather mere style, neither Doric, nor Ionic, nor Korinthian—a kind of eclectic style which we may very properly call the *Attic* style. The Erechtheium of Athens was in this style. There are six principal distinctions in this style, which justify us in treating it as totally distinct from those mentioned under *A*, *B* and *C*:—

1. A particular plinth is wanting in the base.

2. Instead of this, a double contraction is transformed into one, united to the common support by means of a strong circular ovolo. The contractura is expressed on a small scale in the base.

3. The shaft is more slender in proportion.

4. The volutes are more projecting.

5. The frieze is considerably higher than it is generally in any of the other orders.

6. The corona is without the dentated ornament; but the projecting plinth is strongly undercut, and powerfully overhangs the finishing member of the frieze.

In all classifications of this kind a narrow-minded pedantry is to be avoided; canons, of whatever sort, hinder the natural growth of art. Still worse than strict canons is ignorance. Without a correct and thorough knowledge of Greek literature, no man can aspire to an exalted position in poetry and science; and without a correct and thorough study of Greek art, no man can become an artist. We do not recommend a slavish imitation of the Greeks, but a thorough understanding of their slow development, through the phases of unconscious reproduction and systematically conscious creation, to the philosophical appreciation of beauty, which enabled them to reflect in their works of art the eternal types of Nature in an idealised form.

The same gradual development which we remarked in their architecture also took place in Greek keramic art. The oldest pottery was coarse, the material generally taken from the most recent formation of the soil, the Cainozoic period. These older specimens are very much alike amongst all the Aryan nations. The forms are undecided, and made by the hand; the ornaments, as in pre-historic times, consisted of points, zigzags, spirals and knobs. At a very early period, however, the Greeks as Pelasgians, Achaians, Danaians and Argeians, possessed more defined outlines, and a more perfect symmetry, even in their very coarsest pottery.

In the oldest, so-called Tyrrhenian, vases we have already a decided plastic improvement. The ornamentation takes its patterns from metallotechnic, and we recognise Asiatic influences in the winged horses and lions, stamped in the clay as flat ornaments. The Greek taste improved; leaves and flowers were treated with a delicate, idealising conventionalism; the vine, ivy, anthimion, and masks and festoons, were used for decorative purposes, and gave to the well-shaped vessel a high artistic value. This was the most successful period of pottery for Greece. Samos appears to have been the principal place for its manufacture. The use of the wheel was long dispensed with; the Greeks trusting more to the delicacy of their touch than to the technical accuracy of a machine. In Asia the wheel had long been known, and it had exercised rather a detrimental than an improving influence on pottery, as the forms, settled by religious prejudices, or venerable custom, did not change, but remained stationary. As soon as the Greeks adopted the wheel—it must have been in use before Homer, for he speaks of it—their better-trained minds brought a new spirit into the handicraft of the potter, which was then turned into real art.

Korœbos, of Athens, a mythic person, is said to have elevated keramic art to high perfection. Dibutades is said to have been the first modeller in clay, and Talos, his nephew, is mentioned as the inventor of the potter's wheel in Hellas.

With reference to the process of colouring we have two distinct classes of Greek pottery:—

1. The *oligochromatic*, from ὀλίγος {oligos} (small), and χρῶμα {chrôma} (colour).

2. The *polychromatic*, from πολύς {polus} (many), and χρῶμα {chrôma} (colour).

I. The *oligochromatic* class of Greek pottery may be divided into two distinct styles: *a.* The Archaic; *b.* The Hellenic.

A. As soon as the wheel became generally used, a finer paste was required, fit for exposure to a greater heat, and for the production of a greater variety of vessels. In the beginning the paste was coarse-grained and of a yellowish-grey; later it was fine, and the colour homogeneous. The glazing was without lustre, brownish-black, and spotted, proving a want of experience in baking. We have violet, brownish-red, and white tints badly fixed on the black glaze. With the exception of Pithoi (wine jars) found at Thera, the vessels belonging to the Archaic style are generally of moderate size, broad and compressed, with sudden and bold interruptions of the curves, and abrupt unions of the extremities. The ornament is not yet an integral part of the vessel. The general forms are cups, pots, flasks, &c., all being entirely black. Some are ornamented with yellowish or white points, or with simple lines drawn all over the vessel. By degrees a clearer understanding of the laws of ornamentation is perceptible; the ornamentation becomes restricted to the bulge, whilst rings, meanders, and floral ornamentations mark the upper and lower parts of the vessel. A further progress may be seen in the treatment of ornamentation in the animals which surround the vessels in parallel circles. Highly interesting are the flowers, balls, and *crosses* on these oligochromatic vases. With the progress of civilisation we find the human figure introduced, surrounded, however, by monstrous combinations of Asiatic origin. Genii, with and without wings, make their appearance; then divinities amongst lions, panthers, ostriches, and a profusion of symbolic representations. Swans are either tamed, chased, or killed. The spirit of Persepolis and Nineveh, of Phœnicia and Egypt, animates these pre-Homeric compositions; they are entirely incomprehensible. This pottery of the Greeks is of the very highest interest; we may advantageously study in it the progress of civilisation amongst them.

We have a period in which monster chases monster; then a period in which men kill monsters; then, when men begin to settle down, and to pass from the barbarous state of mere hunters into a more settled mode of living, freed from obnoxious wild animals, they fight against men. The conquerors have decidedly Aryan features, whilst the conquered have unmistakably Turanian faces. (See the work of Lord Hamilton.) At length we suddenly surprise them before the walls of Troy; the incidents of the Iliad are known, and furnish the potters with heroic subjects. Achilles and Hektor, Penelope and Ulysses, may be recognised; the first two in deadly combat, the two latter meeting after a long separation. The subject, in these Archaic vases and vessels, is not yet thoroughly purified, for amongst the heroes we see Gorgons with spread wings and lolling tongues. Other monsters, destroying animals, surround the principal actors of the drama as mere unconcerned 'dummies.' We accompany the development a step further, and observe that the monsters have a share in the action; they seem to take part *pro* and *con*, like the gods in the Iliad, and, later, they appear in yet more purified forms as protecting divinities. It is as if the Iliad had first been drawn in clay by potters and improved upon, till at last it was shaped in its divine form, and edited under the name of Homer.

B. The Hellenic, or classic, style of Greek pottery, based on the Archaic, shows great improvements in every direction. The paste is harder, finer, and well glazed, and the colours are less discordant. The red is of a fiery brightness, and the black without any spots—sometimes with a greenish hue. In the decoration great delicacy of shape and feeling is prominent. The figures are laid on with anatomical accuracy. The limiting frame is dispensed with, giving ampler scope to a freer and still more connected ornamentation. The curves are less protruding, and the transition from concave to convex lines is gentler. The canon of this period, that the vessel had to form in all its parts one continuous line, rendered these products sometimes stiff and over- regulated. The influence of the progress in the Attic style, however, soon corrected this evil, and the potters of Greece vied with the very best sculptors and painters in beautiful works. The Asiatic types of winged or unwinged monsters were merely used as grotesque or comical friezes, and soon began to disappear altogether, to make room for some useful animal, and, finally, to give place to frets or garlands of the most beautiful combinations. For the monstrous creations of an overheated imagination, heroes, gods, and goddesses were substituted. Perseus destroying Medusa; the Forge of Hephaistos; a triclinium with Herakles and Alkmene, Hermes and Athene; diskoboli and their teachers; Aphrodite at her toilette; Ares, Herakles, Athene, and Zeus driven in their quadrigas by Nikê; Elektra at the tomb of Agamemnon; Aphrodite crossing the sea on a swan; the blind Chiron healed by Apollo; the weighing of Cupids—'young loves for sale;'and rows of well- sketched warriors, representing the victories of valour, beauty, and honesty over barbaric roughness, dishonesty, and despotism, form the subjects of pictorial ornamentation. What an immense field for the student of art to peruse, to fill his imagination with lively classical scenes!

II. The *polychromatic* style took its origin in the very first attempts in pottery, when white pipe-clay was painted over. The colours used were red, violet, and yellow oxides of iron. At the period when marble was introduced in architecture, and ivory in sculpture, during the middle of the fifth century B.C., we find these highly-coloured and richly-decorated vases. The paste was very fine, originally white, and the colouring encaustic. Not only mineral pigments and metallic oxides, but also vegetable colours, requiring only a very slow fire, were known and used. The encaustic consisted of a polychromatic paste more or less opaque, containing, in addition to wax, also flint, whether as principal or secondary element it is difficult to decide. This polychromatic treatment is to be observed on some smaller vessels, and vases known under the name of Lekythus (with a narrow mouth), and on saucers of large dimensions, the outsides having reddish figures on black grounds, and the insides, coloured figures on white grounds. Pottery led to fashioning in clay, and this to modelling in bronze and sculpture.

Architecture took its origin in religion, as also did sculpture. Opposed to the inorganic, objective productions of human intellect, as embodied in architecture, is spirit aspiring to a subjective existence in sculpture. The inorganic sternness of architecture is far surpassed by plastic art, which embodies spirit in a less fixed form. Spirit is not yet absolutely free, for it requires a tangible body to show its existence. Unlike music and painting, which by a mere movement of the air, or a mixture of tints, produce bodies, plastic art has to fill the three dimensions of space, and does this by means of coarse matter—with clay, wood, bronze, or stone.

Sculpture stands higher in the scale of art than architecture, for it is not obliged to transform inorganic matter for a utilitarian purpose.

At a certain period the Greeks were contented with shapeless divinities; a pointed stone, a square piece of wood, the deformed root of a tree, a pillar with a circular finish, or a cone, sufficed for their piety. Even Plato indulged in the untenable proposition that art was mere mimicry, and therefore a falsehood, and detrimental to virtue; as truth ought to be the only aim of humanity. The Beautiful with Plato was a mere abstraction, applicable exclusively to the absolute 'good'; artistic beauty was looked down upon by him as something bad and altogether objectionable. The Kynic and Kyrenæic schools held to a certain degree the opinions of Plato. The Kynics said that anything good was beautiful—anything bad ugly; whilst the Kyrenæics propounded that everything beautiful must be good—anything ugly must be bad; and in this way the notions, good and bad, beautiful and ugly, changed places. This dialectic difference led at last to Aristotle's deeper appreciation of art.

Aristotle, who rarely started from pre-conceived, *à priori* ideas, but attached his deep reasonings and admirable inductions to something tangible and really existent, pronounced, in opposition to the idealistic Plato, more correct thoughts on art. Imitation, mimicry (μίμησις {mimêsis}), is with him the subjective formation or creation of an idea, and therefore a process far superior to that of imperfect reality; in fact it is a sublimated, idealised representation and reproduction of reality. Next to the 'mimesis' he required purification from all passion (κάθαρσις {katharsis}) to be the aim and purpose of art. Genius and imagination were the means by which alone a work of art could be produced. The principal element in every work of art was with him ἦθος {êthos}, and wherever Ethos, the ethic or moral principle, was wanting, the product failed to be artistic in the highest sense of the word.

The development of Greek sculpture has borne out the sublime views of Aristotle on art. As soon as the merely naturalistic and sensational began to rule supreme, the Katharsis was neglected, the Ethic no longer swayed works of art, and the Antique died out.

The priests at Delphos, at a time when Greece abounded with the most exquisite Apollo-statues, still held to a pointed pillar as the emblem of the god of wisdom and the leader of the muses. Anthropomorphism was long opposed by the hierarchy of Delphi, but they encouraged the artists to produce beautiful vessels, tripods, lamps, sacrificial basins, &c., which had to be made according to certain prescribed forms. By degrees the Asiatic idea 'that God created man in his own image' was inverted by the Greeks, 'and man began to create the gods in his own image.' This one sentence embodies the cause of the progressive development of Greek sculpture on the one hand, and the ever-stationary forms of the East on the other. The Greeks had also idols that dropped from heaven, puppet-like forms or symbolic carvings, like the Artemis of Ephesus or the *four-armed* Apollo of the Lakedemonians, reminding us of Vishnu.

The discoveries at Athens, Kyprus, and most recently at Hassarlik by Dr. Schliemann, prove the gradual and slow progress of Greek sculpture in all its different phases. The first Parthenon, destroyed by the Persians, was adorned with divinities entirely different in shape from those which surrounded it after it had been rebuilt 444 B.C. The dresses, ornamentations, jewels, and pearls are of Assyro-Egyptian and Indo-Persian patterns. The faces of the divinities show far more of the Turanian than of the Aryan type. The eyes are protruding, the cheek-bones high, the drapery is extremely stiff, the anatomy doll-like, and the features bear a kind of repulsive grin. In the gigantic, rock- hewn bull, near Smyrna, we have a proof that the Indian Nundi and the Egyptian Apis must have had their worshippers in Greece.

Of Daidalos it is reported that he was the first who improved upon these symbolic carvings. He made winking gods and walking images by means of mechanical contrivances. He is said to have been a contemporary of Theseus; both belong therefore to the mythical period. Though a statue of Herakles, holding in his right arm a club, whilst his left extended bears a lion's skin as a shield, is attributed to him; and though Homer mentions Daidalos, of Krete, as having wrought a dance in metal for Ariadne, which formed the model for that wrought by Hephaistos on the shield of Achilles; the fact that the very word to 'embellish' is taken from his name, points less to a distinct person than to the period in which Greek art began to free itself from Asiatic bondage.

The historical periods into which we may group Greek sculpture correspond to those of their architecture.

First period, from the 8th century B.C. to the Persian wars, 470 B.C.

Second period, from Kimon to the end of the Peloponnesian war, 470 B.C.-400 B.C.

Third period, from the delivery of Athens to the conquest of Greece by the Romans, 400 B.C.-146 B.C. This third period comprises Greek sculpture in its decline.

Struggle into existence, growth and development, acme and decline, follow in rapid succession. Wood-carvers and potters begin; then we have a transition to bronze-works under *Glaukos*, who was the first to solder the separate parts of the statues, which prior to him had been always beaten into union. Following up this improvement, the artists of Samos succeeded in making a clay-model, and then in covering it with the fluid metal. As if by a supernatural charm the bright metal statue grew out of the gloomy clay, and formed an everlasting monument to adorn temples, squares, and streets. *Rhœkos* and *Theodorus* of Samos, with *Smilis*, built the Labyrinth at Lemnos, which they adorned with 150 columns, which were turned out by an ingenious mechanism, an improvement on the art of casting in bronze. Pliny describes a bronze figure by *Theodorus*, which held in its right hand a file, and in its left a quadriga with a charioteer, which was so small that the car, with the four horses and the driver, could be covered by the wing of a fly. The celebrated ring of Polykrates, admirably wrought gold and silver sacrificial vessels, and a vine with golden leaves and grapes of precious stones, were also attributed to this artist. At Chios, the birth-place of Glaukos, the family of *Mêlas* worked for the first time in Parian marble; whilst *Byzes* of Naxos cut marble into thin slabs for architectural purposes, giving a more exquisite finish to the houses of the gods. On every side a marked improvement took place. The head-dress of Apollo was still that of the Egyptian sphinx. The faces of the statues were placid, mask-like, as if modelled separately and then fixed on; the eyes looked as if first cut out, and then placed into their sockets; but the anatomy of the body was treated with greater care and a more refined feeling. The legs were close together and the arms hung down perpendicularly, with a prescribed stiffness, but there were details in the treatment of the stone surface, which promised well for the future of Greek art, and the promise was most faithfully kept.

The struggling art freed itself from the fetters of stern canons. Custom, struck by the lightning of genius, had to vanish, and life, truth, and beauty as essential elements ruled the Greek mind. To blend the isolated perfections of the two sexes into one became the aim of Greek art. Women were sculptured with the colder lines of manly firmness, and men received gentler forms through a less angular treatment. The artists conscientiously purified their works from all passions and second thoughts, expressing nothing that could divert the mind from the simple admiration of idealised nature. At this period they only succeeded in animating the limbs of their statues: action was expressed with great power in strained muscles and swelling veins. The faces were still without life, and without a comprehension of those emotions which vibrate electrically in the countenances of excited humanity. They could not yet petrify the thinking soul, but they undoubtedly already succeeded in sculpturing the animated body to perfection.

The *second* period was ushered in by the versatile and productive talents of Onatas, Ageladas, Kalamis, Iphikrates, Pythagoras of Regium, and Myron. Greece had attained her independence, the Persian hordes of despotism were vanquished, and Athens enjoyed her hegemony. Freedom and national exultation produced Sokrates, Plato, and Anaxagoras in philosophy; Kimon, Perikles, and Themistokles in politics; Æschylus, Sophokles, and Euripides in dramatic poetry; and Pheidias, Praxiteles, and Skopas in sculpture. If we add to this fourfold triad Herodotus, Thukydides, and Xenophon, we have given an array of names each of which singly would have filled the world with its fame, and become a landmark in the progressive development of humanity. Athens was at this period the most brilliant centre of intellectual and artistic life. Men were inspired by the general animation; they began to modify old thoughts, to transform eîdola, and to give birth to numberless productions which in beauty and striving for truth surpassed anything attempted before. Schools of arts vied with the schools of wrestlers, poets, and thinkers, and all excited the dramatists to their grand conceptions, which again reacted on plastic art. Under these influences the imaginary theogony yielded to a more scientific inquiry into the origin of all things, which led to the recognition of the first incomprehensible, immutable, eternal cause, no longer based on mere belief, but on the immovable rock of scientific conviction. No wonder that art was also inspired by this spiritual movement. The conceptions of the priests and philosophers were to be loudly proclaimed in visible forms, and the sculptor, from a deep feeling of veneration for the Supreme Artist of the Universe, became the expounder of the divinity, and the exclusive high priest of beauty and truth. Instead of singing Vedantic hymns or Egyptian psalms and litanies to the glory of God, the Greek sculptors hewed the gods in majestic forms, and every touch of their chisels on the lifeless marble, every blow of their hammers, became an eternally resounding prayer in honour of God.

Wood, metal, clay, precious stones, and marble had by degrees yielded to the creative power of the Greek masters; and matter could no longer resist in any way their ruling intellectual force. At this moment, under these circumstances, Pheidias, the son of Charmides of Athens, the pupil of Hegias and Ageladas, stepped forward, and was raised by the superiority of his genius to the dignity of king of Greek plastic art. The Zeus of Olympia and the Athene of the Parthenon qualified Pheidias as *the* sculptor of the concrete *form* of the divinity; for if the father of the gods had had a visible form, and his wisdom and intellect had been incarnate in Athene, both must have looked as they were sculptured by Pheidias. In symbolic emblems he poetically expressed the powers of the two divinities; and used the mineral, the vegetable, and animal kingdoms to glorify their power.

Nothing is left us of these two master-pieces but the glowing descriptions of those who saw and admired them. That which a combination of thousands of our artists, with all our technical advancement, can scarcely accomplish; the drawing of thousands and thousands of *intellectual* human beings together to admire their works of art; was done by Pheidias. Men flocked from all parts of the world to see and admire his statues, and to offer fervent thanks to the Father of all for having endowed one of his creatures with the power to give a correct form to Homer's lines:

He (Zeus) spoke, and awful bends his sable brows;
Shakes his ambrosial curls and gives the nod,
The stamp of fate, and sanction of the god;
High heaven with trembling the dread signal took,
And all Olympus to the centre shook.

We possess in the Vatican a copy of the original head of the Jupiter, and what a master-piece even this *bad* copy is! What a power in the bold, arched brows; the large eyes with their benevolent, forgiving, and yet commanding glance; the full, parted lips ready to bless and to forgive; the luxuriant beard, the mighty locks inspiring veneration, and the beautifully-rounded cheeks, expressive of creative force and eternal manly beauty! The independent works of Pheidias were very numerous. Besides the two colossal divinities of bronze (Athene Promachos, 50 feet high, and Athene ἡ Ληµνία {hê Lêmnia}), we find twelve others mentioned: of these, six were statues of Athene; one colossal Apollo of bronze, 70 feet high; one marble Hermes; three of Aphrodite (two of marble, and one of ivory and gold); a mother of the gods, material unknown; and an Asklepios (Æsculapius) of gold and ivory. Of sacrificial statues, a group of thirteen bronze figures, in commemoration of the victory of Marathon, is mentioned as having been executed by him. In this work twelve mythical characters surrounded *one* historical figure—that of Miltiades; a proof that the Greeks attributed their victory far more to the help of the gods than to the exertions of their leaders. They were much more inclined to adorn the courts of their temples and their public places with the statues of orators, wrestlers, poets, artists, and philosophers, than with those of men who, in defending their country against invading hordes of barbarians, did their duty and nothing more. What a scope for our artists if we were to adorn our town-halls, courts of justice, our museums, universities, academies, public places, and churches with the statues of those who had devoted their energies to religion, oratory, science, art, politics, and the general welfare of their country! If gratitude were to prompt us to do this, and not childish vanity or egotistical pride, we should shortly have many Pantheons with excellent sculptures.

In no town in Europe can the artist study the sculptural splendour of ancient Greece with greater ease than in London. Of the ninety-two metopes which adorned the Parthenon on the Akropolis at Athens we possess seventeen; of the frieze of the cella 3–1/5 feet high and 524 feet long, representing the Panathenaic procession, we possess fifty-three plates and casts of the whole western side. In all these sculptures what a clear power of grouping, what a variety of characters, what handsome men and women! The flower of Athens is seen assembled to do homage in joyous excitement to the supreme divinity of the State, the embodiment of wisdom and intellect. Some are crowned with wreaths; others carry sun-shades, chairs, splendid pitchers, ornamented vases, or decorated pateras; some are ready to start; others, preparing in animated haste to take their places, are in the act of mounting their prancing horses, or, already mounted, eagerly await the arrival of their friends. On the eastern side, under the entrance to the temple, there was an admirable group of gods and goddesses, in whose presence *peplus*, or sacred veil, is delivered to the authorities of the temple; animals are led to be sacrificed— flute and kythara-players follow. Amongst the hundreds and hundreds of figures not one is like the other; the exquisite variety in the folds of the dresses of the sitting, standing, walking, riding, driving groups is in general unsurpassed for beauty of design, and perfection of execution. None of the figures are raised more than *three* inches from the background, and yet the most correct perspective is observed. There is such a softness and truthfulness, such a firmness and ideal vitality in this frieze, that we may at least attribute the composition to Pheidias himself. Some plates of the western side are less excellent in execution; the forms are marked with roughness and dryness, and some faults in the outlines are also apparent to the critic. Some of the horses have legs too long, and bodies too thin; in one of the horses, which is bending its neck to rub its head against one of its fore feet, the curves are much too stiff. The execution of these reliefs must have been left to some inferior artist. What we must admire is, that there are so few faults. The correct study of this frieze ought to serve us as an example in grouping, and would teach us how to arrange a marble strip round some monument for the sake of decoration. Little of this influence, however, is to be observed in our sculptors. We intend to evolve sculpture from our own inner consciousness, and neglect these ancient books with their glorious poems in Pentelic marble; we prefer '*going to nature*' as the popular phrase runs, and ignore or despise the study of the antique. Now the Greeks had an opportunity of going to real nature—not with the darkened eye of Asiatic prejudice, despising matter and exalting *spirit*—but with a prejudice in the very opposite direction, cultivating spirit only so far as it served to embellish and to reproduce form. In this they attained perfection, and to surpass them in sculpture is after all impossible; we can only try to equal them, and to learn from what they have left us, to produce other combinations. In this spirit we ought to study the nine figures from the eastern pediment of the Parthenon, in the British Museum. What forms, what exquisite drapery! The finest tissue of pliable stuff is reproduced in hard Pentelic marble. The drapery disguises, and at the same time reveals, the beautiful forms of the human frame. Softness and sensationalism were equally avoided by Pheidias and his school. The study of anatomy was not yet degraded to coarse realism. It was not yet the aim of Greek sculptors to distort the human body so as to exhibit expanded muscles, over-strained sinews, and swelling veins, as expressions of pain, grief, distress, or contortions of the death-agony. Anatomy served Pheidias as a mould, into which he poured his beautiful conceptions—the spiritualised forms of gods and men. Katharsis was the principle of his school. The very heights of perfection were reached by Pheidias, Polykletus, and Alkemenes. Gods and goddesses were the subjects of their chisels. They were not only the high-priests of art—but inspired prophets, to whom divine beauty was revealed in all its brightness and splendour.

The existence of the Greek State was suddenly shaken to its very foundation. Internal dissensions weakened the safety of the citizens; sophistry destroyed philosophy, and mannerism grasped Greek art, dragged it down from its heights of idealised beauty and hurled it into the abyss of sensational realism. The best specimen of this school is the frieze from the temple of Apollo at Bassæ, near Phigalia in Arkadia. (Found 1812, now in the British Museum.) It represents Kentaurs fighting with Amazons. The old Indian Ghandarvas, the moist and heavy clouds that hinder the sun from breaking forth in all his glory, and are conquered by his fiery shafts, became in time monsters, half-men, half-horses, fighting against loveliness and civilisation. The Amazons in this instance represent fair Greece rushing into civil strife. Passion is predominant in action and expression. Amazons are dragged by the hair and by the legs from their horses; a Kentaur is seen biting a warrior in the shoulder. Bold naturalism and vulgar realism go hand-in-hand in these sculptures. How sensitive art is—how faithfully it reflects the social condition of a nation! and the feelings by which the artists were pervaded may be studied in this frieze. The nude is treated with exquisite truthfulness, but there is heaviness in the sudden, too violent movements. Action and expression lose the balance of the symmetrical. The women are common; their drapery floating and yet stiff, deranged for the sake of effect. The artists worked no more with love and security. The political party spirit troubled their imagination. The chisel trembled with rage or fear, with hatred or passion, in their hands; they saw prophetically the national downfall of their country, and with it science, art, poetry, and philosophy were to be rendered for thousands of years houseless and homeless.

Once more art revived under Skopas, Praxiteles, and Lysippus, but in a totally different shape. Greece had lost through her civil war the proper balance between her moral and intellectual forces. Simplicity and refinement of thought had vanished. In literature metaphors prevailed; in politics Aristides had to yield to the double-tongued Alkibiades; in tragedy Sophokles was superseded by Euripides; in sculpture the immortal Pheidias was followed by Praxiteles. The national spirit of the Greeks, inspired by common interests, swayed by the very highest aspirations in arts and sciences,

suddenly collapsed into a narrow-minded, particularising egotism. Tribes cared only for tribes, parties for parties. The public buildings began to be neglected, whilst the private dwellings gained in ornamentation and comfort, what was denied to the grand national enterprises. The public places were no longer adorned with the statues of those who had gained the general approbation of the masses. The artist, doubtful whom to please, tried to please everyone, or to satisfy the individual fancy of a paying patron. Art was no more the chaste virgin sacrificing to beauty, but became a courtesan seeking general and special favour at all hazards. The divinities were no more the representations of a spiritual eîdolon, but a glowing sentiment of sensual love was poured over their frames; they were no longer ideal conceptions in marble, but beautiful flesh forms in stone or bronze. They lost all generalisation, they were more correct in the anatomical outlines, but a passionate sentiment of sensuality thrilled through every point. Kephisodotus (the elder), probably the father of Praxiteles, embodied the change in Greek thought in a beautiful group. Eirene (peace) fondles the child Pluton (riches)
—a splendid allegorical representation of the political condition of Greece at this time. 'Let us put an end to our quarrels; let us have peace, and enjoy life once more.'

Skopas, born on the island of Paros, expressed the modern flow of ideas in Greece with greater clearness. Violent scenes of deadly struggle filled the pediments of the temple of Athene Alea at Tegea. In front, the hunt of the Kalydonian boar by Herakles, at the back Achilles fighting with Telephos was represented. An under-current of thought, a kind of allegory, may be traced in this composition, for the boar to be hunted was the opposition. Art was no longer to exalt the mind unconditionally, but to fulfil another purpose—to irritate, to excite to hatred, and to arouse passion; thus placed, art must lose its civilising influence, and it did this step by step. Even the divinities sculptured by Skopas were not to inspire veneration, but to please by little allegorical additions; his Apollo (Smintheus) stood on a mouse; Apollo, the leader of the muses, the representative of vivifying light in art, science, and the universe, degraded to a beautiful 'mouse-killer.' Aphrodite, the mother of humanity, was sculptured sitting on a goat—the vilest emblem of passion in union with the purest eîdolon of tender love. Another Apollo was represented in the long waving robes of an elegant Grecian lady playing the lyre; this was still more objectionable. Though the drapery excites our admiration by its exquisite softness and finish, the statue appears to have been chiselled to show the artist's skill in carving a heap of waving drapery. Whenever art condescends to such tricks it is on the high-road to degradation. Skopas composed a splendid group for a pediment, representing Achilles receiving from his mother the arms forged by Hephaistos. The principal figures are Thetis, the queen of the bright green waves, Poseidon, and Achilles; they are surrounded by a crowd of Nereids and Tritons, all in harmonious arrangement. Richer in grouping are some marble reliefs (now in the Glyptothek at Münich), representing the wedding of Poseidon and Amphitrite. The mother of the bride, Doris, is seated on a Hippokamp (sea-horse), holding two torches towards the couple; Tritons play on shells and lyres a merry wedding tune. Nereids surround them. One rides on a sea-bull, led by a mischievous-looking Eros, standing on its left fore-foot; another, mounted on a fantastic sea- monster, is accompanied by another, borne by a Triton; other Nereids follow, pointing towards the principal group, one sitting on a Hippokamp, with an Eros on its curled tail; a dragon carrying a Nereid is led with self-conscious pride by another Eros, whilst a Triton carries another sea-nymph on his winding body with placid and contented looks. The composition in general, and in all its details, is perfect. Without over-crowding the allotted space, it could not be better filled up. There is a striking freedom in the lines, and lively contrast of forms. We may consider this relief the prototype of all those fantastic compositions of the pure renaissance style, in which we see dragons and monsters, bulls and horses, entwined with plants and flowers, nymphs and gods, everything real and imaginary, beautiful and graceful, united into one great dissonant harmony. Skopas was the first (so far as we know) who sculptured Venus in the full beauty of her nude body. Pheidias would have considered such a treatment of the mother of mankind blasphemy. In a group of Eros, Himeros, and Pothos (Love, Longing, and Desire), we find a classification of a general feeling into three distinct subdivisions, executed with conscious discernment in order to produce a sensational effect. A raving Bacchante appears to rush away with dishevelled hair, in flowing robes; the head is thrown backwards in delirious delight; the marble lives and breathes maddening joy, but is vivified with sensual feelings, and not inspired with the elevating spirit of artistic simplicity and purity.

Of this period we may study another master-piece in the British Museum; the frieze of the tomb of Mausolos at Halikarnassus. The greater part is in London and the remainder at Genoa. The subject is a battle between Greeks and Amazons. The composition is nearly as good as that on the Parthenon. There is a continuous symmetrical stream of action and reaction, as in the dashing waves of a stormy sea. *Skopas* worked the eastern, *Bryaxis* the northern, *Timeotheos* the southern, and *Leochares* the western side. Many mistakes may be found in the details, but the whole is a master-piece of manly thought;—it may be said to have been the *last manly* product of the period.

Praxiteles altogether turned the scale; Aphrodite, Demeter, Persephone, Flora, Eros, Dionysius, and Apollo, are the divinities mostly sculptured by him. Everything is smooth, young, and effeminate. All harshness of line is avoided, all loftier ideas discarded. The flesh become stone is placed before us in charming and full roundness. Aphrodite was no longer draped—but with the concealing drapery the higher conception of the divinity fled. Venus, conscious of her charms, with a smile on her lips, and a coquettish movement of her hand, sinks to the level of an every-day woman. Venus had eaten of the tree of knowledge; with the consciousness of her particular womanly charms the ideal of divine universality was gone.

We possess of Praxiteles, an Eros in the Vatican, and his celebrated Apollo with the lizard (Saurokthonos) in the Louvre. Both these statues are more women than men. The lines are too soft; the bodies as though without muscles or bones, composed only of flesh and fat. It is true that the older artists also softened down the too marked lines of the sexes, and in blending them together created ideal forms of beauty; but now the mere surface of the woman's body was used for both sexes, to affect the senses exclusively.

Three groups (the one probably for the pediment of a temple, the other two forming independent works of art) deserve special mention.

The group of Niobe and her dying children, attributed to Skopas or Praxiteles. Greece was fast sinking. *Niobe-Greece* sees her children struck down one after the other by the inexorable decree of the gods, who are bent on punishing the *proud mother* who only cared for the *outward* beauty of her children, and neglected their moral *inner* grandeur. Niobe, amidst a harmonious confusion of misery and endless woe, stands erect, and presses the youngest child to herself, turning her proud looks upwards, her eyes filled with tears of heroic resignation—for she knows the gods have willed her downfall, and their will is unalterable. This moment of agony, of mental rather than bodily suffering, makes the group a master-piece of antique beauty and grandeur.

This cannot be said of the sensational Laokoön, the joint work of Agesander, Athenodorus, and Polydoros (of which there is a copy in the Vatican), and the so-called 'Farnese Bull,' the joint work of Apollonios and Tauriskos (a copy of which exists in the museum at Naples). Bodily anguish is the dominating element in these two groups. If it were the province of art to depress the soul, and to fill us with pain and horror, nothing could surpass the technical skill with which these two are arranged.

In the first we have:—

1. In the father a stifled *death scream.*

2. In the younger son, to the right, the last *convulsions* of a dying boy.

3. In the elder son, to the left, an unbounded *horror* at witnessing the

frightful death of father and brother.

There is no psychological necessity in this group to indemnify us for the pathological and anatomical truthfulness of so great an amount of horrible suffering. Art has never to serve as a hospital ward, and to force us to witness the contortions of a poor family dying poisoned by strychnine or arsenic. Not less objectionable is the revenge of a mother and her two sons on a defenceless woman. In this group we have:—

1. The horror-stricken, half-dying, half-imploring look of poor Dirkê.

2. The merciless glance of the jealous Antiope, wrapt in placid satisfaction to see herself revenged on her rival.

3. The ferocious anger of the two passionate sons; and, lastly,

4. The wild look of the furious bull, ready to dash the beautiful frame of a frail woman to pieces. Dramatic justice is here meted out by the artist in a most revolting way. A bull is called in to help to punish; it is the vulgarity of the cruel revenge that degrades the technically masterly work of art. The free grouping of marble statues is one of the most difficult tasks, and was never attempted during the classic period of ancient art. A mixture of men and animals is even more to be avoided.

As soon as the gods of Egypt changed their architectural and monumental position, they lost their sway over the superstitious masses; as soon as the Greeks lost that balance of morality, which, in the form of the beautiful, regulated their life, science, and art, they lost at the same time their productive power. Form and idea as in Asia came into conflict; the *formal* had attained the extreme of perfection, and the new *ideas* had not yet ripened.

Art was either to touch the feelings or to speak to reason—it was to be based on a mere imitation of nature, or to be the expression of some thought in some form. This 'either,'—'or,'—or this 'neither,'—'nor,' which divided art-critics during this period, made an end of art altogether. The Asiatics rent the universe asunder with conflicting abstractions based on the phenomena of nature; the Greeks lost their power, when they once recognised that there was something higher than the mere *form*. A new sphere was felt to open new spiritual beauties—but this sphere was to be attained through totally different means. The formal was however so highly developed by the Greeks that we shall see the new spirit, after more than a thousand years, become incarnate in those forms.

We see then clearly that art, the product of the creative force of men, requires a certain moral and intellectual condition, under which alone it can actively live. Change the moral temperature through the superstitions of a

terrified populace, the aspect of nature, the despotic organisation of government, or the rule of a wild, uneducated mob, and the artistic force will also change or die out altogether. The artist acts only to a certain degree on the public; the public reacts with a greater combined *vis inertiæ* on the artist, who is merely the reflection of certain ideas floating in the intellectual atmosphere around him. Is a man who sees nothing but emaciated, beggarly, or sanctimonious faces, thin limbs, hungry looks, dwellings bare of all domestic comfort, decayed brick-houses and crumbling walls, to paint convivial scenes of happiness and joy? Or let him change this atmosphere and live in a sphere of so-called respectability; having always the same bland smile before him, the same trimmed whiskers, the same business-like self- contentment, the same stiff collars and cuffs; hearing the same stereotyped, insignificant phrases about the weather or the funds, the price of coals or meat
—will he, influenced by such an atmosphere, not draw or paint only caricatures, and never grand and heart-stirring historical paintings, recording in glowing colours scenes full of life, excitement, passion, and dramatic action? In such surroundings it is necessary for an artist to create for himself a world of his own—an intellectual world—by turning to the glorious records of the past, and devoting every spare hour to the study of the ancients and the reading of history. His imagination, deadened by reality, must be fed and nourished by the poets, poetry, works of art, and historical facts of the past. Our meagreness and poverty in artistic productions take their origin in our unpardonable neglect of the study of history; through this neglect we have deprived art altogether of its firmest basis.

The very moment that the Greek artists lost their historical and poetical ground, they took to and excelled in painting barbers' and shoemakers' shops; oyster shells, vases, little combinations of chairs and musical instruments, and small things, with great accuracy. In fact the same causes produced the same pictorial effects; the mind of the Greek nation had dwindled, and their works of art embraced decorations of household furniture and pottery. In these ornamentations the reminiscences of a by-gone age may be traced; they are still symmetrical to the highest degree, plants are still treated with great conventional freedom, but the Greeks only worked as skilful workmen— artists they produced no more.

CHAPTER IX.

ETRUSKAN ART.

The first question that here suggests itself is, who were the Etruskans? Their name Tuskan, from Tuisko, points at once to an Aryan branch of Teutonic race. But ethnologists differ. Some say they were Phœnicians, others assert they were Egyptians; some that they were pure Teutons, and others that they were pure Kelts. Taking their old pottery into consideration, as given in Lord Hamilton's admirable plates, or in the collection of the Museum at Clusium (Chiusi), we are induced to pronounce the aborigines of Etruria to have been Turanians, conquered by immigrant Aryans. This mixture of Aryans and Mongols under the influence of a totally different aspect of nature, on a different soil, under different social and religious conditions, produced a type quite different from the Greek—a kind of transition link between the Pelasgians and the Romans.

Two distinct immigrations of Aryans into Etruria are recorded. The first about 1650 B.C., when Pelasgians and Thyrrenians settled amongst the aborigines; and the second, 400 years before Herodotus, about the times of Thales and Lykurgus. Of the first immigration we have scarcely any relics; the second time the immigrants succeeded in forming an organised social state; they brought with them Greek mythological notions, and a kind of Greek writing. Their language and writing died out after Augustus, and disappeared altogether before Julian, fourth century A.D. Nature forced them to industry and enterprise. The Etruskans had to cultivate their fields by individual exertion; in spring they had to ward off the devastating waters of overflowing rivers, and in summer they had to provide water for their parched valleys. They consequently became masters in constructing aqueducts and irrigating the land, at an early period.

Their mythology was composed of Assyrian, Persian, and Egyptian notions, strongly tinged with gloomy superstitions. Petrifactions of the most astonishing forms abound in the plains where they settled. Near Cortona the bones of a whale have been found. The Arno valley resembles a vast elephant burial-place; and the bones of the mastodon, rhinoceros, and hippopotamus, are scattered broadcast all over old Etruria, and are still used to fence in the fields. Besides the bones of these huge monsters, those of hyænas, panthers, bears, and wolves are found in such abundance, that the peasants to this very day believe they grew like mushrooms over night, having been sown by invisible spirits to give the poor the trouble of picking them up. The aspect of nature and the remains of an antediluvian world gave the Etruskan priesthood an irresistible sway over the minds of the people. Whilst in Greece, under the influence of a happy aspect of nature, the Indian, Assyrian, and Egyptian embodiments of the forces of nature lost their fearful forms; in Etruria they gained even more gloomy and melancholy figures in the presence of everlasting thunder and lightning, and volcanic disturbances.

The Etruskans had two sets of gods.

a. The veiled gods, with '*Asar*' at their head, representing the cosmognical forces of nature; especially fire, water, earth, and ether, like the divinities of India and Egypt.

b. Twelve lower divinities presiding over the order of existing and visible things. Their gods have a great resemblance to those of the Scandinavians, uniting in one distinct chain the Aryans on the Ganges, those on the Nile, and those round the Delphic oracle, with the Hyperboreans of the farthest north. They all believed in an 'inferno,' only with the Greeks this was an Elysium, a land of shadows, a land of happiness. The divinities of the Etruskans were phantoms of horror. The whole of their creed was devoid of a comforting union between gods and men. This despairing faith impressed the people with a ferocious character. Their art under such impressions never could reach the beautiful. A tribe of whom it has been said that their priests attacked the Romans with hissing serpents and burning torches—a tribe that crouched in fear before invisible gods, and hated every other tribe—could never take an interest in the gentler emotions produced by poetry or art. They remembered the Greek expedition against Thebes, and adorned their *burial* urns with scenes from the battle at Marathon; they commemorated the heroic deed of a ploughman, who, in the midst of the battle, took up his plough and drove the Persians before him like a flock of frightened sheep, whilst the Greeks remembered the deed in mentioning *Echetlos* in connection with Marathon, but possessed no record of the fact on any of their monuments. The Etruscans, however, delighted in such scenes. At their funerals they had no dances, but sanguinary fights.

No less than twelve different thunderbolts were known to them. They believed in a thunderbolt of prophecy, one of authority, one of law, one of wish, one of admonition, one of approval, one of help, one of prosperity, one of falsehood, one of plague, one of threats, and one of murder. Every transaction in life, with the best or the worst of mankind, might have been accompanied by an approving or disapproving thunder-clap. They firmly believed the thunderbolts used by the Supreme Deity were all manufactured in the fiery interior of Mount Ætna. They possessed no ritual of the dead like the Egyptians, but a thunderbolt ritual. Every day of the year that brought thunder had its special signification. All the veiled gods, and *nine* of the secondary gods, had the power of thundering.

Their conception of angry, jealous, persecuting, thundering, and lightning divinities has much in common with the Jewish and Phœnician ideals of the Supreme Deity. This peculiarity the Northerns shared in their conception of Thor. The Etruskan belief, that aërolites were thunderbolts sent by the angels against the Titans, has a great analogy with the Persian legends assuming these to have been hurled by the Fervers against the Devas.

Their superior divinities are, like the kings or priests of Persia, Assyria, and Babylon, provided with wings. Jupiter, Diana, Minerva (a kind of female Mercury with the Etruskans, who had wings not only on her shoulders, but also on her feet) and Venus were all winged; others, like Proserpina (Persephone), Amor (Eros), and the Furies, had wings on their heads. White and black winged genii (angels and demons) are plentiful in the subterranean tombs of the old Etruskan town, Tarquinium. According to Dempster, their cars even are often provided with wings. What was a metaphor with the Greeks was turned by the Etruskans into matter-of-fact. Euripides in his 'Orestes' speaks of the winged car of Phœbus, and on some Eleusian coins Ceres is seen sitting in a winged car, drawn by two serpents.

From a gloomy contemplation of supernatural matters the Etruskans turned their minds to extremely worldly and practical purposes. They wished to secure their towns and to protect them against real and imaginary monsters, and they constructed excellent walls and most comfortable houses. The '*cavœdium*' ('cavum œdium'), with the *impluvium* and *compluvium* (the one for collecting and the other for preserving water), was altogether an Etruskan invention, and was called by the Romans who adopted it, *Tuscanicum*. They constructed temples differing only in some details from those of the Greeks. The cella was generally *square*; sometimes they had more than one cella; one in the Postica and one in the Antica (the rear and front of the temple). The portico was often filled with columns. The architectural style was a rough and primitive Doric. They never attained the majestic simplicity which distinguished this order in Greece. The columns had a base, were more slender (about fourteen moduli), stood more apart, and supported a wooden roof with clumsily-protruding beams, an unwieldy cornice, and a high pediment.

Cinerary chests they had in abundance with divinities on them, worked in reliefs of a decidedly Egyptian type. They used brazen tablets representing Osiris and Isis. Little clay figures were put into the graves to protect the dead.

Amongst these has been found a winged Harpokrates or Horus, with the fore-finger of one hand on his lips, a lotus on his head, and a cornucopia in his other hand.

Their ancient pottery is more in the Egyptian than the Greek style. Their jars represent sphinxes and women; their drinking cups are in the form of human legs, with human faces replacing the knee; some are in the form of Mercury with a pointed, attached beard, like those to be seen in Egyptian divinities. Some of the patterns of their ornamentation, in general as well as in detail, are perfectly Mexican. On one of their lamps we have a winged Kentaur holding a rabbit, whilst four rabbits running after one another, form the spirited ornamentation of the border, intermixed with triangles, rosettes, or solar circles.

With their religious notions, it is not surprising that the Etruskans should have devoted the greatest care to their tombs and burial-places.

These tombs were:—

1. *Subterranean*; hewn into the tufa on plains. Steps led underground, where a vestibulum, consisting of several chambers, sometimes provided with columns, led into the vault. The ceiling of this was either horizontal or pointed, in imitation of a wooden roof. Many such tombs are found at Volci, Clusium, and Volaterra.

2. A second species of their subterranean tombs consisted of those *provided with tumuli* above-ground; simple graves as found in Scandinavia and the north of the Western hemisphere, the corpses lying on simple stone beds.

3. *Burial chambers* (cucumella) with artificial hills above them, and provided with a tower-like construction, or with conical columns. They are found near Volci, Tarquinii, and Viterbo.

4. *Chambers, vertically hewn into the rocks*, with a simple or decorated entrance near Tuskania.

5. Rock-hewn chambers *with façades screening the entrance*, as at Aria, or with Doric fronts as at Orchia. Asia furnished patterns for the decoration and construction of these tombs. The reliefs are full of lively scenes, reminding us of Assyrian and Babylonian sculptures. The figures are heavy, the legs short and thick; the upper part of the statues is placed 'en face,' whilst the legs and feet are in profile. The monstrous element predominates. Harpies, chimeras, winged lions, sphinxes, and griffins abound; but they are void of any symmetrical arrangement, and are dry, stiff, and as revolting as possible in their coarse outlines.

With regard to the construction of their walls it is remarkable that they improved very early on the Kyklopean mode, and constructed the very best regular freestone walls. They had arched gates, built with wedge-shaped stones, which produced by their span a firmly-vaulted construction. The Etruskans thus acquired a lasting merit in the history of art by the new epoch which they inaugurated with the introduction of this decidedly progressive element in the technical construction of architectural works. As *potters* and *metal-workers* they distinguished themselves more than either as architects or sculptors. As the Chinese are considered as the potters *par excellence* of the farthest East, the Etruskans may be called the potters of the West. In burning, painting, and fashioning clay they appear to have acquired a speciality, so that their trade in vases extended all over the then known world, and even the Greeks furnished their houses with Etruskan pottery in preference to their own. The gloomy mythology of the Etruskans was far better suited to potters, manufacturing black vases with red figures, or red vases with black figures, or for casting dark bronze figures, than to sculptors handling white marble. They also distinguished themselves in chiselling and founding metal. Innumerable chests, candelabra, metal frames for looking-glasses, and other utensils show their cleverness in working gold, silver, and bronze. Some ivory carvings, described in a report of the Archæological Society at Rome, 1862, are of great interest. They were found at Præneste (Palestrina), where also silver vessels in the purest Egyptian style, and an ivory tablet with Assyrian patterns, were excavated. More important even than these discoveries are four ivory tablets found at Corneto, showing traces of gilding and painting. The carvings represent scenes of every-day life, mixed with mystic figures. We see on the tablets a lady and gentleman sitting at dinner, served by a little boy; a huntsman chasing game; a kind of sea-divinity holding in each hand a fish; and a man in a biga driving winged horses. These figures might have formed representations concerning the zodiac, namely: the Twins, Sagittarius, Pisces, and the Sun (Phœbus or Horus). The receding forehead of the driver and his manner of holding the whip are types which we constantly meet in Egyptian sculptures and reliefs.

About 660 B.C. Eucheir, Diopos, Eugrammos and Demeratos were driven from Korinthum into Etruria, and from that date we note a decided improvement in the artistic productions. The Etruskans began to excel in terracotta and bronze works. Their vases, amphoræ, statuettes, cinerary and mystic chests, prove this. Their mystic chests (cistæ mysticæ, corresponding to the quippa-chests of the Mexicans) were made of embossed bronze. The lids were ornamented with mysterious animals, and the legs formed of the claws or paws of mythical brutes. Foliage and Greek frets in good arrangement were also used. Their candelabra are of a superior design. Other works of art, such as ornamented backs and handles for mystic mirrors, in gold, silver, or bronze, are of excellent technical execution.

There was, however, too much of the aborigine Turanian element left in the Etruskans. The noble and elevating rhythmus of Greek idealisation is everywhere wanting. Cooking utensils, small pieces of furniture, tables, chairs, and couches, aqueducts and viaducts, and even cloacas, were made and constructed to perfection, but as soon as they attempted the production of human forms, or of higher works in architecture, they did not succeed. The heads of their figures are either too small or too large. The legs are short; the drapery in stiff lines hangs down with rope-like regularity. Animals are much better executed; but the human form, in consequence of a scrupulous and constrained conception, and an exaggerated attention to detail, had a cold, lifeless appearance, void of all spiritual animation. Their imagination was one-sidedly directed by nature and religion to take a gloomy and distorted view of creation, and their products bear this spiritual stamp. In everything they touched we recognise the Egyptian mythology with its stifling breath, and the influence of the volcanic ground on which the Aryans were thrown, amongst a number of superstitious Turanians. The rumbling, fire-spitting Vesuvius and Ætna worked on the brains of the new immigrants. The sudden, devastating bursts of fire and water filled their minds with horror; they were forced to ponder over the instability of human things. The beauty of the Italian sky, the exuberant luxury of the vegetation, heightened in them a feeling of dumb despair. The contrast between life and death was too striking, and filled the souls of the artists with awe and dread, reflected in their artistic compositions.

Their representations were often divided into two distinct compartments. On one side were scenes from the lower regions. Mantus, Mania, and furies pursuing the deceased with hammers. Mantus of the Etruskans, probably a descendant of Radamanthus, was an infernal divinity. Mania (whose name we have preserved in the words *mania* and *maniac*) was the mother of the Lares and persecuted the dead. Our readers must begin to see whence many of the horrifying scenes of the middle ages took their origin. On the other side were scenes from life in the upper regions—joyous, triumphal processions and festivities. Drunkenness and licentiousness are always twin-sisters of superstition and bigotry. These arrangements recall the same custom of dividing subjects in antithetical groups observed in Assyria, where we find on the slabs hunts in the upper compartments, and joyous festivities in the row below. The subjects chosen with the Assyrians were undoubtedly much healthier. Hard work first, and joy and happiness afterwards. The Etruskans kept to the old Egyptian customs, reminding man continually of the short duration of his life. The mummy placed in Egyptian banqueting halls, with the inscription: 'Eat and drink; such a one wilt thou be,' had a pernicious ethical effect; instead of sobering man down, it drove him to reckless and despairing gaiety and extravagance. The Etruskans, though filling their imaginations with horrors, could never master art in life. They had the savage fondness for adorning their persons with innumerable trinkets. The desire to shine conspicuously for the short and uncertain time of their existence absorbed their artistic endeavours, and this fashion prevails amongst the peasants in Italy at the present day. The patterns are now filigree Moresque; in ancient times they were in a clumsy Greek style. To wear a ring was considered essential to man's and woman's existence.

This led them very early to cultivate glyptics, or the art of stone-cutting. The subjects were partly mythological, partly heroic; the artists delighted in strong muscles, attitudinizing groups, and theatrical postures.

In the paintings and mosaics, with which they adorned their burial chambers, we may distinguish, in reference to their treatment:

a. An Archaic style;

b. An Etruskan style.

A. In the *Archaic Style* they exhibit a thorough acquaintance with Greek mythology and classical poetry. Orpheus, Homer, Hesiod and Pindar furnish the scenes, but the dead play the most conspicuous part. We have, in another world, festivities in vine bowers and blooming gardens; processions, gymnastic games and races amongst the departed. The grouping is spirited so far as variety is concerned, but the execution is rough, and bare of all higher artistic feeling.

B. In the *Etruskan Style*, stern simplicity and roughness yield to a freer treatment of the human form. The thick-set, short figures are replaced by better drawn and lighter forms; the subjects are exclusively taken from Etruskan mythology. White and black spirits (angels and devils), armed with big hammers, are represented as fighting for the souls of the departed. In one of the graves (see Dempster and Agincourt) we have a soul hanged, and tormented with iron instruments, roasting over a brisk fire. In these products, in spite of the intervention of the Roman period of history, we find the direct connecting link between the old Assyrian, Egyptian, Etruskan, and early Christian arts.

The Etruskans indulged in fantastic conceptions, and rejoiced in forced and cruel scenes, and in bizarre compositions. Art with them was exclusively technical. We may arrange their works into the following five groups:—

1. The original *Tuscanica* (as Strabo has it) or Etruskan works. Heavy in

form and details; dresses very stiff; figures without beards. Of this group we have many bronze figures, very few sculptures in stone, some gems, and some very old wall-paintings.

2. The Oriental group. Imitations of Egyptian, Assyrian, and Babylonian patterns. Tapestry, for floor and wall-decorations, was much used. The imitations were good, but without any effort at originality. Remains plentiful.

3. Caricatures distinguished by grotesque quaintness. This style predominates at periods, when nations look upon art as superfluous; not as one of the most important factors of civilization. Taste degenerates, and the higher aspirations of art are crippled by distorted products. The quaint is preferred to the beautiful, and the dynamic force of the artistic element, driven into this direction, loses itself in a broad grin at everything sacred and elevated in State, religion, and science, fostering a deplorable spirit of vulgar egotism, which looks down upon the sublime exertions of artists, as the mere vagaries of simpletons or madmen.

4. Works in the best Greek style, but only in bronze, as frames and handles of mirrors. Whenever the higher spirit of art is neglected, the power of the artist is directed to small matters; he serves trade and nothing but trade. We have in these 'Articles of Etruria' the prototypes of our 'Articles de Paris.'

5. Mechanical products, such as helmets, weapons, swords, shields, hatchets, clubs, wall-breakers, cooking utensils, pots, pans, and saucers, were of exquisite workmanship, but without any attempt at artistic forms. The utilitarian incubus is as bad as the hierarchical canon; both expel all higher aspirations from the realm of art.

The Etruskans thought, with many of us, that if the house were only built of dry bricks, the carpet thick, the furniture solid and heavy, and the knife sharp, it was unnecessary to care for anything else. Whilst such ideas exist, art, in a higher sense, will remain as little possible, as it was with the Etruskans.

CHAPTER X.

ROMAN ART.

The Greeks, from a poetical, artistic, and esthetical, and the Romans, from a social, legal, and political point of view, are still our masters. Historical art-critics, and a certain class of writers, who would wish to see the whole universe one great court of justice with an infinite variety of crimes, subdivided into felony, misdemeanour, petty larceny, &c., will never agree as to the place that should be assigned to the Romans in the world's history. We are bold enough to assert that the whole of the criminal and sanguinary history of Rome, with her products in literature and art, might be wiped out, and yet philosophically, poetically, and artistically, not the slightest gap in the progressive development of humanity would be found. Socially and legally, we should be sorry to miss a state, which had a mission of its own, which, if well understood, may teach us the causes why the gentler feelings of morality were oppressed, imagination defiled, and every higher artistic aspiration deadened in Rome.

From beginning to end, ROMA, read backwards AMOR, was an ambiguous 'state-abstraction,' which absorbed the individual. The State with the Greeks was a concrete association of freemen. With the Romans, it was the abstract principle of an imaginary union of heterogeneous citizens. The Greeks fostered science and art, poetry and philosophy. The Romans despised science, mocked art, scorned poetry, and never condescended to trouble themselves about philosophy. The Greeks colonised and civilised their colonies, which became the free daughters of a free mother-country, attached to it by the ties of a common worship of beauty and intellectual enjoyment. The Romans conquered, and the conquered provinces were to furnish soldiers or labourers, and were tied by means of despotism to the wheels of the proud state-carriage. The Greeks humanised; the Romans demoralised and organised. The Greeks played at soldiers in a spirit of glorious patriotism. The Romans were soldiers for the sake of conquest, plunder, and vain glory. Spirited youthfulness was the Greek element. Stern and calculating manliness the essence of the Roman. The Greek was free in life, in art, in the worship of his gods, in poetry and philosophy. The Roman was cowed down in religion, politics and life, by the inexorable despotic force of legal phantoms, which turned men into mere machines. The despotism of the East was the despotism of some invisible god, or some visible ruler; and it often overlooked the individual in its almighty position. The democracy of Greece gave fair play to individual talent and genius in art and science; but the Roman self-constituted aristocracy, or rather triple theocracy, invented the inexorable and meddlesome monster authority, to which everything was to be sacrificed. Under the tragi-comical sobriquet, *Salus reipublicæ suprema lex* (in free translation, 'whatever we in authority find good, is good'), they committed the blackest crimes, which no historian could venture to commit to paper in their whole truthfulness.

This triple theocracy presented itself in the shape of seven mythical kings; in the form of a nominal republic, which was in reality a military and theocratic aristocracy; and lastly in the theocracy of the Cæsars, which in course of time was changed into a papal theocracy.

The Romans had to reverence and submit to theocracy under the form of a triple authority—the political authority; the paternal authority; and the legal authority. Wherever the Roman turned to, in that vast empire, which was bounded in the west by the Atlantic, in the north by the Rhine and the Danube, in the east by the Euphrates, and in the south by the deserts of Arabia and Africa, he met his triple crown of authority. He was confronted by some consul or proconsul, some law, some edict, some whim or caprice of an invisible something, that always had a visible *lictor* at its command with a bundle of sticks, ready for flogging, or, in urgent cases, with a well-sharpened axe to sever the head from the trunk. He had to obey a power, with innumerable soldiers, ready to punish whole provinces if they resisted that ever present, ever vigilant, and ever-active State abstraction. Whilst in Greece, the individual man was developed with all his bodily and intellectual faculties in science and art, Rome disturbed and hindered this individual development, concentrating the static and dynamic forces of her citizens on brutal military enterprises.

Rome, through its theocratical spirit, oppressed the conquered by the conqueror, the poor by the rich, the 'nihil habentes' by the 'possedentes,' the client by the patron, the plebeian by the patrician, humanity by priests and gods, and the individual by the State. The Roman as individual was never a self-acting, self-conscious, and free-thinking entity, but a mere cipher after the State unit; a wheel in a large and complicated machine; a drop of water in an ocean; an atom in the universe. The Greek recognised in the State only an agglomeration of men like himself; this sum total of citizens had to serve *him*; the State was to him a means, not an aim. The Greek demanded of the State that it should protect him in the free and perfect use of his bodily and intellectual faculties. He was, if he liked, poet, magistrate, athlete, judge, dancer, philosopher, fighter, priest, wrestler, tragedian, soldier, or singer; all for his own sake, without ever becoming an over-regulated or over-regulating pedant. He worshipped his gods without restraining dogmas; he never allowed his individuality to be absorbed by some incomprehensible, shapeless, universal theocracy; his whole scientific and artistic national career was one glorious struggle against such an accomplishment. All this was the very reverse with the Romans. That Rome had no art or science of her own, was the effect of those causes which we have here tried to sketch in a general way.

The Romans, like the Greeks, were a mixture of Aryans and Turanians, with this difference, that with the Greeks the Aryan element predominated, whilst with the Romans the Turanian, and even the black elements formed a considerable portion of the national State body. The Greek element, which, at the time of the earliest formation of the Roman State, was very powerful, soon became absorbed in the Gallic, Iberian, African, Egyptian, and Syrian elements. The enervating south was not counterbalanced by the energetic north, but, on the contrary, the south predominated; and as in the south-east theocratic despotism flourished, the same principle was adopted by the Romans, and worked into a perfect system.

That the language of the Romans had a common origin with that of the Greeks, Persians, and Indians is evident from the consideration even of a few words. The verbs *sum* (I am), *do* (I give), and the words *pater, mater, frater,* are Sanskrit. The most important pastoral and agricultural expressions are Sanskrit, showing that a certain degree of civilisation must have been brought with them by the settlers, after their separation from their Trans-Himâlâyan brethren, when they peopled the shores of the Mediterranean, and occupied that small coast-land which was probably once connected with the African continent through Sicily.

Pecus, sus, taurus, and *canis* are Sanskrit words. The Sanskrit *agras* (meadow) is the Latin *ager* (Germ. *acker*, acre). The Sanskrit *kurnu* (Germ. *korn*, corn, grain) is the Latin *granum*. The settlers were undoubtedly acquainted with even higher elements of a steady and civilised life. The Sanskrit word *aritram* (ship and oar), survived as *aratrum* the plough, cutting through the ground like the aritram through the waves. The Sanskrit *damas,* δόμος {domos} is the Latin *domus; naus* is *navis; akshas* is axis (Germ. *achse*) a coach or cart; and we have in the Sanskrit *vastra,* the Latin *vestis* (vestment), not only a proof of the connection between the Aryans of the Ganges, and those on the shores of the Tiber, but a living testimony that the former had left off tattooing their bodies and used textile fabrics. The Romans were first called Ramnes. Three races may be said to have furnished the first settlers on the Seven Hills, the Ramnes, Titians, and Lukeres. From this threefold confederation we have the word tribuere, tribus (tribe). Later Pelasgians, Sabines, Albans, Etruskans, and Hellenes joined the first settlers, and formed by degrees the Roman State.

As the Britons at one time earnestly believed that they were the direct descendants of Brutus, the son of Æneas, we need not wonder that the Romans should have indulged in the flattering faith that they were the direct descendants of Æneas himself. They had scarcely attained a settled state, when they began to work out their legends and myths, concerning the divine foundation of their town, which had taken place under *seven* kings.

1. Romulus, a god-man, for he and his brother, Remus, were incarnations of the war-god Mars and miraculously born of a virgin. Their uncle Amulius, fearing that they might deprive him of his throne, had them exposed in the swollen Tiber in a cradle. The river subsided, and the cradle was caught by a sacred fig-tree at the foot of the Palatine hill, and a she-wolf had pity on the boys, and suckled them. The founders of Rome thus mythically imbibed, with their foster-mother's milk, that savage brutality and thirst for blood which distinguished the citizens of the Holy City for thousands of years. Romulus and Remus were found by shepherds, and brought up by them. Subsequently a town was founded by the twins, and Romulus then killed his brother and ruled alone. He divided the people into curiæ.

2. Numa Pompilius enlarged the town and introduced a settled form of worship, not out of piety, but in order to subject the citizens to the will of the State.

3. Tullus Hostilius improved upon the theocratical institutions of Numa, and gave Rome a military organisation, as the secret tool with which her will was to be enforced throughout a vast part of the globe.

4. Ancus Martius commanded the citizens to have taste and to beautify the town, or rather had this done, superintending the improvements himself. He is stated to have been a grandson of Numa.

5. Tarquinius Priscus, of a Korinthian family, showed in his very infancy that he was destined by supernatural influences to become a benefactor of the chosen people, the Romans. When a tender boy sleeping in his cradle, his head was surrounded by a brilliant halo of flames. He conquered many Latin and Sabine towns, and showed himself worthy of his exalted position. He introduced the golden diadem, the ivory throne, the sceptre adorned with an eagle, and the purple toga, as distinctive marks of the supreme authority.

6. Servius Tullius was also of supernatural origin. He was the son of a female slave, and the protecting divinity of the royal castle. He divided the people into five classes or castes; instituted tribunes, and founded the orders

of senators, knights, and commons.

7. Tarquinius Superbus, like the Chinese tyrant Ly-wang, who succeeded the five good emperors, defiled the imperial dignity, outraged all laws, divine and human, and was rebelled against by the patricians, who abolished the regal authority. The innocent Lucretia is said to have been the direct cause of the expulsion of the tyrant, and the establishment of the republic.

In the myths concerning these seven kings we have abundant elements for the most beautiful songs, epic poems, and artistic subjects full of dramatic power and vitality. The remarkable fact with the Romans was, that they preserved these myths as *historical* truths, recorded them in dull *prose*, affixing to them dates, each of which was a flagrant falsehood, and used them in good earnest as the basis of their national existence.

The royal period ended with the seven kings. Rome had prepared in perfect silence her murderous weapons, and, suddenly dashing forward a well-trained prize-fighter, inaugurated the military theocracy. The history of this second period, with its appalling monotony, may be condensed into one terrible word—WAR.

From 342–340 B.C. war with the Samnites. From 340–337 B.C. war with the Latins. From 325–290 B.C. the second and third Latin war. From 288–264 B.C. war with Carthage and Syrakuse. From 264–241 B.C. the first Punic war. Peace was made, and to fill up the leisure hours, there was a Gallic war. From 218–201 B.C. the second Punic war. Peace was again concluded, and during the interval (183 B.C.) Greece and the Makedonian empire were subjugated. From 149–146 B.C. the third Punic war. The world was conquered, and the boundaries of the vast empire extended in all directions; but the warlike spirit of the Romans had not learnt to rest and to enjoy these conquests in peace; industry, arts, and sciences, had no charm for these wild and indomitable conquerors, and wanting a foreign enemy, they quarrelled amongst themselves. The internal dissensions began. There were the Numantian troubles, the tumults of the Gracchi, and the feud between Marius and Sulla. A foreign war happily put an end to these internal struggles. From 112–106 B.C. war with Jugurtha. From 88–80 B.C. war with Mithridates. From 72–71 B.C. the slaves rebelled and called for bread and for revenge. This was the first civil war—individual egotism conspired against the supreme power, faction fought against faction; a dissolution of all law and order threatened the State. From 54–51 B.C. the Gallic war amused the Roman spectators and war-comedians. From 49–48 B.C. there was a second civil war; from 43–30 B.C. a third; and the republic was at last absorbed by a Cæsarian theocracy.

That arts and sciences did not flourish in a state of continual warfare is quite natural. The houses were mean and low, here and there adorned with clumsy Etruskan pillars; the temples had some Greek forms; sculpture was not cultivated, and Greeks had to chisel or to carve the scanty embellishments. On the other hand, high roads of great excellence, and bold bridges with magnificent arches, were constructed, for everywhere the spirit of practical realism was served; in every stone, every column, every pillar, every statue, the spirit of theocratic despotism predominated. The charming gods of the Greeks were turned into haughty military commanders, not inviting love through beauty, but demanding blind obedience with a thundering '*sic volo, sic jubeo*' ('as I will it, so I command it').

The period of imperial theocracy showed Rome in her pomp and splendour, covering inner hollowness and gradual decay with marble slabs. Palaces and temples, basilicæ and arcades, triumphal arches and amphitheatres, arenas and baths (of the latter Rome alone had about 768), naumachiæ and circuses, theatres and arenas, hippodromes and magnificent tombs abounded; but in all these architectural marvels, the monumental spirit of pride, self-glorification, vain ostentation, and theatrical display, is to be traced; the love of beauty, of artistic moderation, and simplicity being everywhere conspicuous by its absence. Roman art and decoration are to be carefully studied, that we may learn 'how not to do it,' if we earnestly intend to produce works of art, and not works of ornamentation, forming a very Paradise for 'parvenus' with bad taste.

We have asserted that the Romans never produced anything original in art and science. Their religion, their literature, and their products of art, bear this assertion out to the very letter.

The word 'religion' is of Roman origin. The Teutons have *faith* or trust in God. The Roman word meant the tying down of everyone to certain formulas or dogmas. They borrowed their dogmas and superstitions, their gods and ceremonies, from all parts of the world; especially from the Greeks and Etruskans, and later from the Egyptians. Everything served their purpose so soon as it helped to overawe the masses. They had augurs, auspices, and sibylline oracles. From the entrails of beasts and human beings they predicted the future. Flashes of lightning, the rolling thunder, the flight of birds, meetings with hares, goats, dogs, or cats, announced the will of the gods. The conceptions of the Eastern gods were disfigured, and they were made more jealous, threatening, merciless, revengeful, and inexorable. Jupiter the thunderer (Jupiter tonans) did not govern by any moral law, but by mere force; he spoke in flashes of lightning and in thunder, in terrifying earthquakes and volcanic eruptions. Amongst the 30,000 deities with which the Roman triple theocracy peopled the visible and invisible world, there was not ONE divinity of kindness, mercy, and comfort.

They had a divinity of peace, to urge them on to war; they had divinities of plague, hunger, fever, mildew, and death. In their practical spirit they went even so far as to have a 'Dea Cloacina.'

What subjects to paint or sculpture!

A pale-yellow woman with dishevelled hair, protruding ghastly eyes, wasted lips, fleshless and emaciated limbs, may represent the goddess of hunger; another woman deliberately and slowly tearing the limbs of helpless creatures from their bodies with diabolical delight, may be a goddess of plague; another, placidly playing with human skulls in a field surrounded by dying men, women, and children, may be the goddess of death.

In the illustration of a Dante or a Milton, a knowledge of the Roman mythology may prove full of suggestive power.

The Greeks had a principle in their anthropomorphic worship; the Romans had no aim. Roman high-priests were spiritual butchers, who tried to appease the angry gods with the smoke of burning bullocks, to nourish them with fat, with which they literally besmeared the statues, and to quench their thirst with blood which they poured over the altars. When already educated enough to consider all these divinities with a cold and sceptic indifference; when the augurs could no longer meet without laughing and sneering at each other and their sacred office, then the Roman mind became eager for a more concrete god than these stone figures, and they found a corresponding living divinity in the person of their Emperors. Earth certainly could offer nothing more divine in the form of visible majesty, recognised and obeyed, as soon as clothed in the imperial purple and crowned with the imperial diadem, than the irresponsible 'god-man,' who sat on the throne of the Cæsars. The creative force of the Universe, and the phenomena of nature, were moulded in visible forms; and now for the first time a political abstraction had become incarnate in the Emperor *pro tem.* The hordes of courtiers, courtezans, flatterers, poets, philosophers, historians, juris consults, orators, prætors, and consuls, supported by the thoughtless mass of the people, rendered *divine* honours to a *mortal*, in whom, however, the *immortal* principle of theocratic authority was concentrated. Not even the Egyptians, crouching in grateful admiration before the crocodiles of the Nile, outraged humanity to such a degree as these polite Romans, rendering divine honour to an Emperor, like Aurelius Commodus, who fought 735 times as a common gladiator in the arena before his enervated people. The Roman religion was, in fact, a cosmopolitan mixture of all the atrocious superstitions of the world.

The Romans also instituted public games in imitation of the Greeks, on the degrading 'panis et circenses' principle. In Greece, Apollo with his nine muses presided over the public games. The Romans had specially-trained gladiators, wrestlers, dancers, and prize-fighters. The competitors at the Greek games were free and independent citizens; with the Romans they were either criminals, runaway slaves, or men condemned to death. Bears, lions, tigers, and elephants were starved, and set against one another, to delight the spectators with their savage brutality. Soon an improvement was effected, and men were arrayed against men with deadly weapons, to amuse men and women, boys and girls, with their skill in murdering; and at last, as a further progressive development in taste, men were pitted against wild beasts. In the Greek tragedy, the ideal sufferings of humanity, struggling in an unequal combat with omnipotent and inexorable fate, were prominently set forth to purify men from their passions by showing the consequences of even unconscious guilt. The Greek tragedy was the national moral conscience brought into the most perfect poetical form. The Romans instituted a cruel reality of *bodily* suffering; *real* blood streaming from *real* limbs; the *real* rattle in the throat, which signals death; and the *real* last gasp of an expiring man, afforded them amusement.

Like their religion and public games, their literature, with the exception of their satires and law-codes, was matter of fact and imitative. The generation of the Roman products of poetry and prose was the following: Homer engendered Virgil, Hesiod—Lucretius; Pindar—Horace; Æsop— Phædrus; Euripides— Terence; Aristophanes—Plautus; Xenophon—Sallust; Thukydides—Titus Livy; Demosthenes—Cicero. Ovid and Tacitus were the only really original writers; the first faithfully depicted the hollowness of Roman ethics; and the other, in unsurpassed language, drew a historical sketch of the Teutons, mercilessly exposing the contrast between noble simplicity, grandeur and honesty, and the demoralised state of his own country.

If art is the outgrowth of the intellectual and moral condition of a people, what kind of art could the Romans have produced? None. And this was the case. Roman art is altogether a misnomer; it is in fact Etruskan, Greek, Assyrian, and Egyptian art, dressed in an eclectic Roman garb by foreign artists. Art with the Romans was never the glorious emanation of the poet's sacred ideal of the gods, or the irresistible civilising power of beauty; it was merely the handmaid of power, wealth, pomp, and vanity. Art was with them a slave, well fed, well clad, well housed, well paid, to make power more powerful, to dazzle the people, to proclaim the universal dominion of Rome over the world. The Roman character was dry and geometrical, and therefore in its artistic taste architectural and monumental. Anything that could serve, by means of technical perfection, to promote art, was encouraged, adopted, and supported by the Romans.

We have given a drastic picture of the evils of the Roman spirit; we must be just to the great mission which it fulfilled unconsciously and against its will. The centralisation in language, customs, and manners produced a cosmopolitan spirit. Greek artists and philosophers spread taste and learning. Distant nations were brought into closer connection. The roads constructed to facilitate the march of legions, bent on devastating a province, served as means of communication; so did their aqueducts and bridges. The wants of an increasing population forced the Romans to improve agriculture, and commerce was found necessary. Corn had to be brought from one quarter, textile fabrics from another; Greece and Egypt were pillaged of their innumerable works of art, and Rome may be said to have been at that period the greatest museum of the universe. The superstition and credulity which existed among the people, by degrees disappeared. Africa had been considered a land of monsters, with serpents large enough to entangle a whole army and to crush it; other regions of the accessible world had been thought inhabited by men without heads. Giants, kyklops, and enchantresses had been said to perform incredible feats, but were found to be without supernatural power; the golden apples of Spain turned out to be mere oranges, and graced the tables of the wealthier, and in time even of the poorer classes. The mouth of hell had been placed on the shores of the Euxine (Black Sea), but when those regions were occupied by Roman soldiers, the mouth of hell had to be removed elsewhere. East and west, south and north, were united under one great Roman vault, the four quarters of the globe were over-arched, and the broad cupola of universalism set over them. Man was made a common slave to one grand and common abstraction, typically foreshadowing the time when men would be brought as free agents under one great dome of universal brotherhood.

For this grand and really majestic soldering of humanity into one total, the Romans found the spiritual as well as the material form in

1. The arch.
2. The cross-vault.
3. The cupola.

Through the *arch*, which was used by the Etruskans, but which under the Romans became a most important part of architecture, the art of constructing was suddenly freed of all hindrances. Courts could be formed with more ease, and the ground-plan drawn with greater variety.

The *cross-vault* may be considered a specially Roman form. Two cylindrical arches were constructed intersecting each other at right angles in a quadrangular space. The intersection takes place at the two diagonal lines, thus uniting the opposite corners. The arches in their cross-form rise from four points of support, and divide the arch into four curved triangles, called calottes.

The *cupola*, a third form of the vault, was called forth in the Romans by their preference for *circular* buildings. The ancient mound was revived by them. It was the application of the arch to a circular ground-plan. A powerful larger or smaller member of decoration was produced, interrupting the flatness of walls, and allowing a rich variety of statuary to be used as ornament. This refers to the use of the half-cupola for semicircular niches and the apsidæ. These merely geometrical constructions would have been monotonous and without grace, like our railway stations; and would have been classed as works of engineering, but never of art; had not the Romans employed Greek forms in the shape of columns and pilasters, to adorn them. The Doric, Ionic, Attic, and Korinthian styles were all used, and a so-called composite or Roman order was added. The composite stood in the same relation to the proto-Korinthian, as Plautus to Aristophanes. The Romans, with arrogant clumsiness, placed a coarser and more contracted form of the Ionic capital on two rows of richly carved acanthus leaves. This was a bad composition, and left room for much improvement, which was effected more than fifteen hundred years later.

Nothing is known of art during the mythical period of Roman history.

During the first centuries of the Republic, the Etruskan style is said to have been prevalent, introduced by Tarquin. Square wooden huts with a rounded and tumulus-like roof of straw, were the first palaces of the Roman citizens. Only after the conquest of Greece 183 B.C., Grecian architecture and sculpture were introduced. From this date we may classify Roman art, under Greek, Assyrian, and Egyptian influences, into the following periods.

a. The *first* begins in the second century B.C., under the Republic, after the destruction of Korinthum by Mummius, and ends with the reign of the Augustan house, and the beginning of the rule of the Flavians, 69 A.D. This was the *Græco-Roman Period* of architecture and sculpture.

b. The *second* period commences with the *Flavians*, 69 A.D. After the tyrannical reigns of Tiberius and Nero, the cosmopolitan Imperial state acquired an apparent stability in new social forms, which found expression in gigantic artistic constructions. This period, which lasted down to Septimus Severus, 193 A.D., has three distinct phases.

α. A phase of powerful development under the Flavians.

β. A phase of brilliant success under *Trajan* (98–117 A.D.)

γ. A phase of revival of classic Greek forms under *Hadrian* (117–138 A.D.)

We may designate these phases of development as the *Romano-Greek* period.

c. The *third* period under the military despotism of the prætorian guards, during which Rome ceased to be the centre of universal dominion, and each province began to feel its own vitality, lasted from *Septimus Severus* (193– 211 A.D.) to Constantine the Great. Art lost every basis—degenerated into luxurious pomp, and became heavier with each new product, and more fantastic in incredible details and impossible executions. We may best designate this as the *Romano-eclectic* period.

A. After the destruction of Korinthum, Rome abounded in Greek immigrants, and in Greek marble and bronze statues, friezes, pillars, and various movable works of art. The spoils of Greek temples and houses were set up in Roman houses built of bricks and mortar. The contrast between the unartistic architecture of the Romans, and the master-pieces of Greek art, was so striking, that they were forced to endeavour to improve their architecture, and art became to a certain degree *fashionable*. The wealthier classes began to study it *theoretically*, and to affect an immense amount of *patronizing* enthusiasm, without any deeper understanding of the laws of taste and beauty, but with a determination to outdo all other nations in the profession of works of art. Such sentiments often engender a *brisk trade*, but they fail to promote real art, or to benefit genuine artists. The walls of the houses of this period were generally white, with red painted ornamentations. Red is the favourite colour with children, savages, and butchers in mind. This led to the making of red bricks, which were mixed with others of different colours, and thus originated polylithic wall-decoration. The spaces between the red bricks were filled in with a black composition in imitation of different textile patterns, and this mode of decoration was called Niello. By degrees, bricks and cement were superseded by marble, and the houses became so rich, that a Puritan party of Roman ιδιώταις {idiôtais} formed itself, and thundered against corruption and enervation, luxury and degradation. The power of this party was so great that Cicero, fearing lest these stern and dull Roman worthies should think him acquainted with the principles of artistic refinement, declared his utter ignorance of art, and expressed his high contempt for all such futile 'allotria.'

The art of ornamentation became more and more universal. The fora and atria were overcrowded with bronze and marble statues and groups. These efforts, however, were not genuine; they did not grow out of the artistic wants and love of the people—the whole movement was strange to their minds— and was altogether a heterogeneous element grafted on their natures by the force of circumstances. They succeeded by degrees in ornamenting grandly, but there was always something in contradiction to, or in conflict with, really good taste. They used patterns meant for floors on their walls, and wall patterns on their ceilings, and that which would have fitted a ceiling, they laid on their floors; creating by this means a sad confusion. Asia always excelling in bright colours, and in a secret talent for matching them correctly, excited the admiration of the Romans, and they began to paint their walls. They often cut out the decorated parts of a pillaged Greek temple, and fixed these pieces at random in their houses, caring very little whether there was a congruity between these and their own wall-decoration or not. We have, during this period, an attempt at 'scenography.' The walls were painted over with architectural views, representing colonnades, interiors, landscapes, and later, Greek mythological and even historical scenes. In these, Perseus and Andromeda, or Medea meditating the murder of her children, or Herkules destroying the serpent, or some other *sensational* deed, formed the cherished subjects. Under the influence of the Greeks of Alexandria, another custom became prevalent. The walls were more and more panelled, and the panels filled with works of art.

This 'mania,' or fashion, became so universal with the Romans that they could find no more works of classic art, and had to engage living artists to reproduce antique cornices, metopes, colonnades, capitals, shields, helmets, tripods, sphinxes, and griffins; but even these artists were so overwhelmed with commissions, that it was impossible for them to satisfy the feverish demand. To produce works of art more quickly, they began to paint the panels, and the Roman empire became a complete manufactory of wall- decorations. Light colonnades of slender reeds, baldachins with pointed arches and fantastic monsters, filled the walls, and sometimes mere combinations of colours were used in a conventional style. Art again sank into mere trade. The panels and walls were not decorated with the works of the good old Greek masters, but with mere imitations. Mannerism supplanted style, and arabesques, flourishes, insignificant chequered patterns, or geometrical puzzles, took the place of historical paintings—poor wall-decorations in a theatrical style, without any attempt at higher art.

The use of marble as a means of decoration was not always customary with the Romans, and was introduced by L. Crassus, the censor, who had his house decorated with six small columns of marble from Hymettus, and was very much blamed for this extravagance. M. Scaurus, the ædile, who built the famous wooden theatre, decorated with 360 pillars of marble, glass, and bronze, and about 3,000 statues and images, had the atrium and peristyle of his private house richly adorned with exquisite columns. Manurra, prefect of the armourers, under Julius Cæsar in Gaul, is set down as the first who had his walls decorated with marble incrustations; whilst M. Catulus could boast of the first marble flooring, and of thresholds in Numidian marble. Of temples, one of the first constructed of marble blocks in a purer Greek style was that of Jupiter Tonans. The temple of *Fortuna Virilis* which rose on a lofty substructure on the banks of the Tiber, was in the Ionic style. The Vesta temple at Tivoli, enthroned on a steep and rocky height above the foaming waters of the Anio, was a circular building in the Korinthian style.

Theatres, public halls, baths, and Fora were found necessary, either to distract the public mind from political matters, or to gain the suffrages of the fickle mob, eager for amusement and excitement. The first theatre in stone was erected by Pompey. Julius Cæsar surpassed all his predecessors and rivals in magnificence. He began the theatre of Marcellus, which was completed by Augustus, and so enlarged and beautified the *Circus Maximus* that it could accommodate 150,000 spectators; he built the beautiful Basilica Julia, a public law-court for the Centumviri or Judges to sit in, and hear causes, and for the counsellors to receive their clients, and had a new Forum constructed, and adorned it with a temple dedicated to Venus Genetrix. The Roman Forum (in imitation of the Greek Agora) was a building about three times as long as broad. The interior was surrounded by arched porticos, and flanked by the most stately edifices, such as theatres, basilicæ, and temples.

These Fora were devoted to special purposes, as Fora *civilia* or Fora *venalia*, and were used for public meetings, or as market-places. Cæsar tried to become a Roman Perikles, but was distanced in this by the Emperor Augustus. Up to the establishment of Cæsarism, Rome had been literally a city of 'bricks;' now it became a 'city of marble.' Temples were profusely built and rebuilt. The Cæsarian theocracy required these abodes of splendour and self-glorification. One of the most imposing specimens of this *Græco- Roman* architecture was the Pantheon, built by Agrippa, the son-in-law of

Augustus. Originally it was to have been an entrance-hall to splendid Thermæ, but on its completion it was turned into a temple, and dedicated to the avenging Jupiter. It was a circular building 132 feet in diameter, and 132 feet high, and triumphantly proclaimed Rome's wealth and might. It contained a statue of Minerva by Pheidias, and a Venus, who it is said had in her ear the half of the pearl left by Cleopatra. The pearl was valued at 125,000*l.* That a Greek marble statue should have been ornamented with part of the *ear-ring* of an Egyptian princess, is highly characteristic of Roman taste in matters of art. One of the most splendid remains in the style of good Greek Korinthian ornamentation is the temple of Augustus at Pola in Istria. Triumphal gates, these Roman specialities, were at this period simple in design, and perfect in execution. Of the Mausoleum of Augustus nothing is left but the substructure, 220 feet in diameter, now used as a circus for equestrian performances. 'Sic transit gloria mundi,' if based on mere ostentation and vain pride.

During this period Nikopolis was planned and built; the Temple of Solomon was adorned with colonnades in the Greek Korinthian style, and at Nîmes (Nemausus) we possess the most complete remains of a prostylos pseudipteros temple of Roman architecture, with the purest Korinthian columns. Under Tiberius the camp of the prætorians was turned into a marble palace. Under Claudius harbours and moles were enlarged, built, and decorated. Nero burned Rome, to reconstruct it with greater pomp. The architects Celerus and Severus had to build the *golden houses*, of which the porticos were miles long. The dining-rooms surpassed in splendour anything dreamt of in Indian poetry. In the decoration of this palace, or rather cluster of palaces, we trace the greatest mistake an artist can be guilty of. The error is of Asiatic origin. It may be designated as a conscious '*lying*' in the constructive elements. They tried to hide the costly material under a cheap disguise; a tendency as bad and objectionable, as a 'lying' in cheap substances to represent costly materials. The Romans used tortoise-shell as veneer for their furniture, and painted it to make it appear like wood; we, on the other hand, use wood, and paint it over to make it appear 'giallo antico,' (yellow marble), or any other costly stone. Ornamentation began to lose all symmetry and proportion. Confusion and profusion ruled supreme. The walls of the rooms looked like exhibitions of oriental carpets, tapestry, and jewelry. Art retrograded to the over-painted, over-decorated, over-ornamented shrouds, in which the mummies of old were buried. For a time art was carried with Asiatic splendour to a grave of tasteless pomposity.

B. With the Flavians, down to Septimus Severus, a new spirit of artistic universalism pervaded the Roman world. The Greek element waned, and the circular forms of the Romans, ornamented with an indiscriminate mixture of

Doric, Ionic, and Korinthian columns, predominated. The Colosseum, a Flavian amphitheatre, begun by Vespasian and finished by Titus, belongs to this period. Three rows of arcades, the first of Doric, the second of Ionic, and the third of Korinthian half-columns, with their entablatures, crowned with a fourth story, adorned with Korinthian pilasters, and furnished with windows, encompassed an oval, 600 feet long by 500 feet broad, capable of holding 80,000 spectators. The circus was so constructed that it could also be used as a naumachy. In this over-decorated pompous building, the great fights of the gladiators took place; here men and wild beasts met in deadly struggle; here men, if killed, were dragged away by ropes fixed in their bodies with iron hooks; here the Imperators sat with all the nobility of Rome, and delighted in sports, which, at a later period of Rome's spiritual dominion, were only surpassed in *cruelty* by the pious 'auto-da-fés' of misguided priests.

The triumphal arch of Titus, on the heights of the Via Sacra; with one arch broken through the massive walls, ornamented on each side by half- columns; was the first to be decorated with the coarser form of the Roman *composite capital*. The ornamentation keeps within certain limits; the inner side walls of the arch have excellent reliefs, referring to the destruction of Jerusalem.

Everything yet enumerated was surpassed in splendour and magnificence by the 'Forum Trajanum' (A.D. 98–117), of which Apollodorus, born at Damaskus, was the architect. The great basilica Ulpia, with its *five aisles*, formed part of it. In a small courtyard, surrounded by pillars, rose the gigantic column of Trajan to a height of 92 feet. The reliefs, which in spiral windings surround the richly ornamented column, are a kind of Imperial record, chronicling with historical accuracy and dryness, scene after scene of the Dacian war. The figures are two feet high and not less than 2,500 in number; they are sculptured in a simple naturalistic style, void of all idealisation, and show the artist's talent for grouping. The heads of the figures, as was generally the case in all sculptures by the Romans, are too small for the bodies.

The triumphal arch of Constantine, with three openings, is undoubtedly the most splendid monument of its kind. It was of Pentelic marble, taken from the fragments of an arch in honour of Trajan. The proportions are noble, and the execution is technically precise; the ornamentation, however, is too profuse. The second phase of this period degenerated very quickly. Cornices began to be fluted; triglyphs and indentations were used alternately in endless rows; even the central volutes of the Corinthian capitals (the caulicoli) were over-decorated. Everything ran wild; rosettes, cassettes, shields, consols, stereobates, and stylobates were used abundantly, without sense and reason, to heighten the effect of the horizontal lines of the buildings. Everything was out of shape, out of proportion, and out of place. An eternal repetition of the same forms proclaimed the same desperate *deification* of the omnipotent power of the theocratic ruler.

Hadrian, the emperor, whose position constituted him a *divine* architect, and who by his very dignity must have known art better than any other mortal, did not share, with many a self-conceited artist of our time, the idea that the 'work and labour done' was all that was required in art, and that any knowledge of correct principles, any feeling of beauty, any acquaintance with esthetics or with art-history, was useless, and that money and power of execution were the only things required. On the contrary, though Emperor of the Romans, he diligently studied the antique, and tried to revive classic art.

We had an *imperial architect*, with an unlimited amount of gold, silver, marble, wood, and precious material at his command, and yet he had to go back to the Greeks for elegant forms in ornamentation. He had Apollodorus executed for daring to find fault with the confused plan of the temple of Venus (*Amor*) *and Roma*, which was a building surpassing, so far as splendour went, any construction of those times. The double temple had certainly something whimsical in its plan. The Emperor was too forcibly struck by the discovery that *Roma* read backwards gave *Amor*, and wanted to express this discovery in an architectural allegory, placing *two* temples back to back so that they made *one*, to typify *two* words with *two* meanings, that yet were *one* word. The success, so far as correctness of plan went, was doubtful. The cassettes of the bronze roof which united the *two* temples into *one*, were most elegantly finished. The court of the temple was 500 feet by 300. Another tower-like circular monument, based on a square sub-structure, formed the Mausoleum (now the Castle of St. Angelo). The diameter of the circular part was 226 feet. The construction vies in solidity and grandeur with the Egyptian monuments. The blocks of travertin are colossal, and the immense building was covered with Parian marble, and crowned with a huge quadriga.

Under the Antonines architecture, and art in general, gradually declined. The people occupied themselves with entirely different topics. Stoicism and Christianity—the old world of heathen formality, and the new world of spiritual redemption—were placed in conflict. A disturbed state of the public mind rarely favours plastic art. A specimen exhibiting this conflict may be seen in the temple of Antoninus and Faustina, built by Antoninus Pius (A.D. 138–161). A second edition of Trajan's column is given in that of Marcus Aurelius (A.D. 161–180), which stands on the field of Mars. The reliefs, winding round the shaft, represent scenes from the war against the

Markomanni. There is a certain liveliness in the execution, but the composition is wanting in clearness and precision, and above all in idealisation. Rivers, fields, and enclosures of walls, are marked with great accuracy; and the reliefs take, in style, the forms of geographical maps. Strict realism is the leading feature in this monument.

C. During the third period architecture and sculpture, ornamentation and painting, had soon to yield to a continual use of arms. The proud mistress of the world no more expanded her sway; she was once more busy in decorating her rich palaces, but in care and sorrow, and with an anxious brow, haunted by the necessity for exerting all her powers to keep what she possessed. The provinces had learnt to do without Rome; the consuls and pro-consuls had so well imitated their *divine* masters, that they thought themselves gods, and the supreme deity, the Imperator, lost his power over them. The State—based on an abstraction—began to vanish like a midnight phantom at daybreak. The one-sided deification of matter, during the old heathen times, had to yield to a totally new mode of feeling, thinking, speaking, and acting. The new times were seeking new forms, and had to pass from a savage state, through that of barbarism, symbolism, and mysticism, into self-consciousness, in order to find such shapes as would express a perfect harmony between spirit and matter. In the meantime, art dragged on its existence in copying what the old masters of Greece and the artists of Rome had done. The chisel, ruler, nay the very stones, trembled in the hands of the artists. They felt that they worked without a basis; that they heaped up blocks to see them soon crumble into the dust; that they constructed streets of pompous columns, some of them 3,500 feet long, to see them empty and deserted; they ornamented, but did it with a heavy heart; their soul was no more in the work. They heard already the deep *spiritual* whisper of other tidings resounding through the world on one side, and the terrible *temporal* shout of powerful barbarians, not yet enervated by luxury and licentiousness, armed with swords and iron clubs, on the other. The footsteps of avenging phantoms were heard in the North; the 'hallelujahs' of redeemed humanity in the South. This period is ushered in with the triumphal arch of Severus, on which the reliefs are placed without any regard to the architectural arrangement. Caracalla (A.D. 211–217) had baths constructed, with gigantic halls, furnished with 1,600 marble seats, with shady promenades, pompous reading-rooms, and places for games of every variety. This was to be a paradise on earth, to detach men from that *spiritual* Eden of love and happiness, the gates of which were opened by Christ. In feverish excitement, streets, palaces, basilicæ, halls, market-places, monuments, and whole towns, were built by the heathens. The pomp of worship was increased. Diocletian constructed baths with 2,400 seats; the principal hall was under three cross-vaults, with a span of 80 feet each, resting on granite columns. Sensationalism seized upon both people and artists; a sensationalism tinged with Roman vulgarity. All the principles of architecture, sculpture, and ornamentation were neglected. Columns and arches were mixed together in doleful incongruity. The arch rested on the architrave, or often rose without interruption directly from the capital. Columns were made in spiral or screw form; the variety of details was oppressive; no rest, no cæsura distinguished their ornamentation. It was, in fact, *an ornamentation over-ornamented*. The technical execution was everywhere splendid, but utterly mechanical; principles were neglected in art, because Roman life had lost even the one guiding principle of its existence—expansion by brutal force. The vulgar in mind and taste will always be charmed by huge and imposing masses, by the richness of the material, the daring of geometrical combination, and by startling feats of mechanical contrivance. The gorgeous mouldings, the friezes of endless decorations, the capitals with their rich foliage, marshalled in precise architectural lines, like Roman legions placed in battle array, have a peculiarly mystic charm for all those, who care more for effect than for taste or severity of style, or more for show than for symmetry and proportion; but if they love the old Roman style, and wish to work in it, let them above all insist on genuine materials. Let them work in real granite, travertin, and marble; let them not work in iron and glass, or in plaster of Paris, instead of Carrara marble; or in wood painted and varnished to represent granite, *lapis lazuli* (azure-stone), or *giallo antico*. An artist's first duty is to know and master his material, and not to try and bring about Roman architectural effects with substances that require an altogether different treatment. Whenever we endeavour to shirk this law, we are sure to produce something small and mean, thin and wasted, notwithstanding gorgeous dimensions. Whilst trying to look grand and haughty, substantial and pompous, we tell 'falsehoods' in bricks and mortar, in painted friezes, sham columns, and meretricious porticos; and we are then astonished that our artistic product, instead of being admired, is laughed at as a caricature.

In Greece the dynamic force was concentrated on the reproduction of *ideal beauty*; in Rome it was exhausted in conquests and politics. Only so long as the moral force of beauty—equivalent to that of virtue— counterbalanced the eccentricities of a wild fantastic imagination, the Greeks were capable of producing models of art. The Romans never cultivated this balance; they disciplined themselves, but in a totally different direction. This technical, mechanical, and military discipline is, at a certain period of an individual's or a nation's life, highly necessary, in order to place the bodily and intellectual capacities under the guidance of some authority, although this may be a mere abstraction. The results which may thus be attained, can be studied in Roman art, in spite of all its shortcomings.

CHRISTIANITY now illuminated the world with its clear light; but, dazzled by the divine brilliancy, everything in art, science and social life appeared at first dark, black, and hopeless. By degrees the minds of men began to grasp the newly proclaimed eternal law, through which alone the disturbed inner and outer, spiritual and material, moral and intellectual, static and dynamic forces of humanity were to attain a perfect balance. In time man became conscious of his nature, and emancipated his spirit in life and in art. He began to strive upwards, to detach himself from mere forms, however beautiful, if there was no meaning, no soul, no sense in them; he sought in everything the redeeming IDEA, without which no *modern* work of art is possible. Thus, ancient art had to yield to different principles. We shall have in future to distinguish between artistic products of *reality*, *feeling*, and *intellect*, till we shall find ourselves obliged to seek for a combination of these elements in order to understand modern art.

CHAPTER XI.

EARLY CHRISTIAN ART.

Historically and philosophically, from the point of view of whatever religious denomination; in the eyes of the devout believer, as well as in the eyes of the sceptic; by the thinker, and by the mere automaton of blood, flesh and bones; it must be admitted, that the two most important events in the history of humanity were the foundation of Christianity, and the great migration of the Northern people. The one was a *spiritual* movement, the other thoroughly *material*.

It is usual, in tracing the historical development of mankind in science and art, to follow the apparent course of the sun, and to assume that progress travelled with Indra, Ormuzd, Horus and Phoibos Apollo, from East to West. This is, however, a mere phrase. To understand and appreciate the history of man, it is better to divide the globe into a southern and northern hemisphere; for we find, that in analogy with this subdivision, the material as well as the intellectual development of life on our globe took place. We may even go further, and trace a distinction between the development of life and art in the south and north of the northern and southern hemispheres. In the farthest south of the southern hemisphere we have animal life and man, in the very lowest scale of progressive development; whilst the further we travel towards the north, the more animal life and the intellectual capacity of man increase. This is also the case in the northern hemisphere, up to the frigid zone, where a reaction sets in. In the south the moral power was more developed than the intellectual. In the south the predominant static force, joined to an ill-disciplined imagination, drove man to the field of metaphysical speculation; the misunderstood laws of nature, and the ignorance of the sluggish and indolent masses, gave free play to superstition and priestcraft. Thus the south (or south-east) was the birth-place of various theogonies, and religious systems. Idolatry, zoolatry, Sabaism, theism, pantheism, astrology, symbolism, mysticism, alchemy, magic, and cabalism originated in the south. The intellectual power in humanity, with a strong tendency to regulate itself by moral force, decidedly prevailed in the north, or north-west of our globe; and we received philosophy, as well as art, in their highest perfection, from Greece, the then most northern dwelling-place of civilized humanity. All the sciences which, through their beneficial influence have promoted the welfare and progress of humanity, were fostered in the North. In the North, astronomy, geography, history, botany, zoology, physiology, anatomy, chemistry, geology, and cosmogony were developed.

The savage of the South, up to our days, does not go beyond an ornamentation with geometrical figures; he can neither produce animals nor the human figure. The Egyptians surpassed the Assyrians and Babylonians in their monumental architecture, but in the plastic reproduction of the human form they never succeeded. Their sitting figures had legs and thighs forming right angles in the side view, while in front they were parallel; the drapery was merely marked by lines, rarely interrupted by folds. In their historical and allegorical bas-reliefs the composition is devoid of elegance and correctness of outlines; but they already showed a remarkable power in drawing animals. The Indians reached a higher stage of progress in sculpture; their mythology and poetry furnished them with a variety of subjects, with which they covered the walls of their shrines and temples; after the doctrines of Buddha became more universal, they attained grandeur in their architecture, combined with a certain degree of elegance. The human form is reproduced with ease; the proportions, though too soft, too sensual, are more correct than with the Egyptians.

So long as the Greek artists worked with reverence and modesty, inspired by faith in the gods, they were capable of understanding God's revelation of beauty in man's outer form. So long as the Romans unconsciously worked in this spirit, they produced their stupendous architectural monuments. When, however, State and citizens were forced by false principles to war with reality for a beggarly existence, or to plunge into mere sensuous enjoyments, man came to an open rupture with his destiny, and humanity might have perished altogether in sin and iniquity, had not Providence mercifully interfered by freeing, through Christ, the 'inner man'—that is, the intellectual and moral force in man—thus preparing humanity for a higher progressive life. The south of Asia had to go through the same religious and artistic phases of development. Buddhism stands to Brahmanism in the same relation as Christianity to Mosaism and Heathenism. Excepting, however, that both religions were reformations of older established creeds, all analogy between them ceases. The proof of the difference lies in the diametrically opposed development produced by Buddhism and Christianity. It is true that Buddhism teaches us not to kill, not to steal, not to lie, and not to be drunken. Christianity does the same. Buddha, in twelve other ordinances, extols self- abnegation, poverty, and commands all to meditate amongst the tombs on the fleeting transitoriness of our earthly existence. Christianity does the same. Christ, however, redeemed and freed our spiritual nature, and brought it into a self-conscious, vivid activity; whilst Buddhism degraded this higher *individual* nature into a nonentity, denying that there was an independent moral agent in us; teaching that we were phenomena of an all-pervading divine power, by which universality we should be absorbed after life. So long as Christianity held, though in a different shape, nearly the same mystic principles as Buddhism, the results in art were the same; for our ecclesiastical art was a revival of Buddhistic temples, with all their divisions and sub- divisions, their pointed arches, their variegated columns and pillars, the triforium, the altar (Daghopa), cloisters, chapels, and crypts.

Christ's divine words resounded at a period when the Greeks had long turned their minds to the licentious worship of the sensuous. The Egyptians, sighing under their Roman taskmasters, had taken refuge in dark mysticism, the meaning of which had been long lost to them; the Jews were divided into quarrelling sects, sunken in religious indifference, or occupied with mere outward formalities, hating everyone and hated by everyone. The Romans knelt tremblingly before an imperial divinity, slaves and poor being considered mere burdens on society; the rich were merciless, debauched, and revelled in amusements; infanticides, suicides, murder and decay, despair and annihilation, were every-day occurrences. At this period, under such circumstances, the divine Master died on the cross, sealing with his death the one great tiding of love: 'that we are all children of *one* Father, who is in heaven.' The god of revenge of the old world was transformed into a God of inexhaustible love. With the Jews and the ancients, he only was blessed who had plenty on earth; now, the pure in mind, whether poor or rich, weak or mighty, beautiful or ugly, was extolled. God was not merely present in the universe as its living soul, or in a burning bush, in thunder and lightning, in growling volcanoes, in an ark, a carved idol, a statue or in a temple. God was present, wherever a kind, loving, and forgiving mind was ready to be His ark or temple. Christ repudiated all local gods; did not require any sacrifices of plants or animals; did not prescribe any diet, or outward sanguinary sign; did not allow polygamy; did not proclaim his followers the only *chosen* children of the *Father of All*; but taught the one and indivisible, and ever-true law of peace, love, and tolerance. This doctrine is as universal as intellect; it must be of as divine origin as intellect itself; it is, and can be, the only faith which must once unite Humanity into one great loving and beloved brotherhood. What a change! Not only a change; it was the building up of a new glorious future; it was the re-establishment of the lost balance between the working forces of humanity; it was the redemption of our individual, moral, and intellectual capacities; it was the enunciation of an eternal law, under which humanity had, till then, unconsciously developed, but of which it became conscious in word as well as in spirit, through Christ. Slavery in body or mind was, at least in principle, for ever abolished; and one of the noblest edifices of

Byzantine architecture in Italy, the church of St. Vitale at Ravenna, was dedicated by Justinian, a Roman Emperor, to the memory of a slave, who was martyred for the sake of his piety and love. Hospitals for the poor and sick, Xenodochia (refuges for strangers) began to be built—architectural constructions of which the whole ancient world could not boast.

The Christian spirit at first struggled to find a corresponding form in art; the new wine was put into the old vessels till it burst the decaying fetters and issued forth in a life-giving art-stream, in two directions:—

(a) As Romanesque art in the West, a decaying continuation of Roman art;

(b) As Byzantine art in the East, a revival of Asiatic art.

The beginning of Christian plastic and pictorial art is to be looked for in subterranean caves; in catacombs, used by Egyptians, Assyrians, Persians, Greeks, Etruscans, and Romans as burial-places. The deep but simple doctrines of Christ were at first hidden in symbols, types, allegories and emblems. In a SYMBOL we try to express a general idea by a special outward sign, totally heterogeneous in form to the meaning. Geometrical figures, plants, and animals, furnish the elements of symbolism. In the ALLEGORY the artist represents congruities, traces connections, unites analogies and separates differences. Imagination has in allegories an inexhaustible field for composition. TYPES are signs, arbitrarily interpreted as meaning something, which they may or may not mean. EMBLEMS with the Greeks were golden or silver figures which could be detached from vessels. With the Romans the word was used as a synonym for symbol or metaphor. They became with us Christians signs in colours. White or blue was the emblem of innocence, red of joy, black of mourning, green of hope, and purple of power or dignity.

MYTHS generally had their origin in symbols and allegories, which found interpreters, commentators, exegists, and expounders in the priests of the ancient world. Later, the myths were taken up by poets and artists, and the dogmatic explanations of mystic signs were transformed into legends, tales, sagas, or even into historical facts. Nothing affords greater delight to the inquisitive mind of man than a mystic sign! The more unintelligible such a sign is, the more welcome it is to the childish creature. Anything veiled in doubt, shrouded in a symbol or type, has a peculiar charm. Anything that can only be guessed at, or dimly felt, is more admired than that which lies clearly before our perceptive faculty. 'Mysteries were taught in symbols, in darkness at night-time; the symbolic itself is to be compared to night and darkness,' says Demetrius. No wonder that symbols were adopted by the first followers of Christ. They were too near to Egypt; the ancient world had not yet altogether lost its hold on the minds of the masses, and they could not have

156

avoided availing themselves of forms which were used by Indians, Greeks, Egyptians, or Romans.

In the old catacombs of St. Sebastiano, St. Calisto, St. Lorenzo, and Sta. Agnese at Rome, extending altogether to about 750 miles, and in those of St. Gennaro de Poveri, Sta. Maria della Sanitá, and Sta. Maria della Vita at Naples, we find some attempts at symbolism; the cross, the monogram of Christ's name XP {CHR}; or an AΩ {AÔ}, symbolical of the beginning and the end of all things; a palm branch, doves, the piscis vesica, and here and there a lamb. But these signs belong to the fourth and fifth centuries A.D. The inscriptions do not go farther back than the second century. The homely simplicity of the early Christians is distinctly to be traced in the absence of all symbolic decoration during the first two centuries. Gradually the Christians passed through the phase of geometrical ornamentation. Triangles and circles, crosses and squares, squares divided into four squares, or the square taken three times, giving twelve points, which number contains the sacred numbers; three (the Trinity), five (the five sacred wounds of Christ), seven (the seven cardinal virtues, or the seven days of Creation), and twelve (the twelve apostles), made their appearance. Seven was a holy and mystic number with all the ancient nations. There were seven planets, and seven colours in olden times; Apollo's lyre had seven strings; Pan used seven pipes for his flute. There are seven days of the week; seven or three times seven are the critical days in medicine; there were seven branches to the candlestick of the Jews in the Temple of Jerusalem. Seven years Jacob had to serve for Leah; and seven others for Rachel; seven were the ears and kine of which Pharaoh dreamt; seven were the gods in Scandinavian mythology; seven were the sufferings of the Virgin Mary; seven the cardinal virtues; seven the deadly sins; seven are the sacraments of the Romish Church. We cannot fail to see in the minutest details of history and art, philosophy and religious systems, an eternally progressing 'one-ness' pervading humanity as a great whole.

Scarcely had the Christians adopted these signs, when they passed on to the next phase, adorning churches and tombs, altars and sacred vessels, with emblems taken from the vegetable and animal kingdoms, to serve as the holy visible outward signs of some sacred inward grace or virtue. What was immortal was to be expressed in mortal forms, and the finite was to embody the infinite. Again, the meaning hallowed the form; again, by degrees, the *form* became all, and the spirit was altogether lost through the mere outward sign. Art suffered for centuries under the gloomy pressure of symbolism, and in striving to disentangle itself, produced marvels, but it was only freed and attained higher forms of beauty again, when humanity had gone back to those laws, which when followed out had produced forms perfect in themselves.

For centuries art revelled in the reproduction of symbolical crows, eagles, peacocks, doves, gridirons, pitchers, beehives, oxen, pigs, bulls, geese, violins, fishes, &c., as the attributes of St. Sebastian, St. John, Sta. Barbara, St. Thomas of Aquin, St. Cyprian, St. Narcissus, St. Bernard, St. Sebaldus, St. Anthony, St. Martin, St. Genesius, St. Chrysogonus, &c. A whole science arose out of these symbols and emblems: *Iconology*, which differs only in form from mythology. The mere phenomena of nature were no longer embodied; the individual spirit that lived in the form, became all in all. We were thus introduced to a two-fold world by Christian art.

(1) Into a spiritual world, in which our intellect moved, as it were, in a circle. We took our beginning in the infinite, lost our transitory bodily form, and returned to the infinite from which we emanated—a kind of idealisation of the corporeal.

(2) A world of external forms, which in their individual phenomena had only a meaning as the fragile temporary vessels of the eternal Spirit; this Spirit was no longer a universal sum total by which the individual was hereafter absorbed, but was assumed to remain *individualised* through all eternity. Artists and men worked not only for this world, but their deeds were to outlast all time to come. In this two-fold world, Christian art went through the following phases:—

(a) Through a *historical* phase, which commenced with Christ's birth, life, death, and resurrection, as the new central point of all things. The eternal Spirit was embodied, worked in a finite form, and freed from it, regained its absolute divinity. This led in time to sublime historical sketches in sculpture and painting.

(b) Through a *religious* phase. The spirit, freed and redeemed by Christ, sought in deeds of harmonious love totally new spheres of action. Crystals, flowers, trees, landscapes, animals and men, were interwoven to proclaim not only outward beauty, as with the Greeks, but a union of the inorganic and the organic, the ancient and the new worlds, in honour of one God in three emanations or personifications.

So long as bishops, priests, elders, deacons and laymen, were occupied in trying to shape the new spirit into words, art appeared to slumber. A too strong storm-wind of dissension on metaphysical niceties, of mystic and dogmatic hair-splittings, hindered a plastic treatment of Christianity. Gnostics, Nestorians, Manichæans, Donatists, Arians, and Athanasians, &c., wasted the energies of the early Christian artists, with their wild distinctions, their incomprehensible differences. Quarrels as to whether a blessing was more efficacious when bestowed with *three* or only with *two* uplifted fingers; whether crosses of equal parts, or crosses in which one division was smaller than the other, were more powerful, did not promote the productive ability of artists. When, under Constantine, Christianity was elevated to the rank of a State religion, churches were built in honour of the new faith. In the West the Roman Basilicæ were given up to the religious worship of the Christians, and in time, mixed with Teuton forms, produced the Romanesque style. In the East a lively revival of Asiatic forms, of Indian, Assyrian, and Babylonian patterns, took place, and from these combinations we have the so-called Byzantine style.

The general characteristics of the early Christian style, in which the form of the Roman basilica predominated, were the following:—The apsis, the seat of the bishop and clergy, was semicircular. Between the apsis and the nave stood the altar, or rather the common table, canopied by a baldachin supported by columns. The walls were covered with figures of Christ. The main body consisted of a broad and lofty central nave, on the two sides of which there were two lower passages, divided by rows of columns, supporting the upper wall of the nave either by a common architrave, or by strong circular arches. The upper wall was provided with large broad windows, some being also placed in the low walls of the side-aisles. The apsis was kept in mystic darkness.

The threefold division of the Indian, Egyptian, and Hebrew temples was carefully kept up. The priests assembled in the apsis; the worshippers in the hall or the galleries; and the penitents or sinners stopped at the entrance. Of this period, we have the Basilica of Reparatus, in Tingitanum (now Orléansville) in Algeria, and another in El Hayz, on a small oasis, in the Libyan desert. In the former the pillars were probably square, and the apsis is not marked outside. The latter is furnished with vaulted aisles, adorned with pilasters and niches in the Romano-Egyptian style.

Under Constantine, Christian churches of larger dimensions were constructed; marble decorations and a profusion of columns were common. The five aisles still predominated, the Athanasians not having yet succeeded in establishing the Trinitarian doctrine. St. Peter's at Rome (rebuilt in the 16th century); Sta. Croce at Jerusalem, and the Church of Sta. Maria at Bethlehem, built by Helena, the wife of Constantine, were splendid specimens of the pure early Christian style. The transept before the raised apsis was an innovation. The central aisle (the nave) rises in independent loftiness. The galleries are dispensed with, as the dimensions of the building are considerably increased. Light is admitted through windows in the lofty central aisle. The lines all tend towards the altar, and the high tribune. The nave is separated from the transept by a lofty arch supported by pillars. The transept is provided with broad windows, throwing the greatest amount of light on the altar, by which means a sublime effect is attained. St. Peter's at Rome, and Sta. Maria at Bethlehem, are provided with cross-beams, which do not accord with the superstructure, which is too heavy. Before these churches, in a court-yard, stood the fountain. These fountains were common to all the Indian, Egyptian, and Hebrew temples, because the *sanctity of water* was recognised by all the religious sects of the Southeast. *San Paolo fuori le mura* belonged to this class of churches. It was constructed by Theodosius and Honorius. 'The mighty apsis, about eighty feet in breadth, is increased in effect by a lofty transept, which stretches in front of it, across the whole nave. The body of the church has five aisles. Eighty granite columns, connected by circular arches, rise in four rows in order to divide the aisles, and to support the upper wall of the central aisle, and the framework of the roof. The main aisle opens into the transept with a broad and lofty triumphal arch, which rests on two colossal columns. A splendid atrium, surrounded with colonnades, was added to the front, completing the plan of this basilica.' The high walls above the central isle fulfilled a double purpose: they vividly expressed an expanding tendency upwards, and filled the soul with the idea of the infinite. This tendency was still more strongly expressed in ecclesiastical or Gothic architecture. Scenes from the life of Christ and his disciples were painted, and, in imitation of Roman decoration, gilded panels and marble pavings were freely used. After the fourth century the five aisles were gradually abandoned, and only three were used, symbolic of the Trinity. We have here a kind of Indian or rather Buddhistic renaissance.

When Ravenna became the seat of the Byzantine Exarchs (viceroys), the Ostrogoth influences which were perceptible under Theodoric vanished, and a freer organisation of the sacred edifices was introduced by the addition of an independent bell-tower, reminding us of the Buddhistic towers or pillars, the Irish round towers, the minarets of the Mahomedans, and the obelisks of the Egyptians. The tower rose in a cylindrical form, without tapering. The roofs of the churches were generally flat. Strong wall pillars, connected by *circular* arches, framed the windows as a repetition of the arcades below. The capitals retained a double row of acanthus leaves, but the imposts became stronger, taking the form of a coffin or a small altar, adorned with crosses, or the monogram of Christ. The churches of St. Vitale and St. Apollinare in Classe, are models of this transition style, which formed the link between the Romanesque and the Byzantine. In these we find Greek marble columns, profuse mosaics on gold grounds, panels and medallions filled with historical scenes, or the portraits of bishops, prophets, saints, and martyrs; the decoration is heavy in outlines, the forms and figures too naturalistic; the taste gorgeous without refinement; and the technical treatment rough and defective.

Whilst the architectural and ornamental styles were receiving fixed forms as the pure Romanesque of the West—through the influence of the Teutons, who became masters of Italy and worked with greater stiffness, simplicity, and angularity—Byzantine architecture assumed, from the time of Justinian, a peculiarly pompous, Asiatic type. The dome prevailed; the ground-plan was composed of squares and circles. Ceremonies and mysteries borrowed from the Egyptians, Persians, and Romans, and the division of priests into different castes, required a different arrangement of the building. There was a place for the high and one for the low clergy; another for the laymen; the galleries were, in the old Jewish fashion, assigned to the women; and, lastly, there was a place for the penitent. These divisions and subdivisions induced confusion and disunion in the whole plan. Many of the Christian buildings have become, in their turn, Mahomedan mosques, just as the Roman basilicæ of old were turned into Christian churches.

The mightiest and the most gigantic of all Byzantine churches is undoubtedly that of St. Sophia, at Constantinople. First the building was a temple dedicated to 'Holy Wisdom,' in the ancient or classic meaning of the word. The edifice was destroyed by fire, and rebuilt by Justinian in five years (A.D. 532–537). Twenty years later it was much damaged by an earthquake. The injured dome was removed, raised somewhat higher upon strengthened counterfoils, and finished A.D. 563. The architects were Anthemis of Tralles, and Isidorus of Miletus. The ground-plan, ornamentation, and construction, aim in combination at one single result—surprise. There is a contradiction between lengths and circles, destroying all effect of simple perspective. The various cupolas, arches, and half-cupolas, connected with great technical skill, have no organically united life. An antediluvian world opens its gates to us. There is everywhere something astounding and gorgeous, but we are unable to discern the necessity for the existence of the parts, to form a coherent total. The galleries with their colonnades puzzle us. The outer square-form, overtowered by a mighty cupola, and by half-cupolas, is as incongruous as the ornamentation of the interior. The shafts of the columns are amongst the finest specimens of Roman architecture. Walls and pillars are adorned with variegated marble panels in mosaic patterns. The roofs of the dome and semi-domes are covered with gold mosaics, set in coloured ornamented frames, interspersed with figurative tapestry-like representations. Christ, saints, and prophets, are suspended in golden clouds. The effect on an untutored mind is perfectly intoxicating. Though we do not underrate the fully developed system of stone-roof construction, we must draw the attention of our readers to the heavy and shapeless capitals with the scarcely recognisable Ionic volutes, combined with Corinthian leaf-work; all outlines being smothered by over-ornamentation, destroying the beautiful effect of the antique by a clumsy impost. Byzantine architecture remained stationary for hundreds of years. The religious spirit went hand in hand with their stiff, lifeless art. Ignorance and credulity engendered in the East a boundless intolerance of all divergence of opinion, to which was added an equally boundless toleration of falsehoods and frauds, so soon as these means served to support the received opinions. An intellectual standstill was the result of these principles, and acted on art, rendering it in general as well as in detail an unwieldy mixture of Egyptian, Assyrian, Greek, and Roman forms, overloaded with Asiatic filigree composed of lines drawn from Christian symbolism. The Byzantine style of ornamentation will always be, like that of China, a strange element to us. However much the ingenuity of the winding, coiling, and recoiling lines, interspersed with small and large jewels, may interest us, though we may gaze at the profusion of gold mixed with gaudy colours with a kind of vague bewilderment, Byzantine art can never appeal to our sense of beauty.

A most important branch of Byzantine ornamentation was the treatment of metals. For flat decoration, in the style of embroidery, nothing can excel the use of metal, be it gold, silver, bronze, or steel, or a combination of all these. There was a fantastic originality in these productions which, when combined with an assiduous study of the antique, may aid us in many instances to produce excellent specimens of book-covers, patterns for ornamented salvers, caskets, cups, candlesticks, crosses, &c. Byzantine art, however, is the very opposite of classic art. Repose, as a consequence of the liveliest vibration of forms, and uniformity through a rich variation of patterns, are the real elements of Byzantine and Oriental art; in contradistinction to classic art, which is based on the authority of purpose and a correct subordination of details. This is the reason why the free but well- systematised ornaments of classic Greece were revived at this period with Assyrian, Babylonian, and Persian textile patterns in metal, stone, or colours. Nothing could be more appropriate for this mode of ornamentation than leaf- work, flowers, creepers, &c., in the arrangement of which, the stern law of a well-regulated distribution of the repeated forms must be observed, to bring about a thorough balance between rest and vibration, variety and uniformity.

Whilst Byzantium was exhausting all its powers, and socially and artistically preparing to fall a prey to iconoclasts and Mahomedans; the movement, next in importance to the establishment of Christianity, viz. the migration of the Northern Teutons, took place.

We intend to group Kelts, Normans, Franks, Ostrogoths, and Westrogoths or Visigoths, Alemanni, Burgundians, Vinilians, Ingavorians, Istavorians, Vandals, Saxons, Anglo-Saxons, Markomanni, Rugi, Ubi, Gurgerni, Herulians, Bojoarians, Gepidi, Quadi, Marsingi, Sclavons, &c., all under the one name of North-European Ayrans. It is an imperative duty, with the art-historian, to group these scattered elements together, according to some visible signs, which serve to prove that, wherever we find an average facial angle of 90°, and an amount of brain averaging 92 cubic inches, we have to deal with the Aryan group of humanity. We avoid by this means divisions and sub-divisions *ad infinitum*, and the danger of losing ourselves in a labyrinth of petty national animosities and jealousies. Art, based on ethnology, and a study of climatological influences, has an immensely Christianising power. We see in the common language of forms, a common bond between those who formed themselves into small political communities, each in turn arrogating to themselves a kind of *'chosen-people' superiority*, and turning their powers against that very mother-stock from which they received life, vigour, a common language, and a common mode of thinking on supernatural matters, and the phenomena of nature. The Kelts, Normans, Saxons, Danes, Swedes, Teutons, Germans (Garmans, Wahrmans, or Wehrmans, Brahmans), are all of the same stock. Separated at different periods from their Trans-and Cis-Himâlâyan ancestors, they lost more or less of their old religious notions, customs, and manners, according to their lesser or greater intermixture with the Turanian substrata of aborigines, who peopled the countries wherein they settled. Next to the aspect of the country in which they established themselves, its climate must be taken into consideration. The Aryan, snowed in for six months in Scandinavia, or living on the coasts of the Baltic, obliged to fight for every foot of fertile ground with a boisterous and obstinate nature, must have developed otherwise than the self-same Aryan who, as Kelt, took up his abode on an island everlastingly green with refreshing verdure, and was insulated from outer influences for long periods, being thus led to look upon this detached spot as the very centre of the universe around which the five parts of our globe, the myriads of suns, stars, planets, and comets revolved. Between the Aryan-Kelt and the Aryan-Frank or Norman, there will be a difference, brought about by the progress of time and a freer intermixture with other branches of the mother-stock who attained a higher kind of civilisation. The Aryans in India lost themselves in metaphysical abstractions, and made of fire, water, and air a theogony in which the anthropomorphic element was altogether effaced. The Aryans in the north of Europe, in their cosmogony, held to the original conceptions. They had to battle with fire, water, and air, in the form of volcanoes, seas, rain, snow, hail and storms; and finding that with their intellectual power they could master these elements, they soon deprived them of their individual godhead, and the whole earth, with its loves and passions, its kindnesses and destructive tendencies, was looked upon as a living being. They also knew of two regions on earth—not of a spiritually created paradise and hell, but of a *Muspel-heim* in the south, and a *Nifel-heim* in the north: the one giving warmth, heat, life; the other cold and death; the one light, the other night; the one summer, and the other winter.

According to the Aryans of the north of Europe the first cosmical heat produced the giant *Ymir*, or *Angelmir*, who was nourished by the sacred cow *Audumbla*, from which ran four streams of milk, the four seasons. Like Brahmă, Ymir had a son and a daughter; the daughter grew out of his arm, and the son out of his foot. The Brahman was the outgrowth of Brahmă's mouth: the Kshattriya sprung from his arms, the Vaisya grew out of his thighs, and the S'udra out of his feet. Ymir's son became the father of the Hirmthursen (giants). By licking huge rocks of sandstone the cow became the mother of Buri. We thus pass from the pastoral into the agricultural state, and have the legend of Jupiter and Io before us. Buri had a son, Bor, who had three sons. *Odin*, Guodan, Wuodan, Wodan, the All-pervader—the 'Allvater' (father of all), *Willi* and *We*—air, fire and water. Wodan was also Baal, or the sun-god, in which capacity he had only *one eye* (the sun); he was also Apollo, the god of poetry, and of all things that love light and goodness. He was also the warfaring god who led the people to battle, and protected the valorous and virtuous. He had to fight against the giant Ymir with his brothers. A reminiscence of the wars of the Greek gods with the Titans, &c.; the Indian Vritaghna or the Persian Veretaghna, with the evil spirits of darkness, or the Egyptian Horus with Typhon. Out of the dead body of Ymir, the sons of Bor created everything. They formed the earth of his flesh, the rocks of his bones, the skull became heaven, and his blood furnished seas, rivers, and streams. They then took four dwarfs and placed Austri (in the East), Westri (in the West), Sudri (in the South), and Nordri (in the North), to guard the four corners of the heavens. Wuodan then embraced the earth, and created his mighty son *Thor*, Donar, Thunder, the protector of his mother-earth, and the enemy of the wicked. He sent his lightnings against giants, purified the air, dispersed frost and cold, killed the demons of heat, silenced the destructive storms, built bridges, made high-roads, furthered the intercourse of man with man, and promoted civilisation. The second son of Wuodan was *Zio* (Ziu, Zeus, Jovis, Síva, also Tyr-Tiu or Tusco), the god of battles, the destroyer. The third son was *Fro* (Froho, Freyr, free), the happy god, the god of love and marriage. Who does not recognise in Thor, Froh, and Ziu—Brahma, Vishnu, and Siva—Jupiter, Apollo and Mars? As with the Aryans on the Ganges, so also with those on the Rhine, the Elbe or the Weser, and in Scandinavia, the passive element of nature was embodied in female divinities. *Hertha*, Nerthus (the earth), corresponds to S'ris, Hera, Ceres, Isis; *Holda* is closely allied with Hilda, Hela, Hell (the hidden), the goddess of death, Durga; and *Freyja* represents Venus, the goddess of love. These Aryans of northern Europe were known to the ancients as Hyperboræans. They were tall, blue-eyed, fair- haired, addicted to fighting, and sport. Some of them erected, in analogy with Buddhists and Egyptians, long thin towers reaching high into the air, pointing mystically upwards. The 'Crux Ansata' is reproduced in the Irish crosses, and their mode of ornamentation, with its twisted rope-like windings, and its serpent-like entanglements, points to Indian patterns of a very ancient type. When these Aryans of the north of Europe first dashed into the south, and destroyed the Roman colossus, they embraced Christianity with all the fervour of their unbiassed hearts. Entirely given up to the culture of the wild powers of nature, free from all metaphysical subtleties—the genuine men of wild oak, pine, and beech forests—they had no Vedas, no Homer, no Zoroaster, no Hermes, and no Moses to forget; they, in fact, only knew of an Allvater, because no two Teuton tribes held the same opinions on metaphysics. They had only one common ground, honest work—*industry* (at those times concentrated on warfare); and therefore they received Christianity with the greatest eagerness, and became the only upholders, expounders, and propagators of a religion for which their hearts were created. They recognised in Christ's words, what they heard in whispers in their legends, and in the experiences of their wild life—that we ought to love others as ourselves. They added some of their old superstitions to the pure faith, which they found already much impregnated with Egyptian, Roman, and Indian signs and symbols. In the beginning, whilst Christianity was spreading all over Europe, they cultivated a mixture of North European and Roman forms in architecture as well as in ornamentation. They constructed their churches with plans borrowed from ancient times, and freely used geometrical symbols—for the sign of the Indian Trimurty, that of the shields of David or Solomon, and that of the Trinity, did not differ. The pentagram is still made on every loaf the Germans bake; it was a Druidical mystic sign, and now serves good Christians to protect their bread from being eaten by evil spirits. If we look at our Tudor roses, or St. Katherine's wheels, we may clearly trace their origin to the Zodiacs of Egypt, used as signs of the *Makrokosm*. The Teuton minds found themselves suddenly dazzled by Christian theology. Greek, Alexandrian, Nestorian, Arian, Athanasian, Jewish and Christian mystics and casuists, already abounded in the sunny Muspel-heim, in which the Teutons settled, and they had to exchange their gloomy, foggy, and stormy Nifel-heim of reality, for a spiritual Nifel-heim of doctrinal controversies. They turned their elfs and sprites, their kobolds and gnomes, their spirits of air, water, and fire, into so many evil spirits. They looked upon the literature of the Greeks and Romans, of which they knew nothing, as the work of Beelzebub. Art was an enchantress of the senses, and sculpture invented by the father of all 'lies,' to deceive us with mock-creatures, to seduce men, and to cheat them of their share in everlasting salvation. In this gloomy spirit the newly converted Teuton Christians built churches, and, sunken in the most atrocious superstition, occupied themselves with the casting out of devils. Nature was, in fact, one grand dwelling-place for demons. Plague, poverty, and sickness, were attributed to the agency of the enemy of mankind. Epileptic fits and insanity were signs that the demon had taken possession of unfortunate wretches, who were either tormented or put to death. Satan, with his legions of devils, continually harassed mankind. To mortify and kill the body by fasting, chanting, whipping, praying, and self-inflicted mortification, was thought the only worthy and cheerful occupation of mankind. In addition to these religious tendencies, wars were waged with merciless cruelty, either in favour of, or against the new Christian superstition. A few so-called *learned* theologians studied the Jewish Cabala, Egyptian mysteries, Zoroastrian magical calculations, Greek sophisms, and Alexandrian Neo-Platonism. How could art have flourished under such circumstances? Incantations, astrological calculations, alchemical experiments, were the order of the day. The few learned men, whether architects or others, as soon as they produced anything astounding, were said to have received their ideas or plans, or their powers, from the devil. Who was to create any beautifully shaped product of art, surrounded by such misgivings?

This struggle lasted for several centuries; until, stimulated by movements in the far East, the Christian world left its secluded haunts in cloisters, monasteries, churches, and castles, and mixed once more with the outer world, and the whole gloomy medley of Christianised northern mythology had to yield to new forms in art.

Of this period we have a quantity of wood and ivory carvings, swords in the form of crosiers, and crosiers in the form of swords, cups and candlesticks, censers and pastoral staffs, diptichs and triptichs, recording scenes from the life of Christ or of some saint. From the third century down to the twelfth, year by year, artistic products of ornamentation grew worse and worse. In the third century there was some naturalness in the drapery, the folds being well executed; but in the fifth century the treatment of the human figure deteriorated; folds became more rope-like; Christ was represented as very young, with or without a beard, often retaining the form of Apollo, or of Hermes, carrying a lamb (the good shepherd). Bodies of saints and holy persons grew more and more emaciated; the anatomy was altogether neglected. After the Crusades in the twelfth century a marked improvement took place, but everything was then impregnated with Mahomedan forms. We should look with deep interest, and a sense of filial piety, on these primitive attempts of Christian art; the execution is bad, but the sentiments spread by their carvings, faulty designs, and poor ornamentations, are always excellent. The artists address us in a rough and unskilful manner, yet some spiritual truth awakens our better nature to exalted feelings of love. This, however, teaches us that a good feeling, a devout spirit, or a religious sentiment in the artists, is not alone enough to produce works of art.

Whilst Europe was expending its powers in the re-arrangement of the disturbed social and religious relations of humanity, a new movement arose which threatened to overwhelm the whole world.

The new movement produced new art forms, which in their turn serve to prove that art is a most important factor of civilisation. Till lately, the erroneous notion that art is a mere superfluous luxury has appeared to prevail with us. Art was placed by the ethicists in opposition to morals, and scientists either altogether ignored it, or regarded it as diametrically opposed to science —a pretty but useless toy. Art is as necessary to man as either ethics or science. For man is endowed with an emotional element, which must be satisfied and cultivated, in order to raise him to the dignity of a human being using his esthetical and intellectual faculties. It is vain to attempt to draw lines of demarcation, between our component material and spiritual elements. We recognise, or become conscious, through our *senses*; we sift the impressions made on our senses by the power of our *intellect*: and we regulate and arrange these impressions with the aid of our *reason*. We may, therefore, strictly treat art scientifically, as well as historically. For works of art may be considered under the following heads:—

(*a.*) As the concrete embodiments of man's thoughts; the importance of the historical study of which cannot be too strongly insisted upon, for through it we can best become acquainted with the past, from a social and religious point of view.

(*b.*) As products that act upon our emotional, intellectual, and reasoning faculties. It is our duty to endeavour to ascertain what forms at different times, and under various impressions, acted most agreeably on us. We must learn to know the causes that produced certain art forms at certain periods, amongst certain people, under certain intellectual, social, and religious conditions. We must inquire why such forms flourished, decayed, or revived at different times.

(*c.*) We may examine the relations in which our subjective impressions stand to the products of art, and learn how far such sensations developed, in time and space, to lead us to the consciousness of beauty.

From pre-historic times to the advent of Christ humanity was always engaged as a busy artist. In studying the history of man we find that art ushers us into life, gladdens the child, inspires the youth, and interests the man. All our public actions, all our religious ceremonies, our Court pageantry, our battles and funerals, all our useful or useless surroundings, pass more or less through an artistic process. In analysing the historical development of humanity at large, or that of a nation, or even that of single individuals, we find that our sensations, intellect, and reason have always been at work to create something in their respective spheres. From the times of Plato to our own all great thinkers have more or less occupied themselves with the endeavour to establish the principles of beauty; just as from Thales of Miletus, and Demokritos to Bacon, Kant, Darwin, and Häckel, they have sought to discover the principle of truth; or from Manû, Confucius, Moses, the Apostles, and Mahomet, to our own theologians, they have striven to decide what is right or wrong. Art worked synchronically with these endeavours, and its products are as numerous and variegated as our philosophical systems, or our creeds and sects. Moreover, works of art are, in many instances, far less perishable than works of mere speculation. It becomes an imperative duty, therefore, to study historically one of the most important branches of human activity and ingenuity, which furnishes us in its very products with a record in lasting forms, with at least the same ardour, earnestness, and veneration, with which we devote ourselves to more varying, changing, and perishable products. One fact must be obvious to every reader of these pages—that real art has so exalted a sphere that it can only exist to perfection wherever sciences and morals are highly cultivated.

In cursorily summarising these pages, we find that wherever and whenever beauty as the *ideal*, truth as the *real*, or goodness as the *ethical* element in humanity, has been one-sidedly cultivated, works of art have not succeeded, for the harmony and union of these three can alone be the aim of humanity. This harmonious union it is difficult to attain, but we must endeavour to become historically conscious of the continuous striving of humanity to bring it about. We find two forces constantly at work in humanity —the one static (morals), the other dynamic (intellect)—bent upon leading us to culture, progress, truth, goodness, and beauty. In the fifth and at the beginning of the fourth century B.C., for once in our development, and then only for a short period, humanity undoubtedly succeeded in attaining a perfect balance of its moral, intellectual, and esthetical faculties. We may well call that period the golden age of mankind in art. We still live on the mere interest of that immense capital which was left by the Greeks as an imperishable legacy to humanity. Whatever the Greeks touched at that period they transformed into pearls of beauty, gold of truth, and jewels of goodness. They mounted the winged steed of imagination, and were taken up to the bright heaven of pure idealisation, where they saw boundless beauty in forms, and acquired an immortal striving after truth and the eternal laws of goodness, based on the very organisation of our complicated double nature. This dream of reality was short but vivid. Humanity lives still in an ineffaceable longing and a burning desire to regain that period. Like diamonds dropped in unknown ages in small crystallisations into the sand of rivers, the works of Greece appear in the stream of time, serving as a fundamental basis of beauty, truth, and goodness.

The well-balanced harmony was unfortunately soon disturbed.

Giddy with victory and joy, the Greeks discarded ethics; truth was made the handmaid of sophistry, superstition, and scepticism; and beauty, in losing her ideal glory, sank into the depths of sensualism and realism. The harmony of the triad, which artists, philosophers, and moral teachers had succeeded in establishing, was destroyed, and a discordant strain of melancholy woe resounded through history, echoing here and there some remnants of the old and charming melodies. The conquests of Philip of Makedon and Alexander the Great brought the East into contact with the Greek spirit. The East furnished mystic incomprehensibilities, and an egotistic hatred of all art that could not be turned into money, or used for serving some deity to buy up its good graces. Buddhistic tenets joined hands with Brahmanic conceits; Egyptian symbols were intermingled with Hebrew practical enactments, without any ideal aspirations. Greek philosophical diatribes were used to prove the impossible possible, and the 'supernatural' most natural. Some Greeks attempted to revive the antique mode of thinking, but they were silenced by the Neo-Platonists, and thus the Greeks themselves became the most successful apostles of unnaturally-shaped superstitions, deadening the vivifying spirit of Christ's teachings.

The Romans had only one aim in history—to regulate their conquests. The State was everything with them; they taught us how to systematise the actions of men, to make them useful citizens in this world, and, when they left their legacy of infallible authority to the Romish Church, how to prepare fit inhabitants for another world. The outward realistic form, proclaiming some inward mystic grace or meaning, became everything. Base hollowness in art and morals, vapid verbiage in philosophy, unnatural profligacy and licentiousness, mean covetousness and heartless egotism, brought humanity intellectually, morally, and spiritually, to the brink of destruction. Everyone thirsted for a change—reality was unbearable.

Men strove, in deadening their bodies, to seek the salvation of their souls. The realistic tendency of the degenerated ancient times gave way to blind faith, which by degrees obtained an exclusive hold on the ideal in man, ignoring his reflective and reasoning nature, working only on the emotional, and burying antiquity under the gloomy ruins of the Middle Ages. For more than 1000 years beauty had to yield to mystic symbolism, truth to superstitious prejudice, and ethics to a morbid sentimentality and a cruel hierarchical despotism. Dogmatic scholasticism sought to foster elegance of forms; to create artistic enthusiasm; but this attempt was vain. When, however, the dogmatic ice began to melt in the burning rays of the rising sun of a freer inquiry; when the Romish Church, anxious for some powerful helpmate to check the rays of this sun, and work on the gloomy, stupified emotions of the masses, called in to aid her the spirit of the Greeks in art, she prepared a bright and happy future for humanity. The reformation in art- forms, and the revival of the antique spirit in poetry, was soon followed by a revival in science and ethics. Philosophy began to unravel the mysteries of nature, and to make natural forces subservient to man's wants and happiness. Ethics, based on freedom of thought, grew day by day more powerful, and Greek forms were used in the purified spirit of Christ, divested of strange and unintelligible dogmas.

Having secured the right freely to store up the results of our intellectual investigations, we must devote our artistic energies, through an assiduous study of the historical development of art, to a corresponding culture of our sense of beauty. This is essential, if we hope to stand as high artistically, as we do technically and mechanically. Without culture we cannot hope to vie with other nations in high art, in historical paintings, frescoes, sculpture, and architecture. A thorough knowledge of art-history will destroy tasteless prejudices, and enable us progressively to develop the past without becoming guilty of anachronisms. Inspired by the firm conviction that the culture of taste leads to the very highest development of ethics, and that art can only flourish in strict harmony with truth and goodness, we can progress, but not otherwise.

In this volume we have brought the reader down to the art of the Mahomedans, and trust in a future work to trace the historical development of art to our own times. What we have said in praise of Greek art, must not be misunderstood to imply that, since it flourished, we have not made gigantic progressive strides in sculpture, architecture, and painting; but we have done so only when we have worked in the Greek spirit, that is, on the principles which stamped their works of art with perfection.

BIBLIOGRAPHY FOR THE STUDY OF THE HISTORICAL DEVELOPMENT OF ART.

Agincourt, 'Histoire de l'Art par les Monuments'. 6 vols. Fol. Paris, 1823.

Asiatic Researches.

Birch, 'Ancient Pottery.'

Blanc (Charles), 'Grammaire des Arts du Dessin.' Paris, 1870.

Bohlen (von), 'Das alte Indian.' Königsberg, 1830. 2 vols.

Bökh, Works, 1811. Leipzig.

Botta and Flandin, 'Monuments de Ninive,' 1849. Paris.

Boutell, 'Arms and Armour.'

Brugsch, 'Histoire d'Egypte,' 1875. Leipzig.

Bunsen, 'Place of Egypt in History of the World,' vol. 5.

Burnouf, 'Introduction à l'Histoire du Buddhisme Indien.' Paris, 1844.

Carrière (Moriz), 'Die Kunst im Zusammenhange der Kulturentwickelung.' 5 vols. Leipzig; Brockhaus, 1871.

Champollion, 'Lettres écrites de l'Egypte.'

'Christy, Museum Catalogue,' 103 Victoria Street. By A. W. Franks, M.A., Curator. Photographs of same.

Cox, 'History of Mythology of Aryan Nations.'

Cox, 'Manual of Ancient Mythology.'

Cox, 'Mythology of the Aryan Nations.' Longmans, 1870. 2 vols.

Creuzer (Dr. Friedrich), 'Symbolik und Mythologie.' Leipzig and Darmstadt, 1836. 4 vols.

Curtius, 'History of Greece.'

Darwin, 'Expression of the Emotions.' London, 1872.

Davis (Sir J. F.), 'China.' John Murray, 1857.

Denon, 'L'Egypte.'

D'Hancarville, 'Recherches sur l'origine, l'esprit et le progrès des Arts de la Grèce.' London, 1785.

Dyer, 'History of the City of Rome.'

Dyer, 'History of Rome.' 1864.

Dyer, 'Pompei.'

Eber (Dr.), 'Ægypten und die Bücher Moses.' Leipzig, 1868.

Egypt, Guide to. Written by Wilkinson. John Murray.

Engelhardt, 'Denmark in the Old Iron Age.' London, 1866.

'Ethnological Society Transactions,' 1869. *Easter Island.*

Fellows, 'Asia Minor and Lycia.'

Fergusson (J.), 'Indian Architecture.'

Fergusson (J.), 'Palaces of Nineveh and Persepolis Restored.' London, 1851.

Figuier, 'Earth and Sea.' 1870.

Flaxman, 'Lectures.'

'Fortnightly Review'—Spencer's articles on *Nature Worship.* Chapman and Hall.

Gailhabaud, 'Monuments de l'Architecture.'

Gau (F. C.), 'Antiquités de la Nubie.' Paris, 1821–27.

Gibbon, 'History of the Decline and Fall of the Roman Empire.'

Gladstone (Right Hon. W. E.), 'Homeric Synchronism.' London, 1876.

Gould (Baring), 'Origin and Development of Religious Belief.' Rivingtons, 1869.

Grote, 'History of Greece.'

Guilleman, 'Heavens.'

Harrison (Charles), 'Catalogue of a Series of Photographs from the Collection of the British Museum.' W. A. Mansell & Co.

Hegel, 'Æsthetik.' Berlin, 1842. 3 vols.

Hegel, 'Philosophy of History.'

Herder, 'Ideen zur Geschichte der Menschheit.' Stuttgart, 1827. 4

vols.

Hirt, 'Monography of the Temple of Solomon.'

Hutcheson, 'An Inquiry into the Origin of our Ideas of Beauty and Virtue.' London, 1729.

Hyde, 'Historiæ Religionis veterum Persarum.' Oxonii, 1700.

'International Congress of Prehistoric Archæology.' 1868.

Jennings (Hargrave), 'The Rosicrucians.' London, 1870.

Jones (Owen), 'Apology for Colouring the Greek Court of the Crystal Palace.'

Jones (Sir Wm.), Works. London, 1799. 6 vols. 4to.

Kant, 'Æsthetik.' Leipzig, 1838.

King, 'Antique Gems.'

Kingsborough (Lord), 'Antiquities of Mexico.' London, 1831–48. 9 vols. Imp. Folio.

Klaproth, 'Nouv. Jour. Asiat.' vol. 5.

Layard, 'Nineveh.'

Lenormant, 'Manual of the History of the East.' 2 vols. Asher and Co., 1875.

Lepsius, 'Denkmäler.' Berlin.

Lewes, 'Biographical History of Philosophy.'

Lubbock, 'Origin of Civilization and Primitive Condition of Man.' Particularly chapters on Religion, and page 119. 1870.

Lubbock, 'Prehistoric Times.'

Lübke (Dr.), 'History of Art.' Smith, Elder, and Co., 1868.

Madsen, 'Afbildinger af Danske Oldsager og Mindesmar.' Ker. Kjöbenhavn, 1872.

'Manual of Ethnology.' John Murray.

Mommsen, 'Römische Geschichte.' Berlin, 1868.

Müller (C. O.), 'Ancient Art and its Remains.' London: B. Quaritch, 1852.

Müller (Max), 'Chips from a German Workshop.' Longmans, 1868.

Newton, 'Second Catalogue of Vase Rooms, British Museum.'

Nott and G. R. Gliddon, 'Types of Mankind.' Dr. Morton.

Oppert (Dr. J.), 'Expéd. scient. en Mésop.'

Parthey (Dr.), 'De Philis insula ejusque monumentis commentatis.' Berolini, 1830.

Philosophy. See Smith's 'Dictionary of the Bible.'

Piper (Prof. Ferdinand), 'Mythologie der Christlichen Kunst.' Weimar, 1847.

Potter, 'Antiquities of Greece.' Edinburgh, 1818.

'Pyramid Builders of the Mississippi.'

Rawlinson, 'Herodotus.'

Rawlinson, 'Manual of Ancient History.'

Rémusat (Abel), 'Mélanges Asiatiques.' vol. 1.

Sandreczki (C.), 'Reise nach Mosul und durch Kurdistan.' Stuttgart, 1857. 4 vols.

Schliemann (Dr.), 'Discoveries at Hassarlik.'

Schnaase (Dr. E.), 'Geschichte der Bildenden Künste.' Düsseldorf, 1866.

Schwegler, 'History of Philosophy.'

Sef (Abd Alla), 'Relation de l'Egypte traduite par Silvestre de Sacy.' Paris, 1810.

Semper (Dr.), 'Die Textile Kunst.' Frankfurt a. M., 1860.

Shaftesbury (Earl of), 'Characteristics.' 1743. 3 vols.

Smith, 'Ancient History.'

Smith, 'Dictionary of Greek and Roman Antiquities.'

Spruner, 'Historical Atlas.'

Squier and Davis, 'Ancient Monuments of the Mississippi Valley.'

Stephens, 'Runic Monuments.' 2 vols. London, 1866.

Stevens, 'Flint Chips.' Bell and Daldy, 1870.

Stuart & Revett, 'Antiquities of Athens.' London, 1827.

Taine, 'Lectures on Art.'

'Traveller's Art Companion.' *Principal Sculptors.* See pages 414 *et seq.*

'Traveller's Companion, The.' Bell and Daldy, 1868.

Tylor, 'Primitive Culture.' London, 1871.

Uhlemann (Dr. Max), 'Thoth oder die Wissenschaft der alten Aegypter.' Göttingen, 1855.

Valeriani (Prof. Domenico), 'Etrusco Museo Chiusino.' Poligrafia Fiesolana, 1839.

Vaux, 'British Museum.'

Vogüé (Le Comte de), 'Le Temple de Jérusalem.' Paris, 1864.

Wilkinson, 'Manners and Customs of Egyptians.' Murray, 1855. Small edition.

Winkelmann, Werke. 2 vols.

Worsaae, 'Norse Antiquities.' Copenhagen, 1859.

Zerffi (Dr.), *Historic Art Studies*, with 1030 illustrations. 'Building News,' 1872–6.